W9-APS-650

Acclaim for Beth Wiseman

Home All Along

"Beth Wiseman's novel will find a permanent in every reader's heart as she spins comfort and prose into a stellar read of grace."

—Kelly Long, author of the Patch of Heaven series

Love Bears All Things

"Suggest to those seeking a more truthful, less saccharine portrayal of the trials of human life and the transformative growth and redemption that may occur as a result."

—Library Journal

Her Brother's Keeper

"Wiseman has created a series in which the readers have a chance to peel back all the layers of the Amish secrets."

—RT Book Reviews, 4 1/2 stars and July 2015 Top Pick!

"Wiseman's new launch is edgier, taking on the tough issues of mental illness and suicide. Amish fiction fans seeking something a bit more thought-provoking and challenging than the usual fare will find this series debut a solid choice."

—Library Journal

The Promise

"The story of Mallory in *The Promise* uncovers the harsh reality American women can experience when they follow their hearts into a very different culture. Her story sheds light on how Islamic society is totally different from the Christian marriage covenant between one man and one woman. This novel is based on actual events, and Beth reached out to me during that time. It was heartbreaking to watch those real-life events unfolding. I salute the author's courage, persistence, and final triumph in writing a revealing and inspiring story."

—NONIE DARWISH, AUTHOR OF *THE DEVIL WE DON'T KNOW*,
CRUEL AND USUAL PUNISHMENT, AND *NOW THEY CALL ME INFIDEL*

"*The Promise* is an only too realistic depiction of an American young woman motivated by the best humanitarian impulses and naïve trust facing instead betrayal, kidnapping, and life-threatening danger in Pakistan's lawless Pashtun tribal regions. But the story offers as well a reminder just as realistic that love and sacrifice are never wasted and that the hope of a loving heavenly Father is never absent in the most hopeless of situations."

—JEANETTE WINDLE, AUTHOR OF *VEILED FREEDOM* (2010 ECPA CHRISTIAN
BOOK AWARD/CHRISTY AWARD FINALIST), *FREEDOM'S STAND* (2012 ECPA
CHRISTIAN BOOK AWARD/CAROL AWARD FINALIST), AND *CONGO DAWN* (2013
GOLDEN SCROLL NOVEL OF THE YEAR)

The House that Love Built

"This sweet story with a hint of mystery is touching and emotional. Humor sprinkled throughout balances the occasional seriousness. The development of the love story is paced perfectly so that the reader gets a real sense of the characters."

—*RT BOOK REVIEWS*, 4-STAR REVIEW

"[*The House that Love Built*] is a warm, sweet tale of faith renewed and families restored."

—BOOKPAGE

Need You Now

"Wiseman, best known for her series of Amish novels, branches out into a wider world in this story of family, dependence, faith, and small-town

Texas, offering a character for every reader to relate to . . . With an enjoyable cast of outside characters, *Need You Now* breaks the molds of small-town stereotypes. With issues ranging from special education and teen cutting to what makes a marriage strong, this is a compelling and worthy read."

—BOOKLIST

"Wiseman gets to the heart of marriage and family interests in a way that will resonate with readers, with an intricately written plot featuring elements that seem to be ripped from current headlines. God provides hope for Wiseman's characters even in the most desperate situations."

—*RT BOOK REVIEWS*, 4-STAR REVIEW

"You may think you are familiar with Beth's wonderful story-telling gift but this is something new! This is a story that will stay with you for a long, long time. It's a story of hope when life seems hopeless. It's a story of how God can redeem the seemingly unredeemable. It's a message the Church, the world needs to hear."

—SHEILA WALSH, AUTHOR OF *GOD LOVES BROKEN PEOPLE*

"Beth Wiseman tackles these difficult subjects with courage and grace. She reminds us that true healing can only come by being vulnerable and honest before our God who loves us more than anything."

—DEBORAH BEDFORD, BESTSELLING AUTHOR OF *HIS OTHER WIFE, A ROSE BY THE DOOR,* AND *THE PENNY* (COAUTHORED WITH JOYCE MEYER)

The Land of Canaan Novels

"Wiseman's voice is consistently compassionate and her words flow smoothly."

—PUBLISHERS WEEKLY REVIEW OF *SEEK ME WITH ALL YOUR HEART*

"Wiseman's third Land of Canaan novel overflows with romance, broken promises, a modern knight in shining armor, and hope at the end of the rainbow."

—*RT Book Reviews*

"In *Seek Me with All Your Heart*, Beth Wiseman offers readers a heartwarming story filled with complex characters and deep emotion. I instantly loved Emily, and eagerly turned each page, anxious to learn more about her past—and what future the Lord had in store for her."

—Shelley Shepard Gray, bestselling author of
the Seasons of Sugarcreek series

"Wiseman has done it again! Beautifully compelling, *Seek Me with All Your Heart* is a heartwarming story of faith, family, and renewal. Her characters and descriptions are captivating, bringing the story to life with the turn of every page."

—Amy Clipston, bestselling author of *A Gift of Grace*

The Daughters of the Promise Novels

"Well-defined characters and story make for an enjoyable read."

—*RT Book Reviews* on *Plain Pursuit*

"A touching, heartwarming story. Wiseman does a particularly great job of dealing with shunning, a controversial Amish practice that seems cruel and unnecessary to outsiders . . . If you're a fan of Amish fiction, don't miss *Plain Pursuit*!"

—Kathleen Fuller, author of The Middlefield Family novels

Home All Along

ALSO BY BETH WISEMAN

THE AMISH SECRETS NOVELS
Her Brother's Keeper
Love Bears All Things

THE DAUGHTERS OF THE PROMISE NOVELS
Plain Perfect
Plain Pursuit
Plain Promise
Plain Paradise
Plain Proposal
Plain Peace

THE LAND OF CANAAN NOVELS
Seek Me with All Your Heart
The Wonder of Your Love
His Love Endures Forever

OTHER NOVELS
Need You Now
The House that Love Built
The Promise

HOME ALL ALONG

AN AMISH SECRETS NOVEL

BETH WISEMAN

THOMAS NELSON
Since 1798

Home All Along

© 2017 by Elizabeth Wiseman Mackey

All rights reserved. No portion of this book may be reproduced, stored in a retrieval system, or transmitted in any form or by any means—electronic, mechanical, photocopy, recording, scanning, or other—except for brief quotations in critical reviews or articles, without the prior written permission of the publisher.

Published in Nashville, Tennessee, by Thomas Nelson. Thomas Nelson is a registered trademark of HarperCollins Christian Publishing, Inc.

Thomas Nelson titles may be purchased in bulk for educational, business, fund-raising, or sales promotional use. For information, please e-mail SpecialMarkets@ThomasNelson.com.

Scripture quotations are taken from the KING JAMES VERSION, public domain and the Holy Bible, New International Version®, NIV®. Copyright © 1973, 1978, 1984, 2011 by Biblica, Inc.™ Used by permission of Zondervan. All rights reserved worldwide. www.zondervan.com

Publisher's Note: This novel is a work of fiction. Names, characters, places, and incidents are either products of the author's imagination or used fictitiously. All characters are fictional, and any similarity to people living or dead is purely coincidental.

Library of Congress Cataloging-in-Publication Data

Names: Wiseman, Beth, 1962- author.
Title: Home all along / Beth Wiseman, Beth Wiseman.
Description: Nashville, Tennessee : Thomas Nelson, [2017] | Series: An Amish secrets novel ; 3
Identifiers: LCCN 2017017661 | ISBN 9781401685973 (softcover)
Subjects: LCSH: Amish--Fiction. | Life change events--Fiction. | GSAFD: Christian fiction. | Love stories.
Classification: LCC PS3623.I83 H66 2017 | DDC 813/.6--dc23 LC record available at https://lccn.loc.gov/2017017661

Printed in the United States of America

17 18 19 20 21 LSC 5 4 3 2 1

To Cake and Icing Lovers Everywhere

Pennsylvania Dutch Glossary

ab im koff—off in the head, crazy
ach—oh!
aenti—aunt
boppli—baby
bruder—brother
daadi haus—grandparents' house, usually a smaller
    dwelling on the same property
daed—dad
danki—thank you
Die Botschaft—Amish newspaper; translated it means
    "The Message"
dochder—daughter
Englisch, Englischer—a non-Amish person
fraa—wife
Gott—God
gut—good
haus—house

kaffi—coffee
kapp—prayer covering or cap
kinner—children
maedel—girl
mamm—mom
mei—my
mudder—mother
nee—no
Ordnung—the written and unwritten rules of the Amish; the understood behavior by which the Amish are expected to live, passed down from generation to generation. Most Amish know the rules by heart.
Pennsylvania Deitsch—the language most commonly used by the Amish. Although widely known as Pennsylvania Dutch, the language is actually a form of German (Deutsch).
rumschpringe—running-around period when a teenager turns sixteen years old
sohn—son
Wie bischt—How are you? or Hi there
wunderbaar—wonderful
ya—yes

Ashes to ashes, dust to dust.

Charlotte pulled her black sweater snug and looked around at the people in attendance for her mother's funeral, a final good-bye to the woman Charlotte only thought of as Janell despite their shared genes. Almost everyone at the service was Amish, except for a couple of people from the psychiatric hospital where Janell had resided for the past three months. Was it obligatory for someone from the rehab facility to attend or, at the least, considered polite protocol?

Bursts of sunlight penetrated a cloudless blue sky as orange, yellow, and red leaves swirled within a gentle breeze, misting the small crowd. As a groundskeeper fought to corral the fallen leaves into a pile, a tractor in the distance harvested a corn maze in which Charlotte wished she could get lost.

Janell had fled four days ago, apparently found her drug of choice, and overdosed. At least that was what the autopsy results would most likely reveal. She had been found on the outskirts of Lancaster County, lying on the steps of a small church with a syringe in her hand. Preliminary toxicology reports showed large doses of methamphetamine in her system—enough to stop her heart, the doctors said. It would remain a mystery as to how Janell ended up at the church, but Charlotte prayed that she'd brought Jesus into her heart before she left this life.

Janell had been an abusive mother, whom Charlotte had tried to love after reconnecting with her a few months ago. She knew her mother's mind wasn't right, but even after Janell had been weaned off the drugs, she spat abuse like a snake, poisoning anyone who came near her with a large dose of verbal venom.

Charlotte wasn't sure if her mother's passing was unintentional, or if she'd committed suicide, like Ethan. She couldn't help but worry since she had the same DNA makeup as the rest of her family. A father killed in a barroom brawl. A mother hooked on meth with mental problems and a mean streak. And a brother whose heart was too tender to endure heartbreak, so he'd taken his own life. *I miss you every day, Ethan.*

Trembling, she forced herself not to cry. A part of her wanted to weep for the mother she'd never had, but stifling her tears protected her from an onslaught of emotions that might derail her. Despite her odious childhood, a few tender memories crept to the surface, comingling loss and anger into a knurly ball of grief.

Daniel reached for her hand and squeezed, a particularly endearing gesture since the Plain People weren't big on public displays of affection. Charlotte loved him for embracing her shaky hand at that moment, but she also loved Daniel Byler for the many ways he'd calmed her soul since she moved to Paradise, in the heart of Lancaster County.

A few moments after the pastor said the final prayer, Hannah Miller and her new husband, Isaac, walked up to Charlotte and Daniel. Hannah's face was moist, her cheeks flushed. Charlotte eased her hand from Daniel's to hug her. Hannah didn't really know Janell, so Charlotte was surprised by the outpouring of emotion, something else uncommon to her Amish friends.

Hannah held on to Charlotte like her life depended on it. She finally backed away as her bottom lip trembled. "I'm sorry for your loss."

Charlotte nodded, sniffling. Hannah was her best friend, but if anyone knew that Janell's passing was causing Charlotte to have mixed emotions, it was Hannah. And ultimately, the Amish believed that everything that came to pass was God's will.

"Where are your parents?" Charlotte had noticed that Amos and Lena weren't at the funeral, which was odd.

"They said they are sorry they can't be here." Hannah reached into the pocket of her apron, pulled out a tissue, and dabbed at her eyes.

Charlotte waited for Hannah to give her a reason for their absence, but Hannah just hugged her again, then turned and left. Isaac tipped his hat before they both walked away.

"Do you think Hannah is acting funny?" she asked Daniel, staring into the comfort of his soft gray eyes, his broad shoulders a protective shield from the early morning rays of sunshine.

He shrugged. "People handle death in different ways."

"I guess." Charlotte wanted to fall into Daniel's arms. Not only would it be inappropriate, but the bishop was heading their way.

Bishop Miller offered his condolences to Charlotte before he asked to speak to Daniel privately. Michael Miller, a man in his early forties, was the youngest bishop Daniel's district had ever had. As such, he was thought to be more lenient than past bishops and elders in the community.

Charlotte knew more about the Amish folks than she could have ever thought possible. Most of them had welcomed her into their world, although some slower than others.

Daniel walked with Bishop Miller until they were away from the crowd and out of earshot. The bishop sighed as he ran a hand the length of his dark beard, slowing his stride as he turned to face Daniel. "Today is not the right time, but I feel we must talk, Daniel. Can you come visit with me within the week?"

Daniel swallowed hard. Bishop Miller had only been bishop for a year, and so far he'd been fair. But Daniel feared that an ultimatum was heading his way. "*Ya*. Okay." He squinted from the sun's glare, not wanting to prolong the conversation. He searched the area until he saw Charlotte talking with his mother and sister. "Can we just talk now?"

Bishop Miller nodded. "*Ya*. Then we can follow up at another time if you'd like." He paused, stroking his beard again. "I took note of those in attendance today, and they were mostly our people. Charlotte has become a member of our district without being a member at all. She's not even Amish, yet she seems to be living the lifestyle."

Frowning, the bishop raised one shoulder, taking his time to drop it. "But she only practices some of our ways. She has no electricity, but she drives a big red pickup. She attends our worship services every other week, but she hasn't been baptized into the faith. And the entire community knows a romance is kindling between the two of you."

Daniel stood taller, his jaw tensed, ready to defend Charlotte's reputation if necessary.

Bishop Miller chuckled. "Calm down, Daniel. I know what it's like to be in love, and I know that you and Charlotte are abiding by God's rules as you sort through your emotions. But I feel that it's time for her to consider what she wants. She can't have her cake and eat it too, as the *Englisch* would say."

"*Ya, ya.* I know." Daniel eased his stance and shifted his weight from one foot to the other as he scratched his head. "She lives in her *bruder's haus*, and it didn't have electricity when it was left to her after his death."

Daniel had felt comfort in the fact that Charlotte hadn't chosen to put electricity in. At first her decision had been financial, but she'd been at her proofreading job at the newspaper long enough that Daniel suspected she could have installed power if she'd wanted to. "As for the worship services . . ." He sighed. "Hannah and her parents are Charlotte's family, and I think she wants to share in that fellowship with them."

Bishop Miller smiled. "Back in my father's and grandfather's days, an *Englischer* would not be allowed to worship with us on a regular basis. And if a young lad was courting someone in the outside world, he could have expected a good talking-to. But I've let this go on between you and Charlotte because the poor girl has suffered, and I was hoping that the two of you would figure things out. But I fear the time has come to make decisions. If a situation goes on for too long, it becomes the norm, and I can't allow that."

He held up a finger. "Now, having said that, Charlotte must be given time to grieve. But I would like to see this resolved—one way or the other—before the holidays are here."

Daniel nodded as he glanced back at Charlotte again, still talking to his mother and Annie.

"Your *mudder* would also like to see this resolved." Bishop Miller winked at Daniel.

"*Ya, ya . . .*" Daniel said under his breath. His mother had been one of the last people to accept Charlotte into her heart, fearful the *Englisch* woman would snatch her son away and take him into her world. His mother wasn't aware that Daniel would go with Charlotte wherever God's path led them, even if that meant leaving the district. He loved her, and his future was with her.

Bishop Miller put a hand on Daniel's arm. "Please tell Charlotte I am sorry for her loss."

Daniel watched the bishop walk away. If the man only knew how many times Daniel had tried to talk to Charlotte about making a life together. *Too many to count.*

Charlotte held her breath as Eve put a hand on her stomach and cringed. Daniel's mother was eight months pregnant. And in her fifties. "Are you okay?"

Eve nodded. "*Ya, ya.*" After a couple of moments, a smile filled her face. "This little one is more active than Daniel or Annie ever was."

Charlotte glanced at Annie, who was scowling.

"You shouldn't have come," Annie said to her mother before she turned to Charlotte. "Daniel tried to talk her out of attending the funeral. Too much walking, and she's been having these pains, which the doctor said were early contractions." Annie folded her hands in front of her. "But she wanted to pay her respects."

"Eve, I would have totally understood you not coming." Charlotte sighed. "And you shouldn't have ridden in a buggy for sure. I can take you home in Big Red."

Annie chuckled. "Are you still calling that old truck Big Red? I figured you would have bought a car by now."

Charlotte shrugged. "I guess I have a soft spot for that old truck." She'd been so touched when Amos King had given it to her, she couldn't imagine parting with it. "Anyway, I'm happy to drive you home." She paused. "Um . . . Hannah and Isaac left without delay, and Lena and Amos didn't come today. Do you know if everything is all right?"

Daniel's mother and sister exchanged quick looks before Annie cleared her throat. "*Ya, ya.* I'm sure everything is fine." She blew out a big breath. "We have to go. We are so sorry for your loss, Charlotte."

"Don't you want me to take you home?" Charlotte called out to Eve as she and Annie started to leave.

"*Nee, nee.*" Eve waved over her shoulder. "It's not that far."

Charlotte didn't move as her gaze drifted from Eve and Annie Byler to the casket. Three men were waiting, presumably until everyone left, so they could lower Janell into her final resting place. She looked around again. Almost everyone was gone. Daniel waved good-bye to the bishop and headed her way, but he stopped to talk to his mother and sister. Charlotte made her way to the casket, offering a weak smile to the three men.

She pulled a rose from one of the nearby flower arrangements. The Amish didn't believe in flowers at a funeral, but this wasn't an Amish funeral and her friends had made sure there was an abundance of flowers for the service.

The three men all stepped away, giving Charlotte some privacy. Her tears threatened to spill again, but more from guilt this time. *God, forgive me. I feel relieved.*

It was a horrible emotion to have, but when it came to Janell, there would always be more bad than good on which to reflect. Janell's resurrection back into Charlotte's life only picked up where she'd left off, chastising and berating Charlotte at every turn.

During her stay in the mental hospital, Janell had called Charlotte every name imaginable. The nurses had tried to make Charlotte feel better by insisting that Janell was mentally ill, in addition to her drug dependency. They were probably telling the truth, but Charlotte tried repeatedly to have a relationship with Janell, despite everything.

Now, as she stood staring at the casket, she finally cried—deep, wracking sobs she couldn't control. But when she felt a hand on her shoulder, she reached up, laid her hand on Daniel's, and quieted her cries. Again.

"Good-bye, Janell." She fought to keep the quaver out of her voice before she faced the man she loved. Charlotte tried to recall if Janell had ever told her that she loved her, and she couldn't think of one single time.

Charlotte gazed into Daniel's gray eyes as wispy strands of dark hair danced in a soft breeze around his strong face. "I love you very much." It was the first time she'd ever said it. She and Daniel had a secret code between them for the past few months. A triple hand squeeze meant "I love you," but neither one of them had ever said it. For Charlotte, she'd known that it would signify the need to make a decision.

Can I embrace the Amish religion in its entirety to be with Daniel? Something about the finality of Janell's passing made Charlotte think about how short life was. What if something happened to her tomorrow, or the next day?

Daniel pulled her into his arms. Everyone was gone or getting into their buggies. He kissed her on her forehead. "I've been waiting a long time to hear that."

Charlotte smiled through her tears. "I've been waiting a long time to say it."

"I love you too." He held her tighter. "But you know that."

She nodded, finally eased away, and sniffled. Looking over her shoulder, she closed her eyes. *Rest in peace . . . Mom.*

"I'm ready." She latched on to Daniel's hand as they crossed through the cemetery toward Big Red. "I offered to take your mom home in the truck. I don't think she should be riding in the buggy when she's so far along."

"I offered to hire her a driver, but she wouldn't hear of it." Daniel shook his head.

They walked in silence for a few moments. In the far distance a man in a dark suit moved toward them. Charlotte thought it might be someone from the funeral home, stopping to offer condolences or to make sure everything went okay.

"Hannah acted funny when I asked her why Amos and Lena weren't here. And your mom and Annie acted a little weird too." She stopped and looked at him when his hand tensed around hers. "What's going on, Daniel?"

"I, uh . . ." He took in a deep breath.

"I knew it. What is everyone not telling me?"

Daniel opened his mouth, then clamped it shut when the man in the suit came into range a few moments later. They both waited until he stopped in front of them.

"Are you Charlotte Dolinsky?" The guy pushed a pair of black sunglasses up on his head. His short, dark hair was neatly parted, and his ebony eyes pierced the space between them. The man had a boyish appearance and distinct dimples, even though Charlotte suspected he was around her age—late twenties. He raised an eyebrow as he waited for Charlotte to answer. She nodded.

He offered the hint of a smile but stilled his expression. "First, let me offer you my sincerest apologies on the death of your mother."

"Thank you." She prayed the man wasn't a bill collector. Charlotte had done a good job of getting her finances in order, but paying for her mother's funeral, modest as it was, had set her back. Even though Janell was considered indigent and qualified for state assistance, Charlotte didn't have the heart to concede to a pauper's burial. "Are you with the funeral home?"

He smiled a little. "No." He glanced over his shoulder at a black Lexus parked near the curb. "Does the name Andrea Rochelle mean anything to you?"

Charlotte stopped breathing as her heart hammered against her chest. "Who are you?"

The man looked down for a few moments at his shiny black shoes, then lifted his eyes to Charlotte again. "I'm Blake, a friend of Andrea's."

Daniel stayed quiet, but he clearly recognized the name, too, as he glanced back and forth between Charlotte and this stranger.

Charlotte gazed past Blake at the car, and she thought she saw movement from inside.

"So . . . um, I just wanted to make sure I had the right person and if you knew who Andrea was."

Charlotte's knees were weak, and despite the cool fall temperatures, sweat broke out across her forehead. "Yes. I know who she is."

Blake looked over his shoulder again, then scratched his forehead and frowned as he turned back to Charlotte. "She felt like she should be here, but I can't persuade her to get out of the car. She's nervous about seeing you."

A vision Charlotte had fought to forget slammed into the forefront of her mind like a derailed train that had jumped the track and was heading right for her. The memories had haunted her for years, and now the product of those recollections was less than a basketball court away.

"Should I . . . ?" She glanced at Daniel, then back at Blake. "Should I go to the car?"

Blake raised a shoulder, then lowered it, his expression somber. "I guess it's up to you."

Charlotte looked at Daniel again.

"I think you will regret it if you don't," he said softly.

Charlotte took in a deep breath and blew it out in a slow stream.

Two

Andrea chewed on one of her painted fingernails, a lovely shade of pink she'd chosen specifically for today. And now she couldn't even bring herself to get out of the car. She watched Blake, Charlotte, and an Amish man walking toward her. *I'll meet her, confirm what I believe to be true, then put it all behind me and never see the woman again.* Andrea knew enough about her family already.

Charlotte came into view. She was an attractive woman with long brown hair, maybe a shade darker than Andrea's. She was dressed in a black maxi skirt, a tasteful dark-colored blouse, and her black kitten heels were stylish. It wasn't what Andrea had expected. Her sister didn't have any makeup on. It seemed to work for her in a plain sort of way.

She put a hand on the door handle, forced herself to open the car door, then stepped out of the vehicle just as the trio reached her. Leaving her sunglasses on, she tried to smile. "Hello."

Charlotte covered her mouth with both hands as her eyes filled with tears. Then with no warning, she threw her arms around Andrea and squeezed her in a giant bear hug. Andrea tried to hug her back, but it ended up being more of a pat on the back before she pulled away.

"I can't believe you're here." Charlotte put a hand to her chest and smiled. She glanced over her shoulder where the three men were lowering Janell's body into the ground. When she faced Andrea again, she was smiling even more. "I know this should be a sad day, but I can't help but be happy. We have so much to talk about."

Charlotte lifted up on her toes as she looked at the Amish man. "This is a miracle." She turned back to Andrea. "I was going to search for you, but I've been busy with Janell, a new job, and getting my life back together. And I honestly didn't know where to start."

Andrea's heart thumped wildly in her chest as her bottom lip trembled. "You were going to search for me, but you've been *busy*?"

Charlotte's smile faded. "Um . . . I didn't remember you until recently. I only had a faint memory of you after CPS took you away. In one of her vicious rants, Janell confirmed what happened. Trust me, wherever you ended up, you were better off not being with our parents. Ethan and I spent two horrible years in separate foster care homes, and the rest of the time . . . Well, let's just say we didn't have a lot of fond memories. I miss him terribly." She smiled again. "But I'm so happy to meet you, and I have to believe Ethan is smiling from heaven."

Andrea had never understood why she'd been the only one sent away. And she'd always assumed Charlotte and Ethan had each other to lean on, even if times had been difficult. Either way, too much time had passed with too much rough water under the bridge to seek out a relationship with Charlotte. "Listen, I know you just buried your mother, and—"

"*Our* mother."

Andrea took off her sunglasses and peered at the sister she'd never known. Andrea's sense of abandonment had festered for years. Charlotte's explanation wasn't an instant cure-all. "I have parents. Great parents. I came here today for closure. I paid a private investigator to learn about my biological background, mostly so I would have a medical history. And I know enough to be grateful that I was adopted by a kind and loving family. But I'm sorry for your loss."

Charlotte opened her mouth to speak, then shut it. Any hope of getting to know her sister crawled into the car and slammed the door.

Blake shook his head. "Sorry. I thought maybe if she acknowledged that the woman who gave birth to her had really died, that if she saw you in person . . ." He shrugged. "I thought she'd be more interested in knowing her sister."

Blake went around the front of the car, gave a quick wave to Charlotte and Daniel, and started to drive away before she had time to think. Her sister was leaving, and despite the woman's hasty demeanor, Charlotte thrust her hand into her purse and fumbled for a pen. She wrote the license number down on her palm.

"Are you okay?" Daniel pushed a few loose strands of hair away from her face.

"I guess." She dabbed at her eyes. "She said she came here for closure, and I got a definite sense that she's not interested in pursuing a relationship. I'm sure it was hard for her to find out that she was the only one not returned to her biological family, but we were just kids. Actually Andrea was a baby." Charlotte calculated that her sister would be twenty-four. Sniffling, she gazed up at Daniel. "She's pretty, huh?"

"Not as pretty as you, but *ya* . . . she's nice looking." He reached for Charlotte's hand and eyed the number written on her palm. "Are you going to try to find her?"

Charlotte shrugged. "I don't know." She'd been on emotional overload with Janell for months. And she missed Ethan even more today than usual.

Daniel squeezed her hand. "Be hopeful. She chose today to meet you, the day of your mother's funeral. No matter the situation, Janell is the common thread for you both. Maybe Andrea is still sorting things out in her head, the same way you were for months after you found your mother."

"Well, I didn't exactly go looking for Janell. She was squatting in my house—in Ethan's old house."

"Let the dust settle, then you might try to talk to Andrea, if you find her from that license plate."

"Maybe." *Ashes to ashes, dust to dust.* The phrase had been in her head all day, and she was sure the pastor hadn't said anything like that during the service.

"Are you hungry?" Daniel started toward Charlotte's big red pickup truck, and she put her arm through his and leaned her head against his strong arm as they made their way across the cemetery.

"A little." She was disappointed that Hannah hadn't invited everyone over for a meal after the service, which was customary, either at Isaac's and her house or at her parents' home. Charlotte was even more disappointed that Lena and Amos hadn't attended the funeral. *They're my real family.*

The Kings had embraced Charlotte not long after she had arrived in Lancaster County the first time, when she'd been searching for answers about her brother's death.

"I'm going to stop by and see Lena and Amos. Something doesn't feel right, and I have a hunch someone isn't telling me something."

Daniel stopped walking and turned to face Charlotte, and pain glowed in his gray eyes.

"Oh no. What is it? What's wrong?" She took in a deep breath and held it.

"No one wanted to tell you today, but Lena's cancer is back."

Charlotte bent at the waist as she crossed her hands over her stomach. "No. No. No." She recalled all the times Lena had stayed with Charlotte in Houston when she was getting chemotherapy. "They got it all. The chemo. The doctors said she would be okay." She stood up, sobbing uncontrollably. "What stage?"

Daniel pulled her into his arms and stroked her head. "I don't know. I heard Annie and my mom talking, and they said Lena would be having both her breasts removed."

"She probably should have done that in the first place, but it's such a personal choice. I'd never judge her, and I tried hard at the time not to influence her." Charlotte swiped at her eyes. "Someone should have told me. *You* should have told me."

"I was going to. Just not today. I figured you had enough on your plate."

Daniel climbed in Charlotte's truck, and it was a quiet ride to his house. Charlotte analyzed everything, and Daniel knew she was trying to sort things out in her mind. About her sister and about Lena. She'd buried the woman who gave birth to her, but Lena and Amos had slipped into the role of parents a long time ago.

Daniel reflected on how far they'd all come. Charlotte had first arrived shrouded in mystery with questions about her brother. Then she ended up moving here. She'd even

given up her most prized possession—her dog, Buddy—
when she moved to her own place. Amos had taken a liking
to the Chihuahua during the time Charlotte had stayed
with Lena and him, and Charlotte left the dog with Amos.
She'd said at the time that Buddy was better off with Amos
and Lena, but that was Charlotte, always putting others'
wants and needs before her own.

But Daniel's heart was heavy for his own reasons. It
wasn't the right time to ask Charlotte about any future
plans, but it took everything he had not to question her.

"Are you okay?" He took off his black felt hat, a dressed-
up version of the straw hat he usually wore. He set it in his
lap as the old truck rumbled down the road with the windows down, the smells of freshly cut grass, hay, and corn
wafting into the truck.

Daniel and his father had already pulled their harvest
in, but they hadn't planted nearly as much this past year,
making for an easier haul. Throughout his mother's pregnancy, they'd all tried to pitch in to lessen her load, helping
with milking, egg gathering, and the yard. Annie had
assumed most of the laundry, housecleaning, and cooking.

"Yeah, I guess I'm okay." Charlotte glanced at him
before she shifted the gears in the truck.

"It's just weird," she said in a soft voice. "I really was
going to look for Andrea, but I have a full-time job, plus I
was taking care of Janell." Lines of concentration deepened
above her eyebrows and under her eyes. "I don't understand
why she was so indifferent."

Daniel shook his head. "I don't know, but I agree with you, that maybe she's jealous or bitter that she wasn't returned to her family when you and Ethan were."

Charlotte shifted gears again, then tucked strands of hair behind her ears with one hand. "You heard her say that she had great parents, and probably a privileged childhood. You'd think she'd be happy about that, especially if she knew exactly how bad things were for Ethan and me." She blew out a heavy puff of air. "I just want peace, and it seems like every time I get close, something else kicks my heart into overdrive again." She frowned. "And not in a good way."

"Peace comes when our soul is calm. Restlessness divides us from God, from the peace only He can provide." Daniel faced forward and clamped his hands on the dashboard when Charlotte slammed on the brakes to stop at an intersection. He was undecided whether or not Charlotte was a bad driver, or if the truck just made her appear to be.

"I know." She brushed hair out of her face. "I pray for peace constantly."

"It will come." Daniel's mind drifted back to the bishop and his imposed deadline.

"Oh, I forgot to tell you . . ." She hit the gas pedal with a jerk as they shot forward. "I have someone coming to give me a quote about wiring my house for electricity. I can't afford it right now, after paying for Janell's funeral, but I figure it can't hurt to at least get a price. That way I'll know how much I need to save."

Daniel swallowed back a knot that was forming in his throat. Did she realize the implications of what she was saying? "Uh . . . I thought you said you'd gotten used to not having electricity."

"Well, I've gotten used to not using a blow-dryer or wearing makeup, but I don't have an oven, and I miss a microwave." She grinned. "And air-conditioning in the summer."

Daniel was still letting the information soak in when Charlotte spoke again.

"Just think of all the meals I could cook for you if I had a regular oven and not just a cooktop." She looked his way and smiled before she refocused on the road, just in time to hit the brakes again when a car pulled in front of her. Charlotte had said that riding in the buggies scared her, but Daniel was pretty sure they were safer in the buggy than when she was driving.

"But you never cook. You eat at Lena and Amos's *haus*, or at our *haus*, or sometimes with Hannah and Isaac. And you don't need electricity to have an oven. Ours runs on propane, the same way your stove top does. You just need a propane oven."

"Well, if I'm eventually going to get electricity, I might as well wait and get an electric oven then. I can't afford to buy one right now anyway, whether it's propane or electric."

Daniel stayed quiet for a few moments, until he couldn't stand it anymore. "What are we going to do?" He pointed a finger at her, then back at himself.

"When, now?" She didn't look at him, but she chewed on the side of her bottom lip.

"*Ya.* Now." He'd taken his hat off, but he put it back on to protect his head every time she hit a bump, lifting him from his seat. "Now . . . and forever."

Still gnawing on her lip, she shrugged. "I'm just taking things one day at a time. I have a job at the newspaper that I like now. I have to believe that I took care of Janell as best I could. And now I have to decide whether or not to seek out a relationship with Andrea."

"What about *our* relationship?" He narrowed his eyebrows as he stared at her.

"What about it? You know how I feel about you." She cast her gaze his way, then shrugged again. "I don't think there's any big rush to do anything. We've only been dating for a few months."

It seemed like an eternity to Daniel. "Charlotte, do you want a future with me?"

She closed her eyes for a few seconds, which caused Daniel's heart to hammer against his chest until she set her sights on the road again. "Do we have to talk about this right now? I just buried my mother."

"Now she's your *mother*? I thought she was just Janell." He folded his arms across his chest, knowing he was acting like a child.

"Daniel, please. Please not now. I'm upset about Lena's cancer, about Andrea, and, believe it or not, there is a level of sadness about Janell too." She pulled into Daniel's driveway but didn't even put the truck in park. "Can we talk about *us* another time?"

Daniel nodded before he leaned over and kissed her. "*Ya*, sure."

But as he got out of the truck, he thought about what the bishop had said. The clock was ticking. Maybe he should have told her that, but pushing Charlotte on any issue had never won him any points. And this was surely the biggest issue of Daniel's life.

Charlotte pulled Big Red back onto the highway as tears flooded her vision. She blinked, allowing them to trail down her cheeks as she pondered what she was most upset about. *Lena, Andrea, her mother's death, or Daniel's inquiries?* He wanted them to have a future together, but Charlotte would have to adapt to Daniel's way of life. Even though she loved him with all her heart, there was a lot to consider.

It wasn't the clothes she would have to wear, the lack of electricity, or not having a microwave or air-conditioning that she was most concerned about. As she ran her hand along the oversized steering wheel of her 1957 red Chevy truck, her stomach churned at the thought of giving up her gift from Amos, along with her independence.

Amos had made a trade a long time ago with an English man, to satisfy the man's debt. The old truck had been sitting in his back pasture until Amos got it running. She couldn't recall her father giving her more than a spanking—or worse—but Amos hadn't blinked an eye when he so freely gave Charlotte the truck.

She also couldn't imagine driving a buggy around town more than ten or fifteen miles at a time. No more quick trips to Walmart. And her trek to work via buggy was going to be a long haul through all kinds of weather. But giving up Big Red tugged at her heart in a way she hadn't expected.

But even all of those reasons didn't add up to her biggest fear. She was scared of the commitment it involved—to Daniel and to God. What if she was baptized into the faith and messed up? What if her upbringing had left her too scarred to be a good wife? She came from a substandard gene pool. Did she really want to have children? Was she capable of being a good mother?

Large families were important to the Amish folks, and Daniel was no different. He'd mentioned wanting children plenty of times in passing, even before they'd fallen in love. But for now, for today, she wanted to focus on Lena.

She turned onto Black Horse Road and started toward Lena and Amos's house. Bless their hearts for trying to protect her from the news of Lena's cancer recurrence, but she felt detached from them, from the community. Everyone else seemed to know Lena's diagnosis, and funeral or not— someone should have told her.

Maybe I think of myself more as family than they do.

She trudged up the porch steps of the King house a

few minutes later, and Lena answered the door, wiping her hands on her black apron.

"You should have told me." Charlotte didn't try to control her tears. "Everyone knew but me."

Lena pushed the screen open and held out her arms. "*Mei* sweet *maedel.*" She held on to Charlotte for a few moments, stroking her hair. "Surely, you understand why, *ya?*" Easing away, Lena cupped Charlotte's cheeks in her hands. "You said good-bye to your *mudder* today, and we felt that was enough to handle."

Charlotte gazed into Lena's eyes. In a tearful whisper, she said, "You are more of a mother to me than Janell ever was."

Lena stepped back and motioned for Charlotte to come in. Amos was sitting on the couch reading *Die Botschaft* with Buddy in his lap. She still missed the little guy: his shrill bark when she'd get home and the way he'd affectionately showered her with wet kisses as he wagged his tail. But he barely noticed her now.

Amos lowered the newspaper and took off his reading glasses when he saw Charlotte. Amos was a quiet man, but she had learned to communicate with him using few words. His expression usually said it all, and right now, his eyes were dark pools of fear as a muscle flicked in his jaw. Learning Lena was sick again was devastating for him. If Charlotte thought for one moment that she could have what Lena and Amos have, she'd hog-tie Daniel and drag him to the altar.

Amos wasn't an affectionate person, but he locked eyes with her. "We are sorry for your loss."

Charlotte sniffled. Amos assumed she was crying about Janell. "Thank you"—she blinked to clear her tears—"but I'm upset that no one told me about Lena."

Amos lowered his head for a few seconds. "Lena will be fine."

The man said it with such determination, Charlotte felt hopeful right away.

"He's right." Lena smiled as she looked down at her chest. "These breasts have properly nourished two fine children. They've done their job."

Charlotte smiled back at her surrogate mother. Lena had been brave during all the cancer treatments before, and she seemed equally confident about her diagnosis now.

"I'm sorry you are upset that we didn't tell you." Lena folded her hands in front of her. "You are our family, Charlotte, so that had nothing to do with our decision to hold off telling you this news." She pointed to the rocking chair. "Now, sit and dry your tears, *dochder*."

Charlotte happily did as she was told. She wasn't sure she'd ever heard Lena or Amos directly refer to her as "daughter," and it warmed her heart.

"Now, tell us, how did everything go today?" Lena sat in the other rocking chair as Amos cautiously put his glasses back on and lifted the newspaper.

Charlotte crossed one leg over the other and relaxed

against the chair cushion. "Okay, I guess. There were lots of flowers, and I appreciate that."

Lena smiled. "I'm glad you were pleased."

"There was a surprise guest at the funeral. Well, not really a guest." Charlotte took a deep breath. "My sister showed up."

Lena sat taller as she brought a hand to her chest. "The one you only recently found out about, or should I say remembered through your counseling sessions?"

Charlotte nodded. "Yes. It's been awhile since I told you about it, but I'd had a faint vision about Andrea. I wasn't able to put it all together until Janell confirmed that I had a sister who was taken from her when I was three or four." She paused, picturing Andrea's face, the way her cheeks dimpled, even if she wasn't smiling. Just like Ethan's used to do. But Andrea's dark eyes had burned with an emotion Charlotte recognized.

"Anyway, she was there, but she didn't seem interested in us getting to know each other."

Lena scowled. "That's a shame. I'm sorry to hear this."

Charlotte slouched back into the chair a little, kicking her foot into motion. "She paid a private investigator to find out about her background. And it sounded like she was meeting me just to put some sort of closure on the whole situation."

Lena tipped her head to one side. "Will you see her again?"

"I don't know." Charlotte stood and made her way to

the window, then looked back at Lena. "Will you be having chemo again? Are you having surgery soon? What is the plan?"

Lena smiled. "Charlotte, I am going to be fine. The doctors have already said they feel fairly confident that they will be able to get all of the cancer by removing my breasts. If I need follow-up chemotherapy, I'll be having it in Pittsburgh, most likely."

Fairly confident?

"Where does your sister live?" Lena apparently wanted to change the subject too.

"I don't know." Charlotte tapped the windowpane with her finger. "She left before I had a chance to ask her much of anything."

No matter how much her sister cited her great parents and life, Charlotte suspected something was amiss with Andrea. Charlotte had hauled bitterness around for most of her own life, and she had a way of recognizing it in others, no matter how hard a person tried to disguise the emotion. She'd carried around her own despair until she'd found her Amish friends, established a close relationship with God, and fallen in love with Daniel.

Daniel. How could she tell him about her fears? *Is love enough when there is so much to consider?* She'd hoped they could just continue on the way they were for a while longer, but Daniel was antsy. He wanted to know what the future held, and she couldn't blame him for that. She just didn't know.

Three

aniel stood beside Annie, staring out the window in the living room, his chest tightening as he watched their new houseguest slam her car door. The woman carried a red suitcase with cat pictures plastered on all sides and several luggage tags dangling from the handle. A gray purse was slung over her shoulder, a bag so big that it seemed to make her tilt to one side as she wobbled toward the porch.

"How long do you think she'll stay?" Annie brought a hand to her chest, her voice boasting enough panic to cause Daniel to shudder.

"Probably until after the *boppli* is born." Daniel quickly calculated that his mother's baby was due in three and a half weeks. "It's got all its fingers and toes by now. Maybe the baby will come early."

Annie glared at him. "We want the baby to go full term

if possible." She huffed, then refocused on their Aunt Faye, who was now carting two more smaller suitcases toward the bottom porch step where she'd left the first one. "*Ach, dear. Look at all that luggage. This doesn't look *gut.*"

Daniel lowered his head, shook it, then moved toward the front door. "I should help her carry in her things."

"Look!" Annie's voice squeaked as she pointed out the window. "She's bringing in grocery bags. Daniel, what are we going to do?" His sister sounded like a frightened child, as opposed to an eighteen-year-old young woman.

Daniel hesitated, his hand on the doorknob. Aunt Faye was known for her bizarre food offerings, particularly her pickled oysters. He eased open the door, Annie on his heels.

"*Wie bischt, Aenti* Faye." Daniel waved and forced a smile as their aunt stopped short a few feet from the porch, a bag on each hip.

"It's about time you showed up. I'm an arthritic old woman with a bad back, bunions, and corns the size of walnuts on my feet." Hunched over, and almost as tall as Daniel, Aunt Faye's loose strands of gray hair dangled beneath her Mennonite *kapp* on either side of a weathered face.

She thrust the two bags at Daniel when he got close enough to her, then shuffled past him to where Annie was standing. "The rest are in the car. I'm going to go check on your mother. I suspect she's been sorely neglected and needs tending to." She pulled the screen door open, reached for the knob, and turned around. "Annie, dear, take special care with the bag on the passenger seat. I've brought along enough pickled oysters so we can have a few with each meal this week."

Annie nodded as she trudged across the yard to their great-aunt's blue station wagon. Aunt Faye had been shunned over five years ago. Did the bishop know she was coming to stay with them? Annie had stayed with their aunt during a difficult time last year and that visit had reconnected them to Aunt Faye, even though they'd been out of touch since the shunning.

Annie had fought hard to convince their parents that she could keep up with things now that their mother was on bed rest until the baby was born, but it was their father who agreed that Aunt Faye could stay to help out. Did *Daed* have any idea about the woman's cooking?

As he carted his aunt's suitcases upstairs to the guest bedroom, he thought about Charlotte. He hadn't spoken to her since her mother's funeral two days ago, but they didn't usually talk or see each other during the workday, unless Daniel took her to lunch on days he didn't have any jobs scheduled. His part-time work building storage sheds was sporadic, and it would really drop off during the wintertime.

But Charlotte had gotten in the habit of stopping by after work, at least every other day or so. Maybe he'd pushed her too hard about the future. Their father had recently gone *ab im koff* about the usage of cell phones, demanding everyone keep them out of sight and turned off except for emergencies. Daniel had done as his father asked, but he'd tried to call Charlotte the past two nights before he went to bed, and the calls went to her voice mail. He hadn't left messages.

Annie was abusing the cell phone privilege in the evenings too. Daniel had heard her talking in a loud whisper to Jacob King recently. Her former fiancé had fled the community months ago to pursue a life in the *Englisch* world. Annie told everyone she'd gotten over him, but her tears said otherwise. Daniel hoped Jacob was okay, wherever he was, but he was glad that Annie hadn't married Jacob—even if he was Lena and Amos's son and Hannah's brother. Annie might have ended up leaving with him, and Daniel was sure his parents wouldn't survive if Annie fled their community.

What was he thinking when he got involved with an *Englisch* woman—a woman who had the potential to crush his heart—something he swore he'd never let happen again? Edna Glick might not be the woman he'd once thought she was, but she'd left a scar on his heart just the same. Now he was in his second serious relationship, and it seemed to be on shaky ground.

He was going to stay hopeful that Charlotte would be baptized into the faith, opting to share a future with him in the community he had called home his entire life. He wanted to build a life with her and have a dozen *kinner*, or at least a few. And even though Charlotte's childhood had been rough, he was sure she would be a wonderful mother. He'd watched her with the *kinner* in their district, the way she was not only nurturing but patient.

She'd overcome one hurdle after another, and bouncing back hadn't been easy for Charlotte, but over time Daniel had watched her grow into the woman she was meant to be. The woman for him.

Andrea kicked off her shoes by the door, leaving them next to a bag full of trash that needed to be carried to the Dumpster. She hoisted Bella up on her hip and kissed her on the cheek. Her daughter clutched the Hello Kitty purse Andrea had gotten her the week before at a yard sale. She'd only paid a quarter for the purse, and she filled it with thirty pennies. Bella took the purse everywhere. Maybe at eighteen months her daughter already understood the importance of money.

"Thanks for paying Penny, Blake. I think she charges too much, but Bella likes her and she's good with Bella."

"Well, the movie was stupid, so I hope the money for that and the sitter was worth it." Blake pushed a giraffe scooter out of the way with his foot as he made his way toward the kitchen in their small apartment, stomping on a roach with enough force to ensure it was flattened against the yellowing linoleum. "We gotta get out of this roach motel."

Andrea set Bella in the playpen. "Yeah, well, we need jobs to get a better place."

Blake pulled a beer from the refrigerator. "I gotta pick up Randy at the airport." He shook his head, frowning. "Then it's back to driving my tank of a car. I gotta return his jacket too."

"Well, it was fun having nice wheels for a couple of days." Andrea plopped down on the worn blue couch, careful to miss the spring almost poking through on one side. She glanced toward the middle of the floor where a package of diapers and some baby wipes lay, hoping she had enough diapers to get by until tomorrow.

Blake came into the small living room and stared at her. "I still don't get why we had to go through that charade for your sister." He took another swig of beer, then shrugged. "Then you barely talked to her."

Andrea clinched her fists in her lap. "She never even tried to find me!"

"Didn't you hear what she said? She just recently remembered you even existed." Blake picked up Bella when she started to cry, laid her down on the floor next to the diapers, and proceeded to pull down her pink pants. For someone who wasn't always a great boyfriend or Bella's father, he'd been decent to Bella. Then she started to scream.

"She's cold. And you can't just lay her on the tile floor, it's hard. Use a blanket or something." Andrea closed her eyes as Bella started to really wail. With a loud sigh she leaned her head back against the couch. She loved her daughter, but sometimes Andrea wished she had the freedom to just take a nap at will.

"I don't think you should be telling me how to take care of Bella since you wouldn't even get up to change her diaper." He put the new diaper under the baby, carelessly sprinkled some baby powder, and got Bella's bottoms back on. "You're a crappy mother, Andy."

"I've told you before not to call me that. And I'm not a crappy mother! I didn't know she was wet." When Blake wanted to hurt her, he tossed out the bad mother stuff. Andrea knew she wasn't perfect. She hadn't had very good teachers. But she'd taken care of Bella the best she could. After he finished the diaper change, Andrea cursed at him. "Just get out!"

"Gladly." He put Bella back in the playpen, still scream-ing. His face turned red as his jaw clenched. "You know, I was hoping you'd make some sort of connection with your sister, but instead you tell her about your wonderful life and parents—all a bunch of bull. Why didn't you tell her the truth? It didn't sound like she had an easy go of it either. Maybe she'd have thrown her little sister some cash, and we could have looked for a better place."

"Quit defending her. I doubt her life was anything as bad as mine."

"Well, you'll never know, I guess. I'm just glad you didn't really spend money to find out about your past and instead researched your family on your own. But I guess that little add-on lie just amped up your fake status at the moment. You're a piece of work, *Andrea*." He shook his head as he moved toward the front door, kicking the package of diapers on the way as he swigged the beer, then nodded at Bella. "Try taking care of your daughter."

I do take care of her. Andrea held her breath as he slammed the door and disappeared. *Though no one ever takes care of me.* She heard the gentle hum of the Lexus as Blake started it up. What would it be like to actually own a car like that? But Andrea would be happy with any car.

She tuned out Bella's crying. Maybe she'd made a mistake by tossing her sister to the curb. Maybe Blake was right. Her sister had been dressed in nice clothes at the funeral, probably not borrowed duds like Andrea's. She glanced around the apartment she could barely afford on government assistance. Charlotte had a job at a newspaper. What kind of money did she make?

Her gaze drifted to the front door. Andrea always wondered if Blake would come back, and so far, he had. Sometimes she picked a fight just to test him. *One day, he won't come back.* Everyone eventually left her.

Andrea picked up Bella and carried her back to the couch with her. She slouched into the seat with her baby still sobbing on her lap. Andrea rubbed Bella's back, trying to console her but was unsuccessful.

After a few seconds Bella's sobs grew louder. Andrea closed her eyes and cried along with her daughter.

⌣

Charlotte waited at the pizzeria for Daniel. He'd called her last night, and they'd agreed to meet for lunch. She'd gotten there early and used the time to proofread a project she hadn't been able to finish at work.

"*Wie bischt?*"

Charlotte looked up as Daniel slid into the bench seat across from her. She'd already ordered him a sweet tea. "Hey." She smiled, hoping he could just enjoy their time together and not question her about the future.

"You look pretty." He winked at her. "I've missed you this week."

She pushed her dark hair behind her ears, wishing she could lean over and kiss him across the table, but she knew better. Local eyes were all around them, and even most tourists visiting Paradise would find it odd for an English woman to show outward affection to an Amish man.

"I've missed you too." She sipped her Diet Coke from a straw.

"What's that?" He took off his hat and put it on the seat beside him as he nodded at the paperwork in front of her.

"An obituary I brought from work to finish proofreading. The woman lived to be 106, raised four children, had eleven grandchildren, and seven great-grandchildren." She eyed the woman's name in the headline—Lucille McAdams. "How wonderful that must feel to have lived such a long and full life, surrounded by such a big family."

Daniel leaned back and stared at her. "We can have a full life too."

Charlotte looked down for a few seconds. When she looked up, she said, "You know how I feel about you, right?" Daniel nodded once. "*Ya.*"

"And I've been making lots of progress with my new therapist, though I don't see her as often as I probably should." She bit her bottom lip as he nodded again. "I told you that I needed to be right in the head before I can be good for someone else. And I am better each day." She shook her head, grinning. "That makes me sound crazy, but you know what I mean. I want to put my childhood, Ethan's death, my parents, and everything else I've been carrying around to rest so I can feel peace. It just takes time."

Daniel scratched his forehead, avoiding her gaze. "I know."

Charlotte had sworn off lying a long time ago, and she did her best to tell the truth, but right now, she was avoiding a big chunk of truth. Fear of commitment to Daniel—and to God—kept her from taking the next step. She tried to live by God's laws, and she considered herself to be a daughter of the promise. But marriage to an Amish man would require baptism into the faith, and that seemed overwhelming.

"The bishop is putting a little pressure on me." Daniel rubbed his chin as his eyes continued to avoid hers.

Was he telling her the truth? But Daniel had never lied to her; it's not how he was raised. "What kind of pressure? I didn't think Bishop Miller put pressure on anyone. Hannah said he's the youngest and most lenient bishop you've ever had."

"He is. But he feels like you are living a semi-Amish life by attending our worship service and not having electricity. Yet you drive and aren't baptized." Daniel looked down as his cheeks flushed. "And everyone knows we are seeing each other. He wants to know what our intentions are." He finally locked eyes with her. "I'd like to know too."

"I don't think he should be putting any pressure on us. We've only been seeing each other a few months." She took another long swig of her drink.

"Charlotte . . ." He sighed. "It's not our way to be involved with someone who hasn't committed to our faith, and at the very least, that person should be thinking about being baptized. You brush off the conversation every time I bring it up."

A toned-down version of the truth was in order. "I'm just nervous. What if I'm like the rest of my family?" *And incapable of being a good wife and mother?*

"*Nee.* You are who you are meant to be in God's eyes."

They both got quiet when the waitress showed up, and Charlotte used the time to think up a response that would satisfy Daniel. After they'd ordered a pepperoni pizza and a side of bread sticks, she said, "Can't we just keep things the way they are awhile longer, before we make any huge commitments to each other?"

Daniel gazed at her long and hard. "I am already committed to you."

Charlotte couldn't imagine being with anyone else, but in her heart, she wondered if she was worthy of someone like Daniel. She stayed quiet.

He leaned back against the seat, keeping his gaze on her.

She just whispered, "I need more time."

He looked over her shoulder, then waited for two people to pass by their table. "*Ya*, okay."

She doubted he was really okay, but it was her cue to change the subject. "Hey, Hannah came by my office to deliver a cookbook I'd ordered, and she said your aunt Faye moved in." Charlotte brought a hand to her chest, grinning, as she recalled meeting Daniel and Annie's eccentric great-aunt last year, when Annie was staying with their aunt following a fight with her parents. When Daniel had tried to get Annie to return home, Aunt Faye went after him with a baseball bat. "How's that going?"

Daniel let out a soft chuckle, which was nice to hear finally. "We might have starved the past few days if *Daed* hadn't brought home some store-bought cooked chicken and snuck it to me and Annie."

"Is she trying to feed you pickled oysters?" Charlotte remembered trying one of the offerings at Faye's house. She cringed.

"*Ya*, pickled oysters and all kinds of strange stuff. Annie snuck *Mamm* some chicken, too, and put some snacks in the drawer by her bed." Daniel frowned. "But *Mamm* isn't eating much. She looks miserable all curled up in bed with the blinds drawn. Like it's nighttime all the time."

"She's due in a couple of weeks so I'm sure she's miserable, especially being put on bed rest." Charlotte raised her eyebrows. "And she's probably worried about all of you. Why did your father agree to let your aunt stay there?"

"I guess because she'll help Annie with the washing, mending, and pulling in her vegetables from the garden. They're ready to harvest, and it's a big garden. Annie was picking a few things per day, but she needs help. Between my job and helping *Daed* run the farm, it's hard for us to offer her much help in the evenings. Besides, *Aenti* Faye is a *gut* housekeeper. She can't cook but the place is clean, and *Daed* seems to think that's important to *Mamm* and best for when the *boppli* comes."

The lines on his forehead deepened as he scowled. "Do you remember Aunt Faye's cemetery room at her house?"

Charlotte giggled, then waited while the waitress set the pizza and bread sticks in front of them. "Yeah, I remember. A room that she kept keepsakes and pictures in, memories of people who had passed."

"Well, our laundry room is now Aunt Faye's cemetery room. There are pictures of dead people taped to the walls, crosses everywhere, and a bunch of other stuff." He shook his head. "*Mamm* wouldn't approve, but *Daed* said to ignore it."

"Your aunt and uncle were shunned before your uncle

died. What does the bishop think about Faye staying with ya'll?"

"There's that Texas slang that slips out every now and then." Daniel grinned. "*Aenti* Faye said that she spoke to the bishop, saying it was a medical emergency." He chuckled as he reached for a slice of pizza. "And she also told him that a herd of wild buffaloes couldn't keep her from tending to her niece, much less a snappy, new bishop who was still green around the gills."

Charlotte laughed. "Good ol' Aunt Faye."

She took a bite of pizza as her cell phone chirped in her purse beside her. By the time she swallowed and sipped her drink, she heard her voice mail chime, but she finished eating first. When she finally listened to her voice mail, she brought a hand to her chest, hoping to calm her racing heart.

"What is it?" Daniel set his piece of pizza on his plate. "What's wrong?"

She set the phone on the table. "It was Andrea. She said she got my phone number from the rehab facility where Janell had been." Unsure how she felt about the staff giving out her phone number, Charlotte wasn't going to worry about it now.

"Uh-oh. What did your sister want?"

"She wants to come see me tomorrow." She paused, staring at him. "And to introduce me to . . . my niece." She blinked a few times in disbelief. "Andrea has a child."

Daniel reached across the table and latched on to her hand. "That's *gut*. She's making an effort, *ya*?"

Charlotte nodded, blinking back tears gathering in the corners of her eyes. The baby she remembered being yanked from Janell's arms now had a baby of her own.

She let the news sink in for a few moments before she squeezed Daniel's hand and smiled. "Maybe there is hope for Andrea and me."

A baby? What had Andrea named her? Did she look like Andrea? Maybe she even looked a little like Charlotte. She smiled. Tomorrow wouldn't get here soon enough. *But why Andrea's sudden change of heart?*

Four

Daniel stared at the pork on his plate, hopeful that Aunt Faye had prepared a normal meal, but when he cut into the slab of meat, pink juice pooled and flowed into the mess of pickled oysters nearby, then found its way to a slice of homemade bread. Annie had made the bread that was soaking up the blood like a sponge.

He looked across the table at his father, who had been cutting his meat since they all sat down. Lucas Byler was a man who usually voiced his opinion, but he was quiet about the meal, even though Daniel hadn't seen him take a bite. Annie had been wise enough to move her bread far away from the pork chop before she cut into the meat, so she was happily slathering butter on her slice.

Aunt Faye wasn't eating at all, mostly moving food around her plate. Daniel feared they'd hurt her feelings, so he stuffed a large bite of oysters into his mouth, forced himself to chew, and swallowed the slimy critters. "We're blessed to have you here, *Aenti* Faye." It was the best he could do. He didn't want to lie, but to be truthful about the oysters would hurt his aunt's feelings.

But Aunt Faye didn't look up from her plate right away. When she finally raised her chin, she stared at Daniel's father.

"Lucas . . ." Aunt Faye sighed, her lip trembling a little. "I think something is wrong with Eve. I should cart her to the doctor tomorrow."

Daed stopped cutting the meat and lifted his gaze to hers. "She's supposed to be on bed rest, and she is doing that. What do you think is wrong? Is the *boppli* going to come early?"

Daniel's aunt set her mouth in a fine line. "I thought she was looking a little puny, and she said she wasn't hungry. I felt her forehead, and she was warm. So I took her temperature. She has a low-grade fever. I also took her blood pressure like the doctor instructed. And that's what has me the most concerned. Her blood pressure is way too high."

Daed's eyebrows drew inward as a pained expression filled his face. He nodded. "*Ya.* I would be grateful if you can take us both to the city tomorrow. I wonder if the doctor is in on Saturday."

"I'll call first thing in the morning. I'm sure there is a backup or emergency number if the office is closed." Aunt Faye's forehead wrinkled.

They were all quiet for a while, and Daniel was sure everyone was silently praying, as he was, that everything would be okay. Annie excused herself, crossed through the living room, and knocked on her parents' door.

Annie had been gone a few minutes when Aunt Faye looked around the table and smiled, her gaze landing on Daniel. "More oysters?"

He glanced at his father, whose head was down, then back at his aunt. "*Ya.* Sure." He looked at the napkin in his lap, a handy tool to catch food for disposal, if need be. He hated wasting food. But he disliked his aunt's oysters even more.

After struggling to finish supper, he went to check on his mother. She was sleeping, so he went upstairs to shower. On his way back to his bedroom, he heard Annie talking to someone. He wasn't normally one to eavesdrop, but he slowed his steps and listened.

"I don't know what to do to help you, Jacob. We need to tell someone what is going on, though."

Annie's voice was barely above a whisper, so Daniel pressed his ear against the door so he could at least hear her side of the conversation. Everyone in the community still worried about Jacob, and as far as Daniel knew, Jacob wasn't keeping in touch with anyone. Except Annie.

"I don't have that much money," she said, followed by a long silence. "But I'll figure something out." Annie sniffled a little. "I need to tell you something. It's about your *mudder.*" She paused for a few moments. "Her cancer is back."

Another long silence ensued. "I think everything should be okay, but she is going to have surgery soon."

Would this news cause Jacob to return home? *And what does the boy need money for?* Daniel thought he'd secured a good job selling pharmaceuticals. At least, that's what he'd last heard.

He tiptoed down the hallway when he heard Annie saying, "Okay, *ya*, we'll talk again when you are able to call."

Daniel wanted to ask Annie what was going on, but with his mother being ill, Lena's cancer returning, lack of a commitment from Charlotte, and Charlotte's sister showing up he wasn't sure he wanted to know Jacob's status. Yawning, he crawled into bed, his thoughts all over the place, but mostly he was worried about his mother.

Annie extinguished the flame on her lantern, then lay back against her pillow. Closing her eyes, she tried to see Jacob's face in her mind's eye, attempting to see him as an *Englisch* man wearing clothes that had been unfamiliar to him prior to a few months ago. What kind of haircut was he sporting now that he was no longer required to have the standard bob with bangs that men in their community had worn for generations? And, most importantly, did Jacob still love her as much as she loved him?

She'd tried to push him from her thoughts, and sometimes she could temporarily. But her ex-fiancé was still in her heart, despite her best efforts to get over him and move on. She'd accepted dates from two other suitors in their district, and both had been painfully boring. Jacob was a mess, but he was *her* mess. And he'd never been boring.

But Jacob was in real trouble, and Annie wasn't sure whether to go to his parents—who were battling their own issues with the return of Lena's cancer—or whether she should confide in her own parents, who were also going through a challenging time with her mother's bed rest until the baby arrived.

Annie threw back her sheet and blanket and sat up, dangling her legs over the side of the bed. She would confide in the one person she'd always trusted. A minute later she tapped on Daniel's door.

"Can I come in?" She pushed the door open a couple of inches. "Are you still awake?"

"*Nee.* I am sleeping. Come back tomorrow."

Annie eased the door open and gently closed it behind her. "Light your lantern. I didn't bring mine, and I can't see."

Daniel huffed, but a few seconds later a match flickered and the glow from her brother's lantern lit the room. "Can't this wait until tomorrow?"

Annie shook her head as she sat in a chair in the corner of the room. "*Nee.* I need to talk to you now."

Daniel fluffed his pillows, folded his arms across his chest, and yawned. "What about?" He held a palm up. "Wait, don't tell me. This is about Jacob, *ya?*"

Annie took a deep breath and nodded. "He's in real trouble, Daniel."

"That's what happens in the *Englisch* world." Daniel yawned again. "What kind of trouble?"

"There was some sort of problem with his last job. The company relocated, and there was a big layoff or something. Jacob ended up losing his job, and he had to take another job, but he isn't making much money. He doesn't even have a cell phone anymore. He had to borrow a phone to call me. I think he wants to come home, but he's too proud." Annie hung her head. "I know pride and vanity aren't looked highly upon." She slowly lifted her head and held her brother's gaze. "But he needs money."

Daniel stared long and hard at her. "I know you still love Jacob, Annie. But that lad can't seem to keep his head on straight." He scowled. "Did he ask you for money?"

"*Nee.* Not really." Annie shifted her weight in her chair and crossed one leg over the other. It wasn't a lie. Jacob hadn't come out and asked for money. "I told him about his mother but that I felt like everything would be okay."

The truth was, Annie knew otherwise. She'd overheard their mother talking to Aunt Faye, saying that Lena's cancer was at stage four. The women had lowered their voices to a whisper when Annie passed by the bedroom where they were chatting. But Annie couldn't bring herself to share that news with Jacob. Not yet, anyway. He had enough to worry about. And instead of telling Daniel what she'd overheard,

Annie planned to keep praying for Lena. Maybe with prayer, the cancer would reduce to a better stage.

"All you can do is pray for Jacob and hope that the boy makes good decisions." Daniel let out a heavy sigh, and they were both quiet for a few moments.

"You're worried about *Mamm*, aren't you?" Annie pressed her lips together, keeping her gaze on her brother.

"*Ya*. But *Aenti* Faye will cart her and *Daed* to the doctor tomorrow. I'm sure everything will be okay."

Annie wasn't tired, but when Daniel yawned again, she stood. "There's too much going on. Lena's cancer, *Mamm*'s risky pregnancy, and Jacob's predicament."

Daniel scratched his cheek as he fought to stifle another yawn. "Jacob's predicament is of his own making."

"I know." Annie thought back on everything she and Jacob had been through. She'd been tempted to stop taking his phone calls, but love wasn't an emotion you could corral or control. She shuffled toward the door.

"Annie."

She turned around and raised an eyebrow. Daniel patted the end of his bed, so she walked across the room and sat down. Daniel reached for her hand and squeezed.

"Let's pray about all of this. For Lena, for *Mamm*, and for Jacob." Daniel lowered his head. Annie did too. It wasn't their way to pray aloud, but she was glad when Daniel chose to do so. Annie's bottom lip trembled as she fought the tears threatening to spill as Daniel prayed for those they both loved. When he was done, she stood, kissed him on the cheek, and made her way back to her room.

By the time she climbed into bed, she could feel the Holy Spirit wrapping around her, the comfort of God's loving arms, and the peacefulness that came from heartfelt prayer. *Now, maybe I can sleep.*

Charlotte woke up early Saturday morning with Lena on her mind. She'd learned that Lena's surgery would be in a couple of weeks. Was there an urgency they weren't aware of, for it to be scheduled this quickly? Or maybe it was just easier to schedule medical procedures in Lancaster, as opposed to MD Anderson in Houston.

Charlotte wished Lena were having the surgery at MD Anderson since it was considered the top cancer hospital in the country, but Lena had assured her that the hospital in Lancaster would be fine and convenient for the family.

After Charlotte let those thoughts soak in, she recalled her conversation the night before with Andrea, when Charlotte had returned her call. Her sister didn't sound like the same woman she'd met at the funeral. She was friendly, said she already knew Charlotte's address, and would see Charlotte at ten o'clock, if that was okay. It was odd, but Charlotte was going to embrace this opportunity. She was also excited to meet her niece. *Bella.*

She picked up around her house, opened some of the windows enough to let a cool breeze swirl around, and drew some of the blinds she normally kept closed so the house would fill with sunlight. She'd come to terms with the fact that she wouldn't be putting electricity in the house anytime soon. The electrician had called her with a bid, and, as she'd expected, it was way out of reach.

Her heart thudded against her chest as her stomach churned. She sat on the couch and watched the clock on her mantel ticking away the minutes. At ten forty-five, she walked to the window and stared past the trickling of orange and yellow leaves floating to the ground. But not a car in sight.

Pacing her living room, she finally got out her cell phone and dialed the number Andrea had called from, and the call went straight to voice mail. After another hour Charlotte made a sandwich and tried to focus on a crossword puzzle. She finally fell asleep on the couch but awoke when she heard footsteps on the porch and a baby crying.

Hustling up, blinking her eyes, and almost tripping over her living room rug, she went to the door, then pushed open the screen. Andrea's eyes were swollen and red as Bella screamed so loudly her cries sounded like she was choking. The baby was clutching a little purse to her chest.

"Come in, come in." Charlotte stepped aside so they could go inside, and she quickly followed them to the middle of the living room. "Does she need a bottle or something?"

Andrea shook her head as she let a pink diaper bag slide off of her shoulder. "She just screams, all the time."

"Hi, Bella." Charlotte leaned down to get a better look at her niece, although tears streamed down the baby's flushed cheeks as she gasped for breaths. Bella's yellow shirt was stained with something purple, and she only had on one white tennis shoe.

"I must have lost one of her shoes on the way in." Andrea bounced the baby on her hip. "Please stop crying, Bella," she said softly, like maybe she'd said it a hundred times before.

"Can she have a peanut butter cookie?" Charlotte was out of her league. She hadn't been around babies much. Andrea nodded.

Charlotte left and returned with two cookies. She handed one to Bella, but the toddler slapped it from her hand.

"Bella, no!" Andrea gave Bella's hand a gentle slap, then put the baby on the floor. Bella rolled onto her stomach, buried her head in the rug, and kicked her feet, still holding tightly to the little purse. "I'm sorry she's acting this way."

Charlotte forced a smile. "Maybe this is the start of the terrible twos?" She wanted to get to know her sister, and she was curious why Andrea had changed her mind.

"Listen, I'm sorry I bolted at the funeral. I'm really sorry about that. I've just been trying to process everything." Andrea shrugged. "You know, about Janell, Ethan's death, and, well . . ." Raising her shoulders again, she spoke louder over Bella's wails. "It's just been confusing." She looked around the living room. "Can I use your bathroom?"

"Sure." Charlotte pointed down the hall. "Go through my bedroom and you'll see it on your right. Kind of a weird setup, but it's an old house."

Andrea hurried off, so Charlotte picked up the cookie and set it on the coffee table, then she tried to pick up Bella, but the child kicked both legs and wiggled on her tummy. "Hey, Bella," she said in a whisper. "I'm your Aunt Charlotte. Are you thirsty?" *Maybe your diaper is wet?* "Hey, sweetie."

Bella stopped crying, stopped kicking her feet, and rolled onto her back. Then she just stared at Charlotte, still gasping for breath a little. But it was like someone turned off a faucet. Then she smiled, and Charlotte could see a mouthful of teeth. She had blonde ringlets that hung almost to her shoulders, dimples, and long, dark eyelashes above hazel eyes.

"You are a beauty," she whispered, trying to recall what her sister looked like as a baby. She couldn't remember, though.

"Wow. How'd you do that?" Andrea walked back into the room and stopped a few feet from them.

Charlotte stood up and shrugged. "I didn't do anything. She just stopped crying." She offered Bella the cookie again, and this time she took it.

Andrea quickly helped her daughter sit up. "I don't want her to choke."

Charlotte felt like they were on borrowed time, in case Bella became unhappy again. "So, where do you and Bella live?"

"In Hershey." Andrea sat on the couch. She'd grown into a beautiful woman with thick brown hair and doe eyes that were a deep shade of brown. "Hey, are you Amish? I noticed when I was in the bathroom that there isn't any electricity." Her eyes scanned the room as if to check for power.

Charlotte shook her head. "No. This used to be Ethan's house, and he'd become Amish before he died."

"Oh, yeah. I remember reading that in his obituary." Andrea sat taller, her hands on top of her blue jeans. She had on a yellow shirt almost the same color as her daughter's.

"I know you said you hired someone to find out your background, but what a coincidence that you live so close since we both got our start in Texas." Charlotte glanced at Bella, who'd pulled a magazine off of Charlotte's coffee table and given up her hold on the purse. Bella fumbled as she tried to turn the pages, but at least she was quiet.

Andrea sighed. "I was raised in Houston, but I got curious about my biological family, so I started digging around online. But uh . . . I mean . . . uh, I eventually had to hire someone to dig around. Ethan was the first person the guy found, and unfortunately, it was his obituary that popped up when the investigator Googled his name. From there, it wasn't hard to find you and Janell, since you were both listed in the obit. Anyway, I ended up meeting a guy online—Blake—and we sort of hit it off. He lived in Hershey, so I decided to make the trip."

Charlotte glanced at Bella, who was still content, and looked back at Andrea. "Do you know about our father?"

"Yep. It can be hard to find people online, unless they're dead. Obituaries seem to show up at the top of online searches."

Charlotte heard no sound of remorse in her sister's voice, but she wanted to smooth the way. "I really was going to look for you. I was just dealing with everything, too, and Janell was a bit of a handful."

"Did it cost money to keep her in that psychiatric place?" Andrea leaned back against the couch and crossed one leg over the other.

"Some of it was paid for by the state, but a friend took care of the rest." Charlotte recalled her reaction when she'd found out that Amos was paying for part of Janell's care. *Truly my father on earth.*

"What kind of friend would help Janell?" Andrea grunted a little and glanced at Bella. "Thank God she stopped crying. I was about to lose it."

"An Amish friend helped out." Charlotte finally eased her way into a rocking chair near Bella.

"Are you going to turn Amish? From what I could see from the car, it was almost all Amish people at Janell's funeral."

Charlotte tapped a finger to her lips for a few seconds. "Um, I don't know." She thought about Daniel, feeling like they, too, might be on borrowed time. She'd committed to Ryan, her boyfriend before Daniel, but that hadn't gone well. But being with Ryan didn't require the type of commitment that being with Daniel would. Charlotte would have to be baptized, and committing herself to God was an even larger promise. She was a Christian, loved the Lord, and tried daily to be the best person she could. But in her mind, baptism represented the ultimate commitment, with plenty of room for failure.

"Is Blake your husband?" Charlotte doubted Blake was Bella's father since Andrea made it sound like she hadn't been in Hershey all that long.

Andrea shook her head. "He's been pretty good to Bella and me, but overall, I don't think it's going to work out."

"Oh, I'm sorry. He seemed nice."

Andrea rolled her eyes. "He can be, some of the time. But don't let his good looks and polite demeanor fool you. He can be a real jerk."

"Did you go to college?" Charlotte had a hundred questions. "And was it foster parents who adopted you? You said they were great; I'm relieved to hear that."

Andrea stared past Charlotte, her eyes glassy, her thoughts appearing to stray.

Andrea had hoped to avoid all of this small talk. "Yes, my foster parents adopted me. They were great. And yes, I went to college." *Lying is exhausting.*

"Wow. That's great." Charlotte smiled. "Out of the three of us, I'm glad one of us had a good experience. But

I had friends in school who had awesome foster parents, so I'm glad you did too."

Andrea shifted her weight, not wanting Charlotte to start asking a bunch of questions that would require even more lies. *What did you major in? What was your life like growing up?* She glanced at the clock on Charlotte's mantel. Was Blake awake by now? He'd come in after three in the morning. She glanced out the window at Blake's banged-up Toyota. He was going to be really mad when he woke up and saw that she'd borrowed it.

"Bella must like you because, I swear, I think she's been crying for days."

Charlotte glanced at Bella, then back at Andrea. "She seems content right now. I don't know a lot about young children."

"But you like kids, right?"

"Yes, I do. I just haven't been around babies a whole lot."

Andrea eyed the diaper bag. She wasn't even sure she had enough diapers to get through the rest of the day. Maybe Charlotte would want to go shopping, maybe even pick up a few things for her niece.

"Hey, I think I'm almost out of diapers. Would you feel like going to the store with me?" Andrea had seen what Charlotte drove—a big red truck that was definitely older than Blake's car, but Andrea suspected that Charlotte probably had more gas in her ride than was in Blake's car. Probably more money in her wallet also.

"Sure. Yeah. We can do that."

⌒

Four hours later Charlotte opened the front door carrying three bags, while Andrea followed her in with Bella asleep in her arms.

"Can I just lay her on your bed? I'll prop some pillows around her." Andrea spoke in a whisper, and Charlotte nodded.

After Andrea was out of sight and Charlotte had set the bags on the kitchen counter, she looked at her checkbook. Something was still amiss, and she hadn't been able to figure out where she'd miscalculated. But she was hoping she hadn't overdrawn her account with the purchases she'd made today. Andrea had filled a basket with diapers, baby wipes, a couple of small toys, and snacks for Bella. She'd also asked the cashier for a carton of cigarettes as they were checking out. It wasn't until then that Andrea realized she'd forgotten her wallet.

Charlotte was skeptical, but she wasn't going to deny Bella anything she needed, and she didn't want to get on Andrea's bad side by saying she wouldn't pay for the cigarettes. Although she hadn't known how expensive the habit was.

Charlotte glanced at her wall calendar. She'd missed Sisters' Day today. She tried to attend the monthly gathering of Amish women in the community, but she had opted out this time since it was at Edna's house. She enjoyed the activities: canning fruits and vegetables, working on a quilt or other craft, and sometimes taking food and visiting shut-ins. It was bad enough having to be around Edna every other week at church and the occasional social gathering. She wasn't going to spend time in the woman's home if she didn't have to.

Edna had dated both Daniel and Charlotte's brother, Ethan. Although Edna had been married when she was seeing Ethan. It was a secret Charlotte had kept for the woman, but she wasn't going to be around Edna unless she had to.

"She's sound asleep. I guess we wore her out." Andrea sat down at the kitchen table while Charlotte unpacked the bags. "I'll pay you back. Sorry about that."

"It's okay."

"Wow. We were gone for a while. I'm kinda hungry. What about you?"

Charlotte finished unpacking the bags, then looked in her small pantry. "I can make us some Hamburger Helper."

Andrea frowned. "Hmm . . . is that all you've got?"

Charlotte took a deep breath, tired herself, and said, "Yeah, pretty much."

"Okay, great."

Andrea glanced at her phone. Blake had left several text messages. The last one was more of a threat, something about throwing her out. "Maybe Bella and I can stay here tonight?"

Charlotte whipped her head around, and Andrea suspected she was getting ready to say no.

"I just thought you and I could stay up and talk after Bella went to bed, so we could get to know each other better." Hearing about her sister's life wasn't at the top of her agenda, but it would be better than going home tonight to face Blake.

"Yeah, I guess so."

Andrea smiled. "I'll go check on Bella."

Maybe finding her long-lost sister would turn out to be a good thing after all.

Five

Charlotte took a seat with the other women at worship service, which was being held at Sadie and Kade Saunders' house—actually, in their barn. After she said hello to the women nearby, she scanned the chairs facing their direction, where the men were seated. She had to look around the deacons and the bishop, seated in the middle, but she didn't see Daniel. He'd called her last night to say that his mother had been admitted to the hospital because her blood pressure was high and that he'd try to call later, but Charlotte hadn't heard from him again. Daniel's father and sister also weren't at church this morning.

She kept looking around, happy to see Lena farther down the same aisle as Charlotte, and Amos was with the men on the other side of the room. When she felt eyes on her, she made a slight turn to her left. Bishop Miller was staring at her. As their gazes met, he smiled, but Charlotte made a mental note to beeline home after the worship service. She loved the meal that was served afterward, but she'd skip it this time if it meant the bishop might try to pin her down about her future plans.

Charlotte reached into her purse and turned the volume on her cell phone to Mute, and she checked for a voice mail or message from Daniel. Still nothing. She'd left two messages yesterday, and she'd tried calling early this morning. Her stomach churned as she thought of scenarios. *Is Eve's condition critical? Is the baby at risk? Did the baby arrive early?*

Charlotte had been down this road before, and she was almost sure that Daniel's and Annie's cell phones were dead. Daniel often forgot to charge his phone, and since their father didn't approve of using them, she doubted a charger had traveled with them to the hospital. Usually, someone went to the coffee shop every couple of days to charge cell phones. Even Faye might be toting a dead phone.

Charlotte jumped when someone tapped her on the shoulder, and she twisted around to see Hannah sitting behind her.

"Have you talked to Daniel?" Hannah asked in a whisper.

Charlotte leaned closer to Hannah's ear. "Not since yesterday. Eve was admitted into the hospital for high blood pressure, but I haven't heard from him again."

"*Ya,* I know. I was at the coffee shop late yesterday

afternoon, and the owner—Sherry Winston—said a friend of hers was working at the hospital when Eve was admitted. I hope everything is okay."

"Me too." Charlotte was worried about Eve, but Andrea and Bella were on her mind too. Andrea had been sprawled out on the couch when Charlotte was ready to leave for church. Bella was sleeping in Charlotte's bed. When it became late the night before, Andrea had asked if she could just lay Bella on Charlotte's bed since the baby had slept there so well during her nap earlier in the day. So Charlotte had agreed.

But this morning, Charlotte had woken up Andrea before she left for church. Her sister huffed a little, then had shuffled to Charlotte's bed and climbed in with Bella. Would they still be there when she got home? She wanted to tell Hannah about her time with Andrea and Bella, but the deacons and bishop were starting the service so Charlotte turned around.

Large portions of the worship service Charlotte didn't understand since it was in Pennsylvania *Deutsch*, but the fellowship and closeness she felt with God made up for it. And Hannah and Lena were good about explaining things to her after the service.

She glanced at the bishop, remembering that she was going to skip the meal today. Then she looked back at Lena. She seemed thinner in the face and a little bit pale.

She tuned out the bishop's opening remarks, closed her eyes, and prayed for Lena. Charlotte couldn't stand the thought of anything happening to her. Then she prayed for Eve. And Andrea and Bella.

Andrea carried Bella into the kitchen, grateful that her daughter was in a good mood this morning. As Andrea opened the refrigerator, she tried to recall when Charlotte said she'd be home from church. Did the service last three hours? That couldn't be right. Who could sit in church for that long?

Andrea pulled out a half-empty carton of milk and found some Cheerios. She filled Bella's bottle with the milk, knowing that she should have weaned Bella off a bottle a long time ago, but sometimes it was the only thing that calmed her. She poured some of the dry cereal on a plate, gave Bella the bottle, and carted her back to the living room.

While her daughter munched on Cheerios, Andrea walked from room to room, scoping out her sister's small home, which took about half a minute. There was a living room, kitchen, one bedroom, a bathroom, and a small room in the back that looked like it could be a laundry room—assuming the house had electricity. She sighed and went back to the main room. Normally, she'd turn on the television for Bella while she ate breakfast. But no heat, no television, no lights. *How can anyone live like this?*

Andrea plopped down on the couch and sighed

again. Her sister went to an Amish church, lived like those religious people, but yet . . . she wasn't Amish, and she certainly didn't dress like the Amish.

"Bella, your aunt Charlotte must live like this because of her Amish boyfriend."

Her daughter looked up but quickly refocused on her breakfast.

Andrea glanced around the house. Ugh. She couldn't live in a place like this. She found her cell phone and called Blake.

"Hey, baby." She squeezed her eyes closed, preparing for him to lash out at her. He would threaten to throw her and Bella out. Again. Then they'd make up, and life would return to normal.

"Where's my car?" Blake's voice was frighteningly calm, but his words were clipped.

"I'm at my sister's house. It got late, and she told me I should spend the night. I'm sorry. I'm feeding Bella some cereal, then I'll leave. Maybe we can go eat some Mexican food when I get home."

"I have your stuff packed. It's by the front door. Is Bella okay?"

Andrea's heart started to beat faster. "Baby, I said I'm sorry. I know I can make things right again. Where would Bella and I go?" Blake might be through with Andrea, and that was pretty much okay, but she and Bella needed a place to stay.

Andrea shook her head, having hoped her sister was

better off than she was. Blake loved Bella, or at the least, he cared for her a lot. She'd need to play off of that. "Bella would miss you."

Blake was silent.

"And I would miss you too," Andrea said in as sweet a voice as she could muster.

"You've found your sister. You and Bella can stay with her."

Andrea twisted her mouth back and forth, thinking. She'd never heard him this serious. They'd had fights before and he threatened to throw her out, but they'd always made up. "I can't stay here. There's no electricity or TV."

"Charlotte seemed like a decent person. She'll make sure you and Bella have a roof over your heads and food to eat. Kenny is on his way here to give me a ride. I found Charlotte's address in all of your notes. I'll bring your stuff. And you better not leave in my car. I'll call the police and report it stolen."

She blinked back tears. "Why are you doing this to us?" Her heart wasn't exactly broken, but fear wrapped around her. "I don't even know Charlotte. And how can you expect me and Bella to live in these conditions?"

Blake grunted, followed by a slight chuckle. "Guess you should have thought about all that before you stole my car, refused to answer my calls, and didn't even come home. I'm done, Andy. *Done*."

Andrea's jaw dropped as she searched for something to say that would change his mind.

"See you in about an hour."

Call Ended. She tossed her phone back in her purse. How many minutes did she have left? "What now, Bella?"

Her daughter stood up, walked to Andrea, and offered her a handful of cereal. "Momma . . ." Bella touched her cheek, and the gesture brought forth a wave of tears. She pulled Bella into her arms and cried.

"No cry, Momma," Bella said, her cheek next to Andrea's.

I'm a horrible mother. She wanted to be a better mother, a better person. But right now, she only had survival on her mind. What if Charlotte refused to let them stay with her? *Surely, she won't do that.* Andrea held Bella closer.

"I love you, sweet pea. I'm gonna somehow make things better for us."

Andrea kicked her feet up on Charlotte's coffee table, sighed, and watched the minutes on her data plan click by as she checked Facebook and Twitter. She bought a phone card at Walmart once a month, however much time she could afford, but she usually ran out of minutes before the end of the month. And now she was almost out of battery power.

A cool breeze wafted through the screened window she'd opened earlier, followed by a rustling sound. Andrea set Bella on the floor with her plate of cereal, then walked to the window. An Amish woman was in the yard. With a shovel. From her profile the woman appeared to be in her twenties, maybe close to Andrea's own age. The woman took several strides into the yard, then pivoted to her right like a soldier, before she began walking again. Then she crammed the shovel into the grass and bore down on it with one foot.

What the . . . ? Andrea wiped her eyes with a tissue and picked up Bella. She opened the wooden door, then pushed the screen wide and stepped onto the porch. The woman spun around and brought a hand to her chest, then hurriedly pulled up the shovel and started across the yard.

"Hey!" Andrea hustled down the porch steps. "Wait!"

The woman looked over her shoulder, waved, and then rushed away. A horse was tethered farther down the road. She called out again, but the woman only walked faster.

Andrea set Bella on the porch when she started to squirm. "Bella, what was that woman doing?"

Her daughter squatted down and reached for a lady-bug.

"Don't eat it. Just look at it." Andrea kept her gaze on the woman until she was out of sight.

Even in Andrea's world, people didn't dig up other people's yards. *Unless they are looking for something important.* She picked up Bella, went back into the house, and found a shovel she recalled seeing in the area that resembled a laundry room. She hauled it back through the living room and stopped to check the clock on the mantel. She didn't know when Charlotte would be home, and Blake probably wouldn't be here for over an hour.

Bella sat in the grass while Andrea tried to find the spot where the woman was attempting to dig. She'd barely started to look when a car barreled up the road. She let the shovel fall to the ground. She recognized Kenny's car. A minute later, Blake opened the car door and stepped out. *He must have driven a hundred miles an hour to get here that fast.*

Without looking at her, he opened the trunk and pulled out Andrea's big black suitcase and her checkered overnight bag that she'd had for as long as she could remember. She thought her second foster mother had given it to her. Andrea had loved the six months she'd spent with Lizette and her husband, Bob. She'd prayed every night that they would adopt her. But when Lizette got pregnant, things started to change, and without much warning Andrea was back at the children's home where she'd started out.

She'd been only ten at the time, but she could still remember the way she felt when she realized that God didn't help everyone. Only some people. And she, apparently, wasn't worthy of His help or love.

But as Blake set a brown paper bag on the ground, his face was marked with loathing. One of her shoes peered over the top of the sack.

A suffocating sensation tightened her throat. *It really is over.*

Blake was in his car and leaving before Andrea could cross the yard to get to him, Kenny driving behind him in his car.

"Aren't you going to say bye to Bella?" she asked in a whisper as they drove away, spinning gravel behind them as if they couldn't leave fast enough. *Good riddance.*

But as tears threatened to spill, she sniffled and walked back to where Bella was sitting in the grass, pulling green blades and throwing them in the air. Andrea picked up the shovel, and without much effort, she located a patch of grass, slightly flattened where a shovel had been shoved into the dirt.

Daniel stood next to Annie as they both gazed upon their new sister. Bundled into a cocoon and donning a pink fitted cap on her head, the baby was in a crib at the hospital nursery. Daniel had been told that under normal circumstances, a newborn stayed in the room with the mother. Monitors beeped and other machines hummed and chimed as nurses wove in and out of the maze of tiny infants being cared for.

"She's beautiful, isn't she?" Annie laid a gentle hand on the white blanket that engulfed this tiny new life.

"*Ya*, she is."

The baby opened her eyes and looked at Annie, who smiled. "I hope her eyes stay that dark shade of blue."

Daniel tried to smile, but he was lost in a thick fog of emotion, a place where gratitude swirled and collided with fear. Sorting things out in his mind was giving him a headache, but even worse . . . a heartache.

"I need to call Charlotte, but my phone isn't charged." Daniel rubbed his forehead, stifling a yawn. "Have you heard from Jacob?"

Annie nodded. "*Ya.* I told him about everything." She continued to touch the baby here and there, the tip of her finger caressing the little one's cheek. "He knows his mother's surgery is soon, and he wants to come home. But . . ." She blinked a few times, and Daniel knew that his sister was dealing with a lot of things right now too. "He doesn't have the money to get a ticket home, and he's worried about how his return will be received."

"How much does he need?" Daniel wasn't one to throw money at a problem without giving it some thought, but with everything going on in their lives, this seemed like an easy problem to tackle.

"I'm not sure." Annie withdrew her hand when a nurse headed their way.

"I'll get Jacob the money to come home," he whispered as the nurse eased up to the crib.

"Thank you." Annie smiled, then turned to the nurse. "Is she doing okay?"

A nurse who didn't look much older than Annie said, "She is perfect. And probably a little hungry by now. Do you want to feed her?"

Annie's face lit up. "*Ya*, I would."

Daniel waited while Annie sat in a nearby chair, then the nurse handed their tiny sister to her, along with a bottle. "She should drink two or three ounces, and maybe try to burp her halfway through it." The nurse smiled, pulled a chart from the side of the crib, scanned it, then put it back. "Holler if you need something."

Annie nodded as she gently rocked and fed their new sister. It brought back memories of Daniel holding Annie when he was eight years old. The difference was, Daniel could still remember feeling awkward, afraid Annie might break. But she handled this new baby like a pro. Years of babysitting jobs, he assumed.

"I haven't seen *Aenti* Faye in a while." Daniel eyed the name tag hanging from the crib. *Baby Byler.*

"She went home to clean house and prepare supper. I offered to go with her, but she said I should stay here." Annie glanced up at Daniel and cringed. "Can we maybe get the driver to stop at a burger place on the way home?"

Daniel didn't have much of an appetite, but he nodded. "We can't keep feeding *Aenti* Faye's food to the pigs and chickens when she's not looking."

"It's better than the alternative, death by pickled oysters." Annie grinned, but as Daniel's eyes drifted back to the name tag, so did Annie's gaze, her smile fading. "She needs a name."

"Is *Daed* still in the room with *Mamm*?"

Annie pulled the tiny bundle up on her shoulder and rubbed her back. "*Ya*, as far as I know." Following a tiny burp from their sister, Annie said, "What are we going to do, Daniel?"

He took a deep breath. "I don't know. *Mamm* would

want to make sure that *Daed* was eating, though. I'll check on him before we leave." Despite his best efforts, Daniel's voice shook as he spoke.

"I haven't heard of that thing *Mamm* has . . . eclampsia." Annie blinked a few times, and her expression begged for comforting words from him. "Do you think she'll be okay?"

A heaviness centered in Daniel's chest as he fought the growing lump in his throat. "*Ya.* She will be. Then she and *Daed* will choose a name."

Annie's eyes stayed locked with Daniel's. "What if she doesn't wake up from the coma?"

"She will." *She has to.*

Six

Charlotte pulled Big Red into her driveway, a mixture of relief and disappointment sweeping over her when she saw Blake's car gone. She'd hoped to spend more time with Andrea and Bella, but she was also exhausted, so a nap later didn't sound bad either.

She checked her phone again, still waiting to hear from Daniel, but no messages. Climbing the porch steps, she heard movement inside, and when she opened the door, she heard music coming from her bedroom.

"Andrea?" She took slow, deliberate steps, just in case it wasn't her sister.

"In here."

Charlotte picked up her pace and stopped just over the threshold, slamming her hands to her hips. She opened her mouth to tell Andrea to get off her bed and how dare she go through her stuff, but when her sister lifted her head and held up a picture of Ethan, Charlotte eased closer to her. Bella was lying on the bed sucking her thumb, her eyelids heavy.

"Bella got in your closet when I went to the bathroom, and when I returned to get her, I saw these pictures stacked in this hatbox, some of them with names on the back." She glanced at the picture for a long while, smiling. "Ethan was handsome."

Charlotte sat on the foot of the bed, tucked her legs underneath her, and picked up a picture of their brother in a pair of swim trunks at the beach. "Yes, he was."

They were both quiet as they looked through the large collection of photos. Some were Charlotte's, and some were pictures Ethan had. She'd recently put them all in one place. She glanced at Bella when she caught movement out of the corner of her eye. Bella edged closer to Charlotte and lay her head in her lap. "Aw," she whispered as she ran her hand the length of Bella's hair.

"Wow. You're really good with kids. She doesn't normally cozy up to someone this fast." Andrea pulled out another handful of pictures from the hatbox, then took her time flipping through them. "What was Ethan like?"

Charlotte put one hand on Bella's back, and she picked up another picture of Ethan, this one also on the beach. She fought the lump forming in her throat. "He loved the water. Beaches, lakes, rivers—it didn't matter. And he was kind, thoughtful, and probably as messed up as I used to be." *And I loved him very much.*

She dug a few more photos out of the box. "I told you,

we weren't as fortunate as you. Our parents didn't know how to parent, and foster care was no picnic either." A shiver ran down Charlotte's spine as she recalled the foster family she'd been with, then she closed her eyes and forced the memory away. "Anyway, I've seen a counselor most of my adult life. I have a therapist here, but I probably don't go as often as I should."

"You don't seem messed up." Andrea looked up, her expression stilled. Maybe she was waiting for Charlotte to elaborate.

Charlotte shrugged. No need to infuse survivor's remorse into her sister's psyche by explaining the pains associated with Ethan's and her upbringing.

"Well, I like to think that I've come a long way, partly through counseling. But I've learned a lot from Daniel and my Amish friends about faith, hope, and the power of prayer." Charlotte kept her gaze on a picture of Ethan sitting in front of a fountain somewhere. "And someday, I'll see Ethan again in heaven."

"I don't believe in heaven or hell." Andrea made the statement as definitively as if she'd just spoken the truth instead of voiced an opinion. "But before you go all righteous and religious on me, let me say this: I do believe in a higher power." She waved an arm around Charlotte's bedroom. "Someone is responsible for all of this, the planets, the earth, our existence . . . I just don't think there is anything after this." She shrugged, picked up another picture, then whispered, "Ashes to ashes, dust to dust."

A chill ran the length of Charlotte's spine as she recalled the poetic words she'd heard at Janell's funeral. But she'd run into this type of nonbeliever before, and while Charlotte had always believed in God and an afterlife, it wasn't until after she'd invited the Holy Spirit into her life, accepted Jesus in her heart, and developed a real relationship with God the Father that everything changed. People could tell you about it until they were blue in the face, but knowing God was personal. Understanding beyond a shadow of a doubt that there was a heaven and a hell was an all-knowing feeling that's hard to explain.

But Andrea was Charlotte's sister, and she could only dream of a day when they would be united with Ethan in heaven, so she was going to try. But people got funny about the subject if you preached at them. *Show me, God. Tell me what to say.*

"If you believe a higher power is responsible for all of this"—Charlotte imitated Andrea's wave of an arm—"then how can you be sure there isn't anything after this life?" It was a poor start at a conversation Charlotte didn't know how to have, but she stared at her sister and waited for an answer.

Andrea flashed an expression filled with disdain, her dark eyes slicing the space between them. "The Bible is fiction. No one can prove that it's real. And yes, believe it or not, I've read it—cover to cover." She paused. "Don't you think I want to believe?" She nodded at Bella. "Don't you think I want to spend eternity with her?" She stared long and hard at Charlotte. "It just doesn't exist. And there is nothing you can say to make me believe otherwise."

Oh, how I hope you're wrong. Charlotte searched her heart and soul for the right words, but how did anyone explain the love of God and the sureness not only of His existence, but of life after death? Charlotte wasn't qualified. And as she pondered this dilemma, her thoughts drifted to her fears about commitment to Daniel and the promises she wanted to make to God, the commitments that terrified her.

If she was as strong in her faith as she thought, why couldn't she be baptized and confident that she would do her best? That she would still sin but that God would forgive her? She'd faced so many demons in her life, it should be easy to embrace the facts she knew to be true and incorporate them into a life and future with Daniel.

Charlotte picked up another picture, her heart heavy with memories. She wanted to get to know Andrea better, and preaching to her about faith and the reality of heaven might push her sister away. "Aw, look at this one." She handed Andrea a picture and also noticed that Bella had fallen asleep in her lap. "That's Ethan's baseball team. It's the only sport I remember him playing, and only for a year."

Andrea gazed at the picture, then lifted her eyes to Charlotte. "I guess you believe he's in heaven."

"Yes, I do."

"I thought even holy rollers didn't think suicide won you a trip to heaven." Andrea raised an eyebrow.

Charlotte lifted one shoulder, lowered it slowly, and sighed. "Yeah, I guess some people think you go straight to hell if you kill yourself, but I'm not one of them, especially since I think mental illness often plays a part in someone choosing to take his own life. Like in Ethan's case. I don't think he could handle the rejection of a woman he was in love with, and I think that, combined with his childhood and depression . . . well, I just think he couldn't see his way past it all."

⤖

Maybe Charlotte doesn't really believe in a heaven or hell after all. Andrea was disappointed that her sister hadn't tried to convince her that there was a heaven.

"Do you think our parents are in heaven?" Andrea wasn't sure where this sudden interest in this subject was coming from, but an unwelcomed sense of curiosity poked at her mind like a cattle prod snapping her to attention, as if she wasn't going to have any peace until she had more information.

"I don't know. That's for God to decide." Charlotte eased Bella's head out of her lap and onto the bed before she stood and folded her arms across her chest. "So, anyway . . . I'm guessing Blake picked up his car. Do you need me to take you somewhere? Where do you plan to stay?"

Apparently Charlotte wasn't going to try to push her beliefs on Andrea, which she should be happy about, she supposed. "I don't really have anywhere to go." She kept her eyes down, but then she glanced at Bella before looking up at Charlotte. "Maybe we can stay here for a while?"

Her sister's face turned pale. "Um . . . I don't have an extra bedroom or a crib or . . ."

"We've never had much. We don't need much." Andrea squeezed her lips together and avoided Charlotte's gaze as she contemplated a way to take back her words. Charlotte thought she'd had a great childhood. Why had she felt the need to lie about it before? "I mean, when we moved here from Houston, we didn't bring a lot with us."

"Don't you have a job?" Charlotte frowned a little.

"No. The only jobs I could find didn't pay enough to justify day care for Bella. But I'll get a job." Andrea swallowed hard. She could practically see the wheels in Charlotte's mind spinning.

"Andrea, I'm glad you and Bella found me, and I want us to all get to know each other better, but I should probably tell you . . . I was struggling financially when I moved here. I don't make a whole lot at my job at the newspaper, even though I love it. And I had to pay for most of Janell's funeral, so I'm going to try to get my finances in order even more than I had before."

She paused, as if waiting for Andrea to say that it was okay, that she'd find somewhere else to stay. "And I don't even have an oven or a microwave. Luckily, I get invited to supper most nights by either Daniel, my friend Hannah, or her parents, Lena and Amos." Charlotte got a faraway look in her eyes. "I don't know how I'll ever pay them all back for the kindnesses they've shown me." She refocused on Andrea. "I just think your parents can take better care of you and Bella than I can."

"I can't go back there."

"Where? To your adoptive parents? Why?" Charlotte tipped her head to one side, frowning again.

"Um . . . they are just too strict." *Partially true.* She chose to omit the part about getting thrown out of the house a couple of years ago for stealing her mother's diamond ring. That event had earned her a bloody nose at the hand of her father before he tossed her out. Time in a women's shelter and an unplanned pregnancy had followed.

But those days were behind her. Having Bella had changed all of that. She'd reached out to her parents after Bella was born, since Andrea had changed, but their clipped tone and refusal to help their adopted daughter and granddaughter had stung too much.

Charlotte lowered her head as she scratched her forehead, then looked back up. "Do you really want to sleep on my couch every night?"

I've slept in much worse places. "I don't mind at all." In truth, she'd woken up with a stiff back.

"I, uh . . . I guess it's okay for a few days."

Andrea breathed a huge sigh of relief. "We won't be any trouble." She smiled but recalled an earlier event. "Hey, on a different note, there was an Amish lady digging in your front yard today."

"What?" Charlotte eased herself back onto the bed next to Bella. "Digging for what? Digging up a plant or something?"

"No. She was in the middle of your yard with a shovel. Maybe she's crazy or something."

"I don't have any *crazy* Amish friends."

Andrea shrugged. "I don't know then." She picked up another picture of Ethan. "Look, this is weird." She handed the photo to Charlotte. "There are butterflies all around him, and even two on his arm."

Charlotte smiled. "I know. Isn't that something? Ethan always attracted butterflies. Some people believe that they're angels or messengers from heaven trying to get our attention. I don't know if that's true, but I love this picture. It was taken in our parents' backyard during one of the more tolerable summers we had as kids." She handed it back, and Andrea waited for Charlotte to elaborate about heaven again, but she didn't.

Andrea had an answer to every religious question that had ever been thrown at her, a zillion ways to rebuke the theory that there was life after death. But she wanted nothing more in the world than to believe she'd spend an eternity with Bella, that she'd have an opportunity to be a better person and a better mother in another life.

When Charlotte's phone rang, she rushed to the living room and found her purse, where she'd slung it onto the couch when she got home. "It's Daniel," she said in a loud whisper. "I gotta take this."

She answered, then walked onto the porch, down the steps, and into the yard, far enough away that Andrea hopefully couldn't hear her conversation.

"*Wie bischt*, I'm sorry I haven't called before now. *Mei* phone was dead, but I finally borrowed a charger."

Charlotte's chest hurt as she listened to Daniel explain about Eve, how she was in a coma after delivering a healthy baby girl.

"*Mei daed* won't leave her side. And he said we aren't naming the baby until *Mamm* wakes up. I don't think he's been to see the baby in the nursery since she was born."

Charlotte swiped at a tear. "I'm so sorry." She thought about how unqualified she'd felt to lead Andrea into God's light. Charlotte still struggled with her own faith sometimes. Despite his strong faith, Daniel was hurting— whether he believed his mother's condition to be God's will or not. "What can I do?"

"Annie and I need to go home for a while. We don't really want to leave, but *Daed* said that Annie needs to help Aunt Faye, and I have plenty of chores to do this evening and early tomorrow morning before I go to work. We've got a couple of small jobs." He took a breath. "I can hire a driver, but I was wondering if—"

"Of course. I'll pick you and Annie up at the hospital. I want to see the baby anyway." She looked over her shoulder. "Speaking of babies, I have a lot to tell you too."

Daniel listened to Charlotte's brief rundown about her sister and her sister's child. He wanted to be happy for Charlotte—that they'd all reconnected. But one thing Daniel knew about Charlotte was that she sought order in her life, and upheavals caused her to lose her sense of God's peace. He'd explained to her before that the more God challenged us, the more blessings would be forthcoming. But even as he had the thought, Daniel felt a restlessness he couldn't identify about the situation with his mother.

"I need to go back inside, but Annie and I will go outside in a few minutes and wait for you."

After he ended the conversation, he went to his mother's room. His father hadn't moved from his chair by the bed, and he barely glanced at Daniel when he came into the room.

"*Daed*, Charlotte is going to pick up Annie and me in a little while. Have you eaten?" Daniel's gaze drifted to his mother. A long tube in her throat seemed to be breathing for her. Her cheeks were sunken in, her color pale, and someone had put on her *kapp*. It was lopsided, but his mother would be grateful, not wanting people to see her without her prayer covering.

"*Ya*, I ate." His father's elbows were resting on his knees as he cupped his chin, the length of his beard nearly to his knees.

Daniel stroked his clean-shaven chin. When would he have the honor of growing a beard? *When I'm married.* He was starting to wonder if that was going to happen. He thought about the bishop's nudge recently. In his heart Daniel knew Charlotte loved him, and that should be enough, but he feared that for Charlotte, it might not be.

He glanced at a half-eaten bag of Doritos on the bedside table. "Do you want me to get you something from the cafeteria?" Daniel looked out the window as it started to sprinkle.

"*Nee.* Tend to the needs at our home. I will be fine here with your *mudder.*"

Daniel rubbed his chin again. "Do you want to go see the *boppli*? Annie was able to hold her and feed her earlier."

Daed shook his head, his eyes staying on his *fraa.* "I will see her later."

Daniel took a final look at his mother before he turned to leave. He was almost out the door when his father called his name.

"The next time you come to visit, can you bring some of Faye's pickled oysters?"

Daniel nodded, although his father despised the oysters. As he walked down the hospital hallway to find Annie, he recalled what the doctor had said. "*You can talk to her. We don't know how much a comatose person can hear, but there have been all kinds of things that snap a person to consciousness.*"

Daniel smiled to himself. A whiff of Aunt Faye's oysters might be exactly what the doctor ordered.

But when he rounded the corner, his smile faded. Annie rushed to him in tears.

Seven

nnie pulled a handkerchief from the pocket of her
black apron, blotted her eyes, then blew her nose.

"What's wrong?" Daniel's eyebrows furrowed as the
lines across his forehead deepened.

Sniffling, Annie stuffed the hanky back in her pocket
and lifted her chin. "I'm fine."

Daniel stiffened. "You don't look fine."

"It's Jacob. He's having some financial problems, and
he wants to get home before his mother's surgery." Annie
wasn't going to lie, but she wasn't planning on telling her
brother the entire truth—that Jacob was also on the run
from some bad people he owed money and that she was
afraid for him.

"You already told me that, and I told you I'd help. How
are you going to get Jacob the money though?" Daniel
relaxed his stance a little as he looped his thumbs beneath

his suspenders. He reminded her of their father when he did that.

"He said there is something called Western Union." She swallowed back the knot in her throat. "But I need to get the money to him quickly. And he's still worried about how his return will be received."

"He wasn't baptized, so it isn't like he was shunned. He's free to come back at any time."

Annie's bottom lip trembled a little. "I know. It's just that he hasn't kept in contact with his family, only with me." She recalled what she'd overheard at the market. "I think Lena is sicker than anyone is letting on. They are proceeding with her surgery so quickly. My friend at the bakery said it took almost two months before they scheduled her mother's stomach surgery. And Lena didn't look good the last time I saw her, which was at Sisters' Day. She'll be okay, Daniel, *ya*?"

He nodded. "*Ya*, she will be okay. And *Mamm* will wake up soon, too, and be able to hold our new sister."

"Speaking of sisters . . . have you heard any more about Andrea and Bella?"

"I think they're going to be staying with Charlotte for a few days."

Annie widened her eyes. "Charlotte doesn't really know her sister, and you said the woman didn't have much to say at the funeral."

"*Ya*, but there is a baby involved, so I reckon we would have taken them in also. *Ach*, and before I forget, *Daed* asked if you would bring some pickled oysters tomorrow when you and *Aenti* Faye visit *Mamm*."

"Goodness me. Why?" Annie crinkled her nose.

"He didn't say, but I suspect he's hoping the smell will cause *Mamm* to wake up."

She sighed. "Wouldn't that be something?"

"Charlotte's going to pick us up. I told her we'd be outside waiting."

Annie wanted to see their sister one more time, but Daniel said they didn't have time. "But we're all she has right now. *Daed* won't leave *Mamm*'s side, and someone needs to hold the *boppli* so she knows she hasn't been forgotten." She rolled her bottom lip into a pout. "Just a quick peek?"

Daniel started walking, and Annie got into step with him. "*Ya*, okay. But we need to make it fast. My phone is dead again, so Charlotte can't call, and I don't want her sitting out there waiting on us. She will probably want to come in and see the *boppli* anyway."

They were quiet as they walked the hallways. A few babies cried from nearby, and a siren was blaring from one of the rooms with a blue light flashing. Daniel was pretty sure that meant trouble for the patient in that room. As they rounded the corner, they came to the nursery, stopped to wash their hands, then punched in the access code they'd been given to enter. A few moments later, they were standing by Baby Byler's crib.

"Let's give her a name, at least for now, Daniel. *Mamm*

and *Daed* can change it when *Mamm* wakes up." Annie gazed upon their new sister sleeping soundly, still cocooned in a pink blanket and wearing a fitted little hat the same color.

"*Ya*, okay. What should we temporarily name her?" Daniel leaned closer. "She's cute."

"Isn't she?" Annie scooped her into her arms. For a long time she'd dreamed about Jacob and her getting married and having a family of their own. But those dreams had become scattered and detached when Jacob fled their community. Jacob was now on the run and nervous about coming home, and Annie was equally as anxious about seeing him face-to-face, wondering if they would resume their courtship. She didn't see how. Too much had happened, and months had passed since they'd seen each other. But her heart still beat faster when she thought of Jacob.

"What about Grace?" Annie breathed in the scent of the new life in her arms, then looked at her brother. "What do you think?"

Daniel nodded as he reached over and touched Grace's cheek. "That sounds nice."

Charlotte leaned her head back against the seat of her truck while she waited for Daniel and Annie, thankful the rain had stopped. Her head felt like it might explode, right along with her heart. She'd been battling the start of a migraine since earlier in the day, and as worry threatened to consume her, the headache reached full force. Daniel and Annie walked out the hospital's front doors just as dusk was settling in.

"The baby nursery just closed for today," Daniel said as he slipped into Charlotte's truck beside her, then Annie climbed in next. It was a tight squeeze for three people, especially with Charlotte switching gears, but they'd done it before.

"Okay. I'll see the baby sometime this week. I'm sure she's precious." Daniel and Annie were quiet, but Annie nodded. "How's your mom?" Charlotte had been praying that Eve would wake up, but Daniel would have gotten word to her if that had been the case.

"The same," he said, his gaze on the road.

Charlotte pulled the knob for the headlights, and no one said much on the way to the Byler house. After Annie thanked Charlotte for the ride, she got out of the truck. Daniel inched away from Charlotte a little, but he didn't leave.

"Are you okay?" She took a deep breath. "It seems like a lot is going on . . ."

Daniel cupped both her cheeks in his hands and pulled her to him, kissing her in a way that would pose great temptation for them if she didn't slow things down. She returned the passion, but only for a few moments before she eased away. She'd barely taken a breath when

Daniel kissed her again, with an urgency Charlotte hadn't felt from him before.

"Hey." She put her hands on his and lowered them to her lap. "Slow down there, big fellow." She grinned, squeezing his hand three times.

Daniel wasn't smiling, but he kissed her gently on the lips, then eased away. "I want to be with you, Charlotte. Forever. And I want to know what you think about that."

She closed her eyes, searching for words, her head really starting to pound. "I don't think we should talk about this now. Not with all that's going on." She held her breath while she waited for him to blast back, but he just slid to the edge of the seat and stepped out of the truck.

"*Danki* for the ride." He closed the truck door. *More like slammed it.* She was tempted to get out and follow him, tug on his shirt, and tell him he needed to have a little patience, but she didn't move. Daniel had a lot on his plate. *God, what should I do?*

She thought she heard a small voice say, *Let him go.* Or did she just imagine that? Did she need God's permission to break Daniel's heart—and hers? How could she marry him when she hadn't been able to commit to the way of life required to have a future with him?

Against her better judgment she opened the truck door, and the loud squeaky hinge called out to Daniel before he hit the porch steps. He waited for Charlotte as she marched across the yard.

"I know you want to know if we have a future together,

Daniel." Charlotte touched his arm, but he stiffened. "I know the bishop is pressuring you about me, but we don't have to decide everything tonight."

Daniel narrowed his eyebrows. "*If* we have a future? I guess I assumed we did have a future, but that you weren't ready to act on it anytime soon. But maybe I'm wrong. So, I'm asking you, Charlotte, do you plan to be baptized into our faith? Yes or no?"

"I—I . . ." She pressed a finger to her temple. "My head is splitting. Can we please do this another time?"

"It's a yes-or-no question, Charlotte."

Daniel held his breath, wishing right away that he hadn't forced the issue. Charlotte was right. A lot was going on. But his heart was at risk, and it had been since the day he let himself fall in love with an *Englisch* woman. It seemed to Daniel that leaning on each other would help them both to get through these difficult times, but as Charlotte's eyes filled with tears, he wanted to take back the question. He wanted to hold her, to pray with her—that his mother would wake up, that Lena would be okay after her surgery, that Annie wouldn't cry about Jacob so much. Daniel was sure there was more, but as a tear spilled down Charlotte's cheek, at the moment her answer was the most important thing in his world.

"I can't believe you are pushing me on this right now. It's not as easy as a simple yes or no."

This was it. She was going to tell him she didn't love him enough to go through the changes necessary to be with him. But he'd never told her that he'd go anywhere with her. Maybe now was the time to do so.

"Charlotte . . ." He pushed back a long strand of her brown hair as the moon dimly lit the front yard behind her. "I'm not asking you to become Amish. I'm asking you if you want to be with me for the rest of our lives."

Another tear rolled down her cheek. "You'd leave all of this for me?" She lowered her gaze, dabbed at her eyes, then looked back up at him, her lip trembling. "You'd be shunned, Daniel. You wouldn't be able to share a meal with your family. You couldn't go to worship service. You would be ousted by the people you love." She stared at him, seemingly holding her breath now.

Was she waiting for him to repeat himself? Hearing her list the realities of his words caused his heart to fall to the pit of his stomach.

"*Ya*, I would," he finally said. "I don't want to be without you."

Charlotte wrapped her arms around him and buried her face in his chest. She clung to him like a fearful child, clutching his shirt as she cried.

She can't tell me. But he knew. She wasn't going to ask him to be in her world, away from his family. And she wasn't going to convert.

"Where does this leave us?" He stroked her hair as she kept her head against his chest. Could she hear the fear in his heartbeat?

"I don't know," she said in a soft whisper.

Daniel felt the ground shift beneath his feet.

$\sim$

Andrea sat on Charlotte's couch with only the light from a propane lamp in the yard illuminating the area around her. Bella was asleep on the couch beside her. She'd tried to light one of the lanterns on Charlotte's mantel, but her lighter was out of juice, and she hadn't been able to find any matches. Bella had thrown up twice earlier from too much orange juice, Andrea suspected. They'd run out of milk, and that was all Andrea could find, except water. And the well water coming out of the faucet was almost the color of milk as she'd poured some in a glass. It eventually cleared, but Andrea wasn't sure whether it was okay to give to Bella.

She glanced around the living room, shadowed and mostly dark. Was this a mistake? And how could her brother, whom she didn't remember, and her sister both live in this little house? It was isolated, there wasn't any electricity, and there wasn't any heat or air-conditioning. And there wasn't much food in the pantry or refrigerator.

She hoped Charlotte would be home soon and that they'd be heading to someone's house—*anyone's* house—to eat. Andrea jumped when headlights hit the window behind her. A minute later Charlotte walked in.

"Thank God." Andrea spoke in a whisper so as not to wake Bella. She eased off the couch.

"Why's it so dark in here?" Charlotte put her purse on the coffee table.

"Because you don't have *electricity.*" *Duh.* Andrea fought the urge to roll her eyes.

"You could have laid Bella on my bed and lit the lanterns." Charlotte pulled a black sweater off and set it by her purse, then she walked to the mantel above the fireplace and picked up a lantern. "Here's where the matches are." She pointed to a little metal thing hanging on the wall.

Andrea walked closer and shone her phone on the yellow box with an opening at the bottom, and sure enough, there were matches.

"This was here when I moved in, the match holder." Charlotte struck one against the stone on the fireplace and lit two lanterns.

Bella moaned a little. "Can I put her on your bed for now?" Andrea was hoping Charlotte would let Bella sleep with her again so Andrea would have more room on the couch.

"Yeah." Charlotte fell into one of the rocking chairs. Her eyes were swollen and red.

After Andrea lay Bella on Charlotte's bed with pillows propped around her, she gently closed the door behind her, then sat back on the couch. "What's wrong?" She was hungry but didn't want to seem insensitive.

"Just a lot going on. Daniel's mom is in a coma. Another friend's cancer has returned. There's more . . ." She sighed as she leaned her head against the back of the rocking chair.

Charlotte had already told Andrea about the problems with her Amish friends, but this felt like something else. "Did you have a fight with your boyfriend?"

"No."

Andrea waited for her to elaborate, but Charlotte just closed her eyes and kicked the chair into motion.

"Will we be going somewhere to eat? I fed Bella some ham you had in the refrigerator, but I think she drank too much orange juice and threw up. Anyway, I couldn't find anything else ready to eat."

"I'll make us something." Charlotte didn't open her eyes or move.

Thank goodness.

Rain pelted against the tin roof on the house, lightly at first, then harder.

"I've got some tomato soup I can heat up, and I can make us some grilled cheese sandwiches."

Andrea had been dreaming of a hot meal somewhere. "What about your Amish friends?"

Charlotte opened her eyes and glared at Andrea. "They are having a lot of problems right now, so that's not an option. Plus, it's raining now . . . and dark." She stood, retrieved a lantern from the mantel, and started toward the kitchen. Andrea followed.

"I'll get some groceries after work tomorrow." Charlotte pulled a pot out of the cabinet, then took out bread and a can of tomato soup from the pantry. Andrea got cheese and butter from the refrigerator and put it on the counter next to the other things.

"That lady was outside tonight, right before dark, trying to dig up your yard again."

Frowning, Charlotte faced Andrea. "What? She was here again?"

"Yep. But same as before. When I opened the door, she took off running back to her buggy down the road."

Charlotte shook her head. "That doesn't make any sense. No one I know would be digging in my yard."

Andrea put a hand on her hip, the rain getting louder. "I didn't make it up."

"I didn't say you made it up. It's just odd." Charlotte dumped the soup in the pot and turned on the burner. Then she pulled out a skillet and put it on the back burner before she started buttering bread. "Would you recognize her if you saw her?"

Andrea chuckled. "They all look the same, wouldn't you say?"

Charlotte grimaced. "No, I wouldn't say that."

"Well, they wear those things on their heads, so not much hair shows." She tapped a finger to her chin. "But now that I think about it, she had dark hair. And she was tall. Not much else to see beneath all those clothes they wear, but she looked around my age, maybe a little older."

Charlotte lit the burner under the two sandwiches, then leaned against the counter and folded her arms in front of her. "Did Blake have a job? Is that how you ate and survived before?"

"Well, yeah, until he lost his job."

Charlotte was quiet as she stirred the soup. Why couldn't Andrea have had a rich sister who was so thrilled to meet her and Bella that she'd pamper them in luxury? Not feed her sandwiches and canned soup in the dark. But she didn't have anywhere else to go. "I guess I can look for a job."

"That would be good," Charlotte said without turning around. "I'll ask around for you, but you can also check the newspaper and online."

"Okay. But my phone is dead, so no Internet for me."

"I have some portable batteries I charged at work. I'll give you one so you can charge your phone, then search online for a job."

Andrea nodded even though she wasn't sure how many minutes she had left. Would a potential employer run a background check? She'd avoided searching too hard for a job, fearing her past would resurface. And those in power usually weren't thrilled about hiring someone with a record, even if it was self-defense.

Eight

Annie sat with Lena on the porch steps of the King homestead. Lena's surgery was scheduled for the following day in Lancaster, after being postponed the week before. The woman who might have been her mother-in-law was weak, her face ashen, and she'd lost weight over the past few weeks.

"Are you scared about the surgery?" Annie shivered, then pulled her sweater snug as she turned to face Lena. November had snuck up on them, and as the holidays approached, the weather was hinting at a mild winter to come. Temperatures had barely dipped into the fifties at night.

"*Nee.*" Lena smiled a little, but her eyelids were heavy and her cheeks drawn in. "The fearless are one with God, and it's in His name that our souls are comforted."

Annie had heard some version of that statement her entire life, but she couldn't help but question if her faith could hold up against health issues such as Lena was facing.

"How's your *mudder?*" Lena laid a comforting hand on Annie's back. "And the *boppli?*"

Annie took a long, deep breath and focused on keeping her words upbeat. "*Mamm* is the same, but Grace will be going home later this week." The hospital had been keeping her new sister in the nursery in hopes that Annie's mother would wake up. Their decision to send Grace home seemed like a sign that the doctors had lost hope in that happening. Or maybe they just needed the bed now for another baby.

Lena rubbed Annie's back before easing her hand away. "A *boppli* is such a blessing."

They were quiet for a few moments. "What if *Mamm* doesn't wake up?" Annie couldn't even look at Lena, fearful she'd see the answer in the woman's tired eyes.

"She will." Lena coughed. Then she coughed several times before she caught her breath. "Is your *aenti* Faye still at your house?"

"*Ya.*" Annie sighed. "We are all learning to like pickled oysters."

Lena laughed, which was nice to hear. "That is *gut.* But"—she pointed over her shoulder—"Hannah has been bringing food for us, but *mei dochder* has brought way too much. I'm going to send some home with you."

"*Danki*, Lena." Annie grinned. "Want me to return the favor and bring you some pickled oysters?"

Lena chuckled again. *"Ach, nee.* I wouldn't dare deprive you of such a delicacy."

Annie's nerves calmed for a few seconds, but then a car pulled into the driveway. Neither woman moved at first, but then Lena stood and brushed the wrinkles from her black apron.

"I need to go get Amos," she said softly as her gaze stayed on the approaching vehicle. She'd already told Annie that Hannah had a doctor's appointment in Harrisburg and couldn't be here for the homecoming. Lena finally went inside.

Annie stood slowly and folded both hands across her churning stomach. It had been almost a week since Daniel had given Annie the money to send to Jacob. It was a blessing that Lena's surgery had been postponed. Now the entire family would be present.

Annie was seconds away from being face-to-face with her former fiancé. Even though she'd talked to Jacob on the phone, she'd lost sleep the past few days in anticipation of seeing him in person. *The prodigal son is home.*

The screen door closed as Lena and Amos stepped onto the porch. Leaves floated on a gentle breeze and swirled aimlessly to the ground as a car door swung open.

And there he was. *Jacob.*

Charlotte finished proofreading a city council article written by one of the staff reporters earlier in the day, then she
looked through the classified ads, hoping to find something for Andrea. Her sister didn't seem to be making
much effort to find work. But they'd settled into a routine
over the past couple of weeks, even though it wasn't a good
schedule. Charlotte would come home from work. Andrea
would be sitting on the couch playing games on her cell
phone. Eventually her sister would whine about her cell
phone being dead. Charlotte kept charging portable batteries at work, then bringing them home for Andrea,
leaving Charlotte to wonder exactly how long her sister
played on her phone daily. Charlotte had added Andrea
to her cell phone account under the family plan, but it
was a limited amount of minutes. On some days Andrea
moaned about that too.

Bella usually needed a bath and her diaper changed.
The sink was usually filled with dishes. Andrea would
say she couldn't find anything to make for supper, even
though Charlotte had gone to the grocery store on Monday
and bought groceries.

Whether it was her privileged upbringing that bred
her to be lazy or just lack of common courtesy, it was
irritating. People weren't necessarily a product of their
environments. She'd been fighting that battle, not to be
like her parents, since she was young.

But Bella was a sweetheart. She didn't wail the way
she did when Andrea and Bella had first shown up. And

Charlotte liked having her niece in the bed with her, watching her small chest rise and fall as Charlotte drifted asleep with the aroma of baby soap and shampoo lingering in the air.

She jotted down two jobs that would be coming out in the paper the following day—a cashier at Walmart on Lincoln Highway and a receptionist position at a nearby hair salon. The first one might be a problem since Andrea didn't have a car, but the salon was on Charlotte's way to work, if the hours jibed.

The distraction over her sister's employment status didn't last long. Her thoughts returned to Daniel. She had talked to him each night before bed, but the conversations were only brief updates about his mother. And there hadn't been any change. He told Charlotte that Jacob was coming home today, so she'd prayed that his reunion with his parents and Annie would go well. And tomorrow was Lena's surgery. Charlotte had already asked for Thursday off to be with Amos, Lena, Hannah, and presumably Jacob.

But after she'd allowed herself to think through the worries swirling around in her mind, she put them in an imaginary bubble—the way Hannah had told her—and blew the bubble to heaven for God to take care of.

But what about Daniel and me?

Charlotte missed him, and she wanted to comfort him through this ordeal with his mother, no matter the uncertainty of their personal situation. She grabbed her purse and clocked out. She'd surprise Daniel with an invitation to lunch. Hopefully he would welcome the visit.

Daniel carried the piece of broken furniture to the work area in the back of the store and set it in a growing pile of odds and ends that needed attention: an extra nail, more glue, another coat of enamel. He did the best he could every Wednesday, but Mr. Cowan really needed to hire someone who could devote more time.

Daniel's father had insisted that Daniel return to work now that Grace was home—a name his father had agreed to. With Aunt Faye still staying with them, Annie had help with the baby, the chores, and the meals. Except today his sister was at the King household awaiting Jacob's return.

He hoped Jacob's homecoming wouldn't bring upheaval and problems between Jacob and Annie again. Always in his thoughts, he missed Charlotte. He wasn't sure which one of them was pulling back from the relationship the most, but the distance between them seemed to be growing. Although right now wasn't the time to push the issue, and Daniel wished he hadn't given Charlotte an ultimatum, forcing her to choose a future that only God could control.

As he pulled a tub of food from the shop refrigerator, he hoped Annie had packed his lunch and not Aunt Faye. When he lifted the lid, he could see it was a joint effort. Chicken salad on the left and pickled oysters on the right—topped with Aunt Faye's signature grape jelly that came from a jar with the name Smucker's on it.

Shaking his head, he set the dish on the small table where employees ate, but the bell on the front door clanked against the glass, so he put the food back in the refrigerator and opened the door to the showroom. He bumped right into Edna.

"*Wie bischt*, Daniel." Her eyes were red and slightly swollen underneath, like maybe she'd been crying. Daniel was used to seeing her this way lately. As much as he tried to avoid his ex-girlfriend, he saw her at worship service and other community gatherings. Although she'd never stopped by the furniture store on a Wednesday before, thankfully.

"*Wie bischt*, Edna. Can I help you with something?"

She took a step closer, the smell of flowery perfume assaulting Daniel's nostrils, and her lips had an unnatural shine as she pushed them into a pout. Both forbidden luxuries, but Edna didn't seem to care about things forbidden. Daniel recalled a time in his barn months ago when Edna had come for a visit. Next thing he knew, she was kissing him.

Daniel had thought he loved her at one time, had even planned to marry her. But that was before she broke up with him, married John, then started seeing Charlotte's brother, Ethan, on the side. Daniel had lost respect for Edna, and any feelings he'd harbored for her had soured.

"I wanted to know how your *mudder* is doing. I thought about going to the hospital to see her, but I wasn't sure how well I would be received by your parents." She bit one of her shiny lips. "Since we broke up, I sense they don't care for me much."

"She is still in a coma. Nothing has changed. But *danki* for asking." Daniel couldn't deny that Edna was not his parents' favorite person.

"My prayers are with all of you. And also with the Kings. I heard that Lena's surgery is tomorrow." She wrapped the string on her *kapp* around her finger. "But I keep hearing different things about her diagnosis. Some folks say she is having a routine surgery and will be fine, and others say it's a bit more serious."

Daniel sighed, keeping his eyes lowered. Most of the folks in their community were aware of Edna's outer beauty, but only a few knew what she was like on the inside. Daniel was one of those people. He'd learned the meaning of the word *temptress* that day in the barn. He accepted his part in allowing the kiss to happen, but he'd promised himself that it wouldn't happen again.

"Lena has looked a little sickly lately, but as far as I know, the diagnosis is still the same—that she will have the surgery and make a full recovery."

"Thank the Lord for that." Edna reached out and touched Daniel's chest as she inched closer to him.

Too close. He tensed as she cupped his cheeks with her soft hands, vowing to stop any advance she might make, but he didn't want to be too rude since it looked like she'd been crying.

Charlotte reached for the doorknob at the furniture store, but before she opened it, she saw movement inside. She eased her hand away and peered through the glass pane, hoping her eyes were deceiving her. She leaned in for a better look, and her heart raced. *No.* Edna had her hands on Daniel's face as they gazed into each other's eyes.

Daniel might have loved Edna a long time ago, but they both knew the truth about her. Charlotte was sure he would never rekindle feelings for the woman, especially because she was married now. But as Edna moved closer and kissed Daniel on the lips, he made no attempt to stop her.

Charlotte was torn between entering the store and smacking Daniel or scratching Edna's eyes out. She squeezed her hands into fists. Her heart was pierced by the betrayal she'd come to expect from men. But Daniel wasn't just any man. He was the man she loved, the man she trusted. *Please God, not this.*

She forced herself from the window, taking slow steps backward, then she ran to her car.

After Andrea put Bella down to sleep, she headed to the front yard with a shovel, to what she thought was the same place the Amish woman had gone. It had rained earlier that morning, so the ground should be soft.

Andrea's teeth chattered even though she'd borrowed one of Charlotte's heavy sweaters. The wind had picked up and a dark cloud hovered in the distance, which caused her to shiver with fear. But the approaching storm looked like it was far enough away for her to seize this opportunity. Maybe there was money buried? A body? That's what people were always digging for in the movies. But an Amish woman? Neither scenario seemed likely, but Andrea was bored.

She jumped up on both shoulders of the shovel until it sunk into the ground, then she pulled back until she had a heap of earth. She dug two more times and jumped when the shovel clanked with something. Rain started to sprinkle, and she was acutely aware that the storm was getting closer. She hoped Charlotte got home soon. *But not too soon.*

Digging around the edges of what appeared to be a metal container about the size of a shoe box, she finally had her hands around the treasure. She brushed away wet dirt mixed with grass and saw a tiny lock, something easy enough to crack open with a pair of pliers.

As the rain began to come down in hard pellets, Andrea set the box on the ground, then did her best to repack dirt into the hole, stomping on it until she was soaking wet.

She picked up the box and quietly went inside, the sound of the rainfall causing her heart rate to pick up. Or was it curiosity about the contents of the box? *Both*, she decided.

She checked on Bella—still sleeping—dried herself off, then searched for a tool to cut the small lock. Once she'd found a pair of pliers, she sat on the couch and got to work.

∽

Charlotte manhandled Big Red into the parking lot at the newspaper, then laid her head on the steering wheel and cried. How could Daniel let Edna kiss him? Again.

He had told her about Edna's one other attempt, before he and Charlotte were in a relationship, and he'd sworn it would not happen again. She let out a low moan. And she had believed him.

If there was a town harlot among them, Edna was it. Or was *harlot* too strong of a word? Maybe Charlotte was wrong about the woman, and Daniel had welcomed Edna's advances. Or perhaps he'd been the one to initiate the kiss?

She finally straightened, blew her nose, and dried her eyes. If counseling had taught her anything, it was to weigh the facts before becoming emotionally entangled in non-truths. Since she was taking tomorrow off for Lena's surgery, Charlotte had to get back to work.

Once inside, she was glad to see everyone was at lunch

except the receptionist, a young girl just out of high school who spent most of her time on Facebook or Pinterest. But Marcy did have a sweet voice and was polite to anyone who came into the office.

Charlotte took a small mirror from her purse to see how puffy her eyes were. Not so long ago, she would have covered any dark circles underneath her eyes with makeup, but those days were gone.

She plugged in her laptop and phone like she did every day about this time, wanting to leave with a full charge on her devices. Leaning back in her chair, she sighed and glanced at the time on her computer. *Four more hours. How will I ever make it?* She scanned her desk for projects that needed to be proofed, but no one had left anything for her.

She rubbed her temples as the scene from the furniture store replayed like a stuck vinyl record, skipping back to the kiss over and over again, and anger nestled itself in a dark cave in Charlotte's mind. Despite squeezing her eyes closed and forcing herself not to see Daniel and Edna kissing, she felt like her heart might explode in her chest.

No matter the circumstances, the fears, the betrayals, and the self-denials, she loved Daniel to the moon and back again. She wouldn't stash him in the shadows forever. But for now, Charlotte retreated to the darkness.

By the time five o'clock came around, Charlotte was exhausted. Too much time in the dismal recesses of her mind, a place her counselor had warned her about. Charlotte hoped that one day that place would be barred up and sealed tight with a big sign that read No Entry.

She started Big Red and headed for home, eager to see and snuggle with Bella. She might be fearful about having her own children and being a good mother, but loving on Bella had been the best thing about reconnecting with Andrea. And right now she needed a hug from her niece.

After parking the truck, she darted through the pounding rain to the front door, feeling guilty, wishing it was just going to be Bella and her tonight. Andrea would greet her wanting to know what was for supper, how long it would take to make, and then Charlotte would bite her tongue as she made her way through the messy house. And each day, music had been blaring when Charlotte got home from work—sometimes from Andrea's cell phone if it wasn't dead, and other times from a portable radio in the kitchen. Andrea was only a couple of years younger than Charlotte, but it felt like a decade or more. She twisted the doorknob and braced herself.

"Hey." Andrea was on the couch with her knees pulled to her chest. Bella was playing with some blocks and toy cars Charlotte had brought home, gifts from Dianda at work.

"Hey," Charlotte echoed as she made her way to Bella.

"How's my precious niece?" She scooped Bella up and smothered her in kisses, then blew air kisses on the toddler's neck until Bella giggled. *A child's laughter. Best medicine on earth.*

She turned to Andrea, waiting for her sister to ask what's for dinner, but Andrea didn't say a word. And to Charlotte's surprise, the house was fairly clean.

"How was your day?" Charlotte kissed Bella one last time before she set her back on the floor with the toys.

Andrea shrugged. "It was okay, I guess."

Charlotte eyed her sister for a few moments even though Andrea didn't make eye contact. "Are you hungry?"

Andrea didn't even look at her.

"Um . . . anything new or exciting happen today?"

Andrea quickly shook her head. "Nope. Not a thing."

Charlotte kept her gaze on her sister awhile longer. *Liar.*

Nine

Annie walked with Jacob to the swing beneath the old oak tree in the Kings' yard. It had been a quiet supper, and while the focus could have been on Jacob and his plans for the future, the quiet tension in the room had centered around Lena and her surgery the following day.

"*Mamm* said over and over that she would be okay." Jacob turned to Annie. "Do you think she will be?"

Annie had a laundry list full of questions for Jacob, but she'd already promised herself to think only of Lena and her own mother right now. "I believe in God's will, and I have to believe that Lena has much more to do here on earth. So, *ya* . . . I choose to believe that everything will be okay."

Jacob lowered his head. He and Annie hadn't shared more than a brief hug before having supper with his parents. When he looked up at her with moist eyes, he asked, "And what about your *mamm*?"

"She is still the same, still in a coma." Annie fought tears, needing and wanting Jacob to comfort her, at a time when he was fighting to harness his own emotions. "But we have a beautiful new baby, Grace."

Jacob lifted his head, nodded, then pulled Annie into a hug. "I've missed you. And now everything is so blundered."

Annie clung to him with all the desperateness she felt in his embrace. "Everything will be okay." She wasn't sure she believed that. Both of their mothers were enduring a health crisis, and Annie hadn't been getting solid answers about anything. *Everything will be okay* had become the norm.

He finally eased away. "You look even more beautiful than I remember."

Annie forced a smile even though Jacob looked terrible. He was thinner, with bags under his eyes she didn't remember him having before. His *Englisch* haircut looked freshly cut, but without the cropped bangs common to their district. His Amish clothes were worn and wrinkled, like maybe he'd pulled them from his suitcase at the last minute.

"How is your *daed* doing?" Jacob rubbed his forehead, looking away from her again.

"Not *gut*. He won't leave *Mamm*'s side, and he's never even held baby Grace." There was no shortage of love for Annie and Daniel's new baby sister. Daniel worked a lot, but Annie and Aunt Faye smothered Grace with an abundance of affection, also whispering to the baby that her mother would be home soon.

"I'm not worthy to be here, Annie." Jacob blinked a few times. "But I wanted to be here for *Mamm*'s surgery." He hung his head. "*Mei daed* couldn't even look at me."

"They are happy you're home, Jacob, and you know what a quiet man your father is." Annie suspected Amos was worried about Lena, just the same way Annie's father was worried about Annie's mother.

"Are you happy I'm home, Annie? I just want peace." Jacob looked at her, but Annie shifted, planning to tread carefully. Jacob had promised to marry her, fled their community, returned, then left again. And now he was back. She wasn't sure how much more her heart could take.

"I'm happy you're home, Jacob, but . . ." When she paused, his eyes watered up. "I still don't think you know what you want. I thought you'd find peace for your soul in the *Englisch* world, but I don't think it matters where you are in this world." She pressed a hand to her chest. "The peace comes from within."

He sighed. "I don't think I'm ever going to have it."

Annie had been through a lot with Jacob, and she'd heard him sound this hopeless before. "You will." She reached for his hand and squeezed. "But you have to want it."

"How can you say that? I've been searching and searching."

"For what?" Annie gripped his hand, fearful he was going to get mad and sprint at any moment.

Jacob scowled, and he did try to pull his hand away, but Annie held it firmly. "For peace, of course."

"And what does peace mean to you, Jacob?"

They were quiet, and finally he said, "Happiness."

"And what will make you happy?" Annie had struggled with this question ever since Jacob had left.

He stared at her long and hard. "I don't know."

"Choose happiness, make it happen. And peace will come." Annie let go of his hand, kissed him on the cheek, and stood. "I have to go. It's getting dark."

She started across the yard toward her buggy, waiting for him to follow her, but the hinges of the porch swing rubbed together as he continued the movement.

"Annie?"

She turned around just as Jacob stilled the swing. "Ya?"

"You're different."

She smiled. "Not really."

As she made her way to her buggy, tears filled her eyes. She didn't know if her happiness was going to be with Jacob, but without him, how would there ever be peace in her heart?

Charlotte watched Bella sleeping on her bed as the rain pelted against the tin roof of her house. It was after midnight when she'd woken up, and she'd been awake for two hours thinking about Lena's surgery later today. Then she realized she had forgotten to tell her sister about the two jobs she'd run across. She couldn't clear her mind.

She rolled onto her side, keeping her gaze on Bella. Each time a lightning bolt lit the room, Bella's sweet face glowed. Should she feel guilty for loving Bella more than her sister? She'd already decided Andrea could stay for a while longer, mostly because Charlotte wanted to be close to Bella.

Daniel. She'd avoided two calls from him. He would have an explanation about Edna, and it would probably be a valid one—how Edna kissed him without his permission, followed up by a convincing conversation about how Edna meant nothing to him. In her heart Charlotte was sure he would tell her the truth. But part of her thoughts were still locked in a dark place, and by keeping them there, she could avoid facing her own future.

As the lightning and thunder became more raucous, she inched closer to Bella, laid a hand on her niece's tiny hand, and closed her eyes.

She jumped when she heard whimpering. Andrea snored, but Charlotte hadn't heard her crying in her sleep. Yawning, Charlotte forced herself from the bed, and with the light of her cell phone, she made her way to the living room, but Andrea wasn't on the couch. Charlotte shone the light around the room until she landed on Andrea, crouched in the corner in a fetal position, crying.

"Andrea, what are you doing?" She hurried to her and

squatted. Her sister had her face covered as she sobbed. "Andrea," she said again, stroking her back.

Andrea gasped, then threw her arms around Charlotte with enough force to knock her over. "I'm scared," she said in barely a whisper. Charlotte felt her shaking.

"It's just a thunderstorm."

Andrea clutched the back of Charlotte's nightshirt as her tears soaked the shoulder of it. Charlotte helped lift her to her feet, but Andrea still didn't let go of her.

"You're okay, Andrea. Come on." It took effort to get her sister moving toward Charlotte's bedroom, but once there, Charlotte pulled back the covers. "Get in."

Andrea climbed underneath the covers and scootched over toward Bella.

Charlotte sighed, needing sleep. But once she was in the bed, Andrea reached around until she found Charlotte's hand, then clung to it. Moments later Andrea was snoring lightly, but Charlotte lay awake staring up into the darkness. She didn't have much room on the bed, and her head was filled with worry about Lena, her relationship with Daniel, Eve's coma, and now she worried about Andrea and Bella's future.

When does peace come? When will I be able to rest in the Lord and not worry about the trials in my life?

But as Andrea clung to Charlotte's hand, even as she slept, Charlotte felt more sisterly toward Andrea than she had since they'd reunited. There was more to Andrea than she was letting on.

Daniel walked into the hospital Thursday morning exhausted from lack of sleep and the continued worry that had latched on to him. But he was surprised to see Amos sitting with *Daed* when Daniel arrived at his mother's hospital room. Daniel paused outside the partially open door when he heard his father's shaky voice say his name.

"Daniel is doing a fine job keeping things together at home." There was a short pause. "Lena's surgery is today, in this hospital, *ya*?"

"*Ya, ya.* Two floors up, but not until ten o'clock. They are getting her ready, so I wanted to pray with you, for both of our *fraas.*"

Daniel lowered his head when the other two men did, even though he was in the hallway, and several nurses scurried past him. Prayer was mostly a silent offering to God, but Amos prayed aloud for the health and well-being of Lena and Daniel's mother.

"*Mei* Eve must wake up," *Daed* said when Amos was done with the prayer. "I can't be without her."

Grief and despair tore at Daniel's heart. His father was crying. Not wanting to embarrass either man, he held his position outside the door.

"She will wake up, *mei* friend."

"I pray for all *gut* things for Lena this morning. May the wise doctors follow God's divine guidance." His father's voice cracked and shook before footsteps moved toward the door.

Daniel took a few steps down the hall, feeling guilty he'd eavesdropped, something he'd also done outside of Annie's bedroom door when she was talking to Jacob. It just seemed there were many secrets among their people lately. And the one Edna had dropped on him was a doozy.

Amish folks in their community didn't believe in divorce, so the fact that Edna was leaving her husband went against the *Ordnung*. The fact that she'd asked him to leave with her turned Daniel's stomach. There was only person he wanted to be with, but Charlotte wasn't returning his calls, although he suspected she was down the hall awaiting Lena's surgery.

Daniel walked into his mother's room just as Amos was leaving, each nodding a greeting, but when Daniel saw his mother, he wanted to burst into tears. He hadn't been to visit in a few days. Could his father see how much thinner she was, that any color was completely gone from her face now?

"*Wie bischt, Daed.* Any more news from the doctors?"

Shaking his head, his father kept his focus on Daniel's mother. "*Nee.*"

"Do you want me to get you something to eat?" Daniel's gaze drifted to the small table by the bed. Another partially eaten bag of chips and a cup of water. His father had also lost weight.

Daed shook his head again, his face turning red,

although Daniel had no idea why. Lucas Byler had a temper, and Daniel and Annie had seen it many times.

"You haven't been to see your *mamm* in over a week." *Daed* turned to face Daniel, his eyes blazing, his nostrils flared.

"It's only been a few days. I thought you wanted me to keep things running sufficiently at the farm, and I've been working."

"It's been a week. Don't you think your *mamm* would want to see you sooner than that?"

Daniel didn't think his mother was *seeing* anyone, and he wasn't sure she could hear anything either, but he wasn't going to engage his father in a confrontation just in case.

"And Annie was supposed to bring pickled oysters. I haven't seen or smelt any yet. Why is that?" His father stood, fists clenched. "Your *mamm* needs family around her. She needs smells and sounds that are familiar to her. Why can't *mei* own grown *kinner* follow instructions?"

"*Daed* . . . I'll visit every day if there is a driver available and that's what you want. And I'll make sure to bring *Aenti* Faye's pickled oysters." Daniel's father had been in the hospital room for too long, so he tried to keep that in mind.

"Where's Charlotte? Can't she be bothered to help out by providing rides?"

Daniel swallowed back the anger that threatened to spew, then took a deep breath. "Charlotte is working. Her sister and niece are also staying with her. And right now, she's probably upstairs with Amos, Hannah, and Jacob waiting for Lena's surgery. Isaac's probably there too."

His father took a step closer to Daniel. "Has everyone settled into the fact that your mother isn't going to wake up? Because she *will* wake up."

"*Daed*, no one thinks that. We all believe that she will wake up." Daniel said the words with as much truth as he could, even though he was losing hope as well. God's will was to be accepted, no matter the outcome.

"She will wake up," his father said in a whisper, his eyes filling with tears. He latched on to Daniel's arm and stumbled slightly before he pointed to his wife. "Those machines keep her breathing."

Daniel nodded. "I know."

Daed took the few steps to the end of the hospital bed, clutched the railing, then lowered his head as his shoulders began to shake. "They want to end her life," he said tearfully without turning to face Daniel. "They want me to kill *mei fraa*. They want me to sign papers that say I will allow them to unplug her from the machines helping her breathe."

His father lashed out in anger when he couldn't cope with the pain he was feeling, and this pain was surely unbearable for him, as it was for Annie and Daniel and all those who loved his mother. But *Daed* had been married to *Mamm* since he was sixteen, a love that had endured great losses and celebrated blessed moments in their lives.

His father swiped at his eyes with a handkerchief before he turned back around to face Daniel, lifting his chin high. "We will not do this pulling of the plug."

For once, Daniel and his father agreed. "Only God chooses when we die. We will not sign any papers to end *Mamm*'s life."

Charlotte gripped Lena's hand. Amos, Hannah, Isaac, and Jacob had all been in earlier to wish Lena well and to pray with her, but Lena had asked to speak with Charlotte privately.

"I have a beautiful *dochder*, and I have a *sohn* who has come home." Lena smiled. "And I have Amos." She paused, still smiling. "And I cherish them."

Charlotte nodded. "I know you do."

"But I love you, too, Charlotte, like one of my own." She let go of Charlotte's hand and reached under the white sheet covering her. They'd already hooked her up to an IV, and Charlotte had been told that she was just waiting for an orderly to take her to surgery. She pulled out an envelope and handed it to Charlotte.

"What's this?"

"It's a Do Not Resuscitate form I have filled out, along with a Power of Attorney for you to make medical decisions if I should become unable to."

Charlotte held the envelope out, pushing it toward

Lena. "No, Lena. This is something your family should have."

Lena smiled again. "You *are* my family."

Charlotte squeezed her eyes shut, savoring the comment and the love she held for this woman. "And you are my family. But Amos should be the one to make any decisions like that. Of course, none will be needed because you'll be just fine."

"*Ya*, I believe I will do all right. But Charlotte . . . if something were to happen, I want nature to take its course. I don't want to be kept alive by machines, and Amos would never let me go." Her eyes drifted away, glassed over a little. "I think about Eve downstairs, unable to communicate what she may or may not want. If and when the time comes, Lucas will have to make such a decision about Eve, but I have the wherewithal right now to dictate my wants. Eve didn't have that luxury." She pushed the envelope toward Charlotte again.

"What is the Amish way? What would the bishop advise?"

"To leave a person hooked up to machines would be viewed by some of our people as okay because if God wanted to call a person home, He could do so whether there were machines or not. But when does it become a time that we hinder God's will with our own worldly technology? Without the machines, I would die, if it had come to that. Isn't that God's will?"

"So, it's a gray area, then?" Charlotte sighed. It seemed

complicated, no matter what religion a person was. She also believed it was a personal choice.

"It's not a gray area for me, Charlotte." She pushed the envelope at Charlotte again, and she took it.

"I will hold on to this, Lena, but only because I know everything will be fine." She leaned down and kissed her on the cheek.

Lena lowered her chin, peeked down her blue hospital gown, and said softly, "Good-bye breasts. You and I will be parting ways." She grinned at Charlotte, then looked back at her chest again. "And good riddance," she said louder, then laughed.

Charlotte chuckled too. "I love you so much."

Lena winked at her. "I know you do. And I love you too. Stay close to Amos. Jacob is a bit of a mess still. Hannah and Isaac have their own lives. I know that both *mei kinner* will take care of their *daed*, but Amos loves you like a *dochder* also. He just doesn't know how to express affection well. But don't ever doubt his love for you."

"Lena, stop it." Charlotte's bottom lip trembled. "You are talking like you're leaving this life, but this is routine surgery."

"Was I?" Lena brought a hand to her chest. "I'm just trying to cover all of my bases, as you *Englisch* would say." She winked at Charlotte. "Speaking of, when are you going to get baptized and marry that handsome Daniel?"

"Hmm . . ." Charlotte sighed. "It's complicated."

"It doesn't have to be. God's blessings on you always, sweet child."

Two male nurses walked in right then. "Are you ready, Mrs. King?" One of the men picked up Lena's chart and studied it for a moment.

"As ready as I'll ever be," she said to the man, the hint of a smile on her lips.

Charlotte was sure she wouldn't be as brave as Lena if the situation were reversed.

"You can wait in recovery with the other family members," the same man said as they started to wheel Lena out of the room. Charlotte loved being referred to as Lena's family.

The two nurses pivoted the portable bed through the doorway but paused as another gurney passed by. Then they started again to maneuver Lena's bed from the end, leaving Charlotte to see Lena's face pass by the opened door last.

And the tear that slipped down her cheek as she tried to smile at Charlotte.

Ten

aniel found the surgery waiting room, and clustered together were Charlotte, Hannah, Isaac, Amos, Jacob, and Annie.

After Daniel greeted everyone, he whispered to Annie that she needed to take pickled oysters to their father and not to forget. Then he asked Charlotte if he could speak to her alone. Under different circumstances, everyone would have eyed him suspiciously and exchanged curious looks. But the others didn't shoot him so much as a glance, and Daniel was sure they were each lost in worry about Lena.

After Charlotte closed the waiting room door, she and Daniel stood in the hallway.

"Are you okay? I've been calling you." Daniel tried to keep the clip out of his voice, but they all had enough going on without Charlotte going silent. Something she did when she was bothered about something.

"No. Not really. I'm worried about Lena." She folded her arms across her chest. "How is your mother?"

"The same." Daniel rubbed his chin. "Are you angry with me about something?"

Charlotte raised an eyebrow. "Should I be?"

He had been around his mother and sister enough to know the female behavior, even if he didn't understand it. "Um . . . I don't think so."

"Okay, then. Is that all?" Charlotte bit her bottom lip and sighed.

"*Nee*, it's not. What's wrong?" He leaned down a little, putting his ear closer to her since they were both speaking in loud whispers.

"I wanted to go to lunch with you yesterday, so I went to the furniture store." Her glare burned into him. "But you had company."

He took in a deep breath, buying some time to think of the right words. "I guess you saw Edna?" Not exactly the words he'd hoped for, but they might as well get it over with. "She's having more problems with John."

"Apparently, since she was kissing you." Charlotte spat the words, her whispering voice a bit louder.

"She kissed me once and I told her to stop. She's leaving John, planning to get a divorce." Daniel couldn't see any good coming out of telling Charlotte that Edna had invited him to go with her.

"What?" Charlotte scrunched her face up, frowning. "The Amish don't get divorces."

"She'll be shunned, but I don't think she cares." He thought about the Edna he'd once dated. She seemed confused back then, but he wouldn't have fallen in love with her if she didn't have good qualities to go along with her attractive looks. "I feel sorry for her."

Charlotte rolled her eyes. "I can't really say I feel sorry for the woman who was kissing my boyfriend." She let out a long sigh. "But I'll pray for her."

Daniel kissed her softly, but she eased away.

"Those lips are reserved for me. I better not catch that woman kissing you again."

He lowered his head before he looked back up at her. "I'm sorry you saw that."

Charlotte grimaced as she folded her arms across her chest. "You're sorry I *saw* that, or you're sorry it happened?"

Daniel grinned. "Both."

"Well, for the sake of everything going on in our lives, I feel like I need to just let the incident with Edna go, but I don't trust that woman."

"I do my best to avoid her."

Charlotte tucked her hair behind her ears, then touched Daniel's arm. "And I know you want answers about us, but I don't think this is the time to focus on that."

Daniel couldn't deny that a cloud of anxiety hovered over all of them, but Charlotte seemed to have dropped the issue with Edna, so he would as well. "Everything will be okay for all of us."

"I know worry is a sin, but I can't seem to control it. I don't know what I'd do if anything happened to Lena." Her bottom lip trembled.

Daniel looked down the hallway in both directions. Two nurses were staring at a computer screen behind a counter, but otherwise, it was quiet. He pulled Charlotte into his arms.

"Nothing is going to happen to Lena." He eased her away, glanced both ways down the corridor once more, then kissed her. "I've missed you."

She smiled a little, leaned up on her toes, and kissed him again. "I need to tell you something."

Daniel held his breath. "What?" He recognized the serious expression on Charlotte's face. She squeezed her lips tightly together, and the lines on her forehead creased. Maybe she wasn't over the Edna kiss after all.

"Andrea told me a woman has been digging in my yard. It's happened twice." She raised an eyebrow. "And the woman is Amish. Who would be doing that? Andrea said the woman parks her buggy down the road, comes into the yard with a shovel, starts to dig, then runs off when Andrea goes outside."

Daniel scowled. "What is she digging for?"

"I don't know. Andrea said the woman's digging in the middle of the grass, not like a flower bed or anything."

He scratched his chin. "Do you believe your sister?"

"I don't really have a reason not to. Why would she make up something like that?"

Daniel shrugged. "I don't know, but I can't imagine why a woman in our community would be digging up your grass."

∽

Charlotte waved away the thought. "Oh well. Who knows? We've both got more important things to think about."

"Will you be at the barn raising on Saturday?" Daniel looped his thumbs underneath his suspenders. He seemed to grow taller when he did that, and Charlotte smiled.

"Yep. I'll be there." She took a peek through the small glass window into the waiting room, just to make sure a doctor wasn't talking to the family, even though Charlotte didn't think Lena had been in surgery long enough yet. "Do you think I should bring Andrea and Bella? Two more English people crashing the event might put the bishop in more of a tizzy."

"The bishop isn't opposed to thoughtful interaction with *Englisch* folks wanting to help with a project like that. He's opposed to courtship with an *Englisch* person"—he grinned—"when it's gone on for months without commitment."

Charlotte had messed up a lot in her life, but letting down God seemed huge. But Daniel was going to keep bringing it up until Charlotte committed—one way or the other. "There's something else I want to ask you."

"Please don't propose to me in a hospital corridor."

Daniel grinned again, and Charlotte was reminded how much she loved his humor.

She chuckled. "No, I'm not. But I wanted to tell you something about Lena. She gave me power of attorney to make decisions on her behalf if anything went wrong with the surgery." She swallowed hard. "Which, of course, it won't." Then she cleared her throat. "But there's also a Do Not Resuscitate form."

"What does that mean?" His eyebrows narrowed into a frown as his jaw tensed.

"Basically, she doesn't want to be kept alive on machines or have anyone resuscitate her should her heart stop." Charlotte paused. "I haven't read it all, but I think that's the gist of it."

A muscle flicked in Daniel's jaw again. "You mean, the way *mei mamm* is being kept alive?"

Charlotte shrugged. "I guess."

"It would be wrong to kill a person, no matter the situation."

"Well, I guess it's a personal choice as to where that line gets drawn." Charlotte tried to recall the way Lena had explained it to her, but the words weren't coming. "Each person should be able to choose what they would want in a situation like that. Lena gave the forms to me because she felt sure that neither Amos nor her children would be able to make that call. And the only reason I would make that decision is because Lena asked me to." She waved a hand in the air and shook her head. "But it's not going to come to anything even close to that, so it's really a moot point."

"Two floors below us it is *not* a moot point." Daniel's face reddened. "*Daed* said folks are saying he needs to think about 'pulling the plug'—as you *Englisch* say—on *Mamm*. We are not going to kill her."

Something about the way Daniel said *Englisch* caused a shiver to run the length of Charlotte's spine. "It's not killing someone; it's being humane. Would you really want to lie in a bed with machines keeping you alive while your family watched your body deteriorating, when your soul ached to go home?" *Thank You, God.* Those words made sense, even to Charlotte.

"*Nee*, of course not. But it's not our choice to make. It is our duty to do the best we can for *Mamm*. God can heal her or take her home."

"God can also keep her alive if you take her off the machines." She touched Daniel's arm, but he backed away. "I would respect any decision that you and your family made about your mother. But you have to also respect Lena's decision, if she were ever in that situation."

He shook his head. "*Nee*. It would be a matter for the bishop to decide."

"I disagree." Charlotte folded her arms across her chest again. "If a person has a legal document stating her wishes, then those wishes should be followed, whether the bishop approves or not."

"What if her *family* disagreed with Lena's choice and

forbid you to do such a thing?" Daniel said the words in a calm, soft voice, as if he was forcing himself not to lose control. He clearly was putting Charlotte on the outside of the family circle, a place she'd grown to love and cherish. And Daniel knew it.

"It would be an awful position to be put in, but I would try to convince Amos, Hannah, and Jacob to do what Lena wanted."

"And what if they couldn't agree to killing her?"

Charlotte's pulse picked up, but she stifled her anger. This was a theoretical discussion about Lena. Daniel, his father, and Annie were living it in another part of the hospital. "I don't know," Charlotte said softly. *The truth.*

The door to the waiting room opened, bumping Charlotte in the shoulder.

"*Mamm* is in recovery," Hannah said, smiling. "And everything went fine. She's doing *gut.*"

"Thank God." Charlotte breathed a huge sigh of relief.

Daniel nodded. "*Wunderbaar* news, Hannah."

But once Hannah was on the other side of the door again, Daniel said, "If you and I were married and you fell ill, needing machines to stay alive, I would not allow anyone to kill you, Charlotte."

She looked at the speckled tile floor in the corridor and shook her head before she looked back up at him. His voice had been so tender, like he would have been doing her a huge favor.

"That's a shame, Daniel. Because I wouldn't want to be hooked up to machines indefinitely."

She pulled the waiting room door open and went back to be with her family.

∽

Two hours later Charlotte pulled Big Red into her driveway. She'd cried half the way home. As grateful as she was that Lena was going to be okay, her heart hurt. She and Daniel were divided on many issues. How would they ever meet in the middle to stay together, assuming Charlotte was even able to commit to that?

But love couldn't be controlled, and no matter the issues they wrestled with, she loved the man and she didn't see that going away. If they couldn't come together on enough issues to keep the relationship from floundering, hearts were going to be broken.

She leaned her head against Big Red's steering wheel, another reminder of what she'd be leaving behind if she chose to be with Daniel. She felt petty for having the thought, but Big Red was more than a mode of transportation to her.

As she walked into the living room, Bella ran to her, arms held high in the air. "Sweet girl." The bouncy toddler filled Charlotte's home with a sense of joy she hadn't known before.

"I live here too." Andrea grinned from the couch where she was sitting.

Charlotte eased Bella onto the floor and zoomed in on Andrea, along with two boxes that came from Charlotte's closet that were in her sister's lap. Large boxes filled with miscellaneous beads that Charlotte had collected for a couple of years when she was heavily into making jewelry. She also had all the tools and wire needed to make earrings, bracelets, and necklaces of all types. But eventually she realized that she didn't have the creative flair necessary to make any real money at it.

"Is this okay? Bella walked in your closet again, and I found these boxes." She pointed to her lap.

Charlotte already suspected her sister snooped, but she lost track of that thought when she eyed the pieces of jewelry Andrea had made using beads and other items in the boxes. Several pieces were laid out on the coffee table.

"Where did you learn to do this?" Charlotte held up a pair of earrings, silver loops with turquoise stones dangling in the middle, that she would easily pay thirty dollars for. "When I was toying around with making jewelry, I didn't make anything that looked like this." She turned her eyes to Andrea. "These are gorgeous." *Who would have known? Andrea definitely has the creative flair that I lack.*

Her sister actually blushed. "Do you really think so?"

Charlotte lifted up two more pairs of earrings. "Uh, yeah. These are amazing, Andrea."

"I'll, uh . . . try to pay for the beads if I can have them. I mean, if"—Andrea shrugged, avoiding Charlotte's gaze—"if you're not using them or saving them for something."

"You don't need to pay me for the beads. I haven't touched them in a couple of years, at least." She picked up a pair of gold dangling earrings with several colorful stones looped around the teardrop. "You can just make me an occasional pair of earrings." She giggled, which felt good, considering her day.

"How's your friend Lena?" Andrea pointed a finger at Bella when her daughter moved to touch the fireplace grate. "No, Bella. Hot."

"Lena did very well. The fireplace isn't hot, though."

"But it will be, and she needs to learn now not to touch it."

Exactly how long are you planning to stay here? But as Bella mouthed the word *hot*, Charlotte knew she wasn't ready for her niece to leave. She wasn't sure about her sister, but they were a package deal.

"I'm going to take a shower." She kicked off her shoes and started toward her bedroom.

"Charlotte?"

She turned on her heel. "Yeah?"

"Do you really think these are pretty?" Andrea blushed again.

"Absolutely. They are gorgeous, and I think you could sell them."

Andrea's eyes lit up. "You mean, like my own business?" She stood, smiling.

"Yep. I'd buy those earrings, especially those teardrop ones, the silver loops." She returned the smile and headed toward the bathroom again, but Andrea was on her heels so she turned around.

"Here." Andrea held the pair of earrings out to Charlotte. "They're your beads anyway."

"I *should* tell you to sell them." Charlotte chuckled. "But I love them too much for that. I'm going to keep them and tell you to make another pair to sell."

Andrea threw her arms around Charlotte's neck. "Thank you."

It was a real hug. From her sister. And as she looked over Andrea's shoulder, little Bella clapped, grinning. Maybe God was blessing her with something she couldn't have foreseen.

Annie sat quietly with her father as *Mamm's* chest rose and fell, the swoosh of the machines filling her lungs, then releasing the air in rhythmic consistency as other devices beeped nearby. Annie heard the sounds in her sleep sometimes. "The doctor said Lena can go home day after tomorrow if all goes well."

Her father nodded but kept his eyes fixed on his wife.

Annie glanced down at her own chest. She couldn't imagine not having any breasts. What if she had been the one to get cancer?

Her gaze drifted to her mother. Each visit was harder

and harder as she watched her mother's continued weight loss, and her face seemed more pallid too. "Grace is such a *gut boppli*. She smiles a lot too. *Mamm* said I smiled early too." She forced a smile, hoping for any response from her *daed*. "*Aenti* Faye and I can't love on her enough." Annie twisted a string from her *kapp* around her finger. "Maybe you should come home for a while and spend some time with her. Somehow I'll make sure *Aenti* Faye doesn't make pickled oysters."

Her father glared at her. "Did you bring pickled oysters like I asked?"

"*Daed*, Daniel just reminded me this morning. I promise to bring some when I come to visit next time."

"I asked him yesterday." His gaze traveled back to Annie's mother, and she decided not to argue with him. He hadn't been home in so long, he couldn't keep track of the days.

"So . . . do you . . . ?" Annie cleared her throat. "Do you want to come home for a while?"

Daed shook his head without looking at her. "*Nee*. Your *mudder* might wake up while I'm gone."

Annie was losing hope that *Mamm* would wake up. Ever. She had cried herself to sleep about it most nights, but it was becoming just as heartbreaking to see her father this way. "I can stay with her, *Daed*. If she wakes, I can call you."

"I don't tote one of the *Englisch* cell phones. You know that."

"I could call Daniel, and he could bring you to the hospital."

Her father cut his eyes in her direction. "You and your *bruder* abuse the mobile telephones."

Annie lifted one shoulder and slowly lowered it. "Lately we've needed them, *Daed*."

They were quiet as Annie's father looked back at her mother. "The Lord hears our prayers, *mei maedel*. Your *mamm* will wake up."

Annie wanted to believe that more than anything in the world, and she was sure that she, Daniel, and their father were all grieving in their own ways, but there was a new life in their world. "Baby Grace smiles when she is sleeping too. She's the most beautiful *boppli* ever."

Daed gave a taut nod before he looked at Annie. "Jacob is back, is he not?"

"*Ya*." But her father's refusal to acknowledge his newborn daughter stung, forcing her to swallow back tears.

"You will not see that boy. He caused you and our family much heartache, not to mention the upset to his own family."

Annie wanted to tell her father that Jacob hadn't been baptized, that he was free to explore the world until he chose baptism. She wanted to lash out at her father, to tell him that she was eighteen years old and could do whatever she wanted.

As she fought the quiver in her bottom lip, she wanted to yell at him that they all loved *Mamm* and that he was an awful person not to hold his beautiful new baby, no matter the situation. But as she studied the expression on her father's face, the bags under his tired eyes, the way his hands trembled in his lap as he stared at his wife—she just sat quietly, fighting off her own tears . . . as machines swooshed and beeped.

Annie didn't know what to pray for with regard to her mother. So she prayed for peace for all of them, entrusting her mother's life to the Lord.

She stood and took a deep breath. "I'm going to go, *Daed*. I will bring some pickled oysters tomorrow." She smoothed the wrinkles in her black apron. "Anything else?"

Her father picked up an envelope from the nightstand between Annie's parents, then held it out to Annie. She took a couple of steps and accepted it.

"Give that to the doctors or nurses on your way out. You can tell them that there will be no unplugging of these machines."

Annie frowned, about to ask what that meant, but her father waved an arm toward the door. "Go, child. Deliver the papers."

She left the room and handed the envelope to a nurse outside her mother's room.

Eleven

Charlotte parked her truck amid all the buggies, like a red-spotted beetle among a bunch of pristine gray ants. For a group of people who defied pride, the Amish had clean houses, impeccable yards, and even their buggies sparkled on a day filled with sunshine, like today.

"This is gonna be weird." Andrea pried open the passenger door. Then she worked to get Bella out of her car seat, which barely fit between two people in the '57 Chevy. "What if they don't like me?"

"They'll like you," Charlotte said before clearing her throat. She'd considered not bringing Andrea to the barn raising. Bishop Miller already had his eye on Charlotte, and considering she never knew what Andrea might say, the entire day might end up a bust. But Charlotte liked the Stoltzfus family, and she wanted to be a part of erecting a new barn for them.

Lightning had hit their farm during the storm, started a fire in the barn, and destroyed most of it. The day before, members of the community had torn down what was left, and now stacks of wood were waiting on the members of the community to rebuild.

"Are we going to actually be hammering nails and all that stuff?" Andrea set Bella on the ground. Charlotte's niece toddled around to Charlotte's side of the truck, lifting her hands in the air. Bella seemed like a different child than she did the first day she and Andrea had shown up at Charlotte's house. She wasn't nearly as fussy, and even if Bella was upset, it was easier to comfort her now.

"No, we're not." She scooped Bella into her arms and walked toward a group of women setting platters of food and pitchers of tea on a picnic table. "We'll help with the meal, get the men drinks, and make sure the younger children stay away from the work area."

"Why don't you become Amish?" Andrea smelled like the cigarette she'd smoked outside Charlotte's house before they'd left home. Now, her sister was smacking on a piece of gum Charlotte had offered her in the truck. Once again, Charlotte thought about the three-year age difference between them and how it felt like much more.

"Quit smacking," Charlotte said as she cut her eyes at Andrea. "And be polite."

"You act like you're my mom sometimes instead of my sister." Andrea spit the gum in the grass.

Charlotte lifted Bella higher on her hip and rolled her

eyes. "I feel like your mom sometimes. Now pick up that gum. Someone will step on it. Here, put it in this."

Charlotte held out a piece of tissue, and Andrea dropped the gum and then shrugged as she shuffled along in blue jeans, tennis shoes, and a red T-shirt she'd borrowed from Charlotte, along with a red jacket. Andrea almost always wore her long dark hair down, but today she had it up in a twist, which made her look a couple of years older.

"You don't have electricity. You're friends with all of these people. And your Amish boyfriend is kinda hot too. Just seems to make sense that you'd convert."

"It's a lot more complicated than that, and you know it."

"It doesn't have to be."

Charlotte stopped walking and glanced at her sister, who had just echoed Lena's words about the same subject. "Well, it is." She scanned the women, most of whom she knew, then unraveled a little when she spotted Edna. They gazed at each other, but Charlotte quickly looked away. This was a day for fellowship and an opportunity to introduce Andrea and Bella to her Amish friends, not a verbal catfight with Edna.

Even if it did mean the bishop might pull her aside for a little chat about Daniel and her. Even if it did mean Andrea might embarrass her to death at some point. But as she snuggled with Bella in her arms, she was eager to show off her niece.

"And who is this beauty?" Lillian Stoltzfus reached

out and touched Bella's arm. Charlotte had been told that Lillian decided to join the Amish years ago, but Charlotte didn't think anyone would ever know. She fit in as if she'd been one of the Plain People her entire life. Lillian had children and grandchildren and was married to a wonderful man, Samuel. After spending a few years in Colorado, most of the Stoltzfus family had moved back to Lancaster County to care for Lillian's mother, Sarah Jane, who had been diagnosed with Alzheimer's disease a few months ago.

Bella played shy and buried her head in Charlotte's shoulder. "This is my niece, Bella." She nudged the little girl. "Say hi, Bella." Charlotte tried to be like the Amish in many ways. She tried to be truthful, helpful, strong in her faith, do for others, and avoid being prideful. But right now, she was proud to be holding Bella in her arms and briefly wondered how it must feel to hold her own child.

Right then, she saw Daniel in a group of men who looked like they were sorting tools and nails. She locked eyes with him and smiled. No matter their differences, Daniel still made her heart flutter.

"And this is my sister, Andrea." Charlotte held her breath.

"Hey." Andrea gave a half wave to Lillian as she smiled at the other women standing nearby. "Nice to meet ya'll."

Charlotte released the breath she was holding, hopeful that Andrea would behave herself today.

❧

Andrea's eyes widened when another group of women began laying out dishes and flatware on the picnic table. She brought a hand to her forehead to block the sun as she studied the ladies, recalling the box she'd found and its contents.

"Hey . . ." She nudged Charlotte, then whispered, "Who's that woman, the one in the green dress?" She pointed to six women.

"Well, that narrows it down"—Charlotte grinned— "since four of them are wearing *green*." She hoisted Bella higher up on her hip.

"Her." Andrea pointed, and Charlotte gently slapped down her hand. "The tall one."

"That's Edna Glick." Charlotte sneered, turning up her nose. "She used to see Ethan."

"Wait a minute. I thought Ethan used to date your friend Hannah."

"Ethan did date Hannah, but I think he was secretly in love with Edna, and they had a thing for a while." Charlotte rolled her eyes. "And Daniel also dated Edna, and she ended up marrying John, the man she supposedly wants to leave now."

Andrea scowled, lifting an eyebrow. "Geez. She gets around." *But why bury the box in your ex-boyfriend's yard?*

"Obviously, I don't really care for her." Charlotte plastered on a fake smile.

Andrea was starting to enjoy living with Charlotte, and Bella had certainly taken to her new aunt, so Andrea didn't want to rock the boat. But she sure did want to question the tall, pretty Amish woman she'd seen digging in the yard—Edna Glick. She sighed and decided to put the issue to rest. For now.

Bella reached for Andrea, so she took her and followed Charlotte toward the house as Amish ladies passed by them carrying more dishes of food and pitchers of tea. Once inside, it was a beehive of organized activity. Andrea figured she'd carry out a couple of platters, then go find a place to smoke.

"You can put Bella down if you want to. Everyone watches all the *kinner.*" Charlotte smiled. "I mean children."

Charlotte even talked like an Amish person. Bella squirmed out of Andrea's arms as if she'd understood what Charlotte said. After Bella moved toward some other children in the living room, Andrea picked up a platter of pickles and olives, then followed Charlotte out the front door.

"So, all these guys will build the entire barn today?" As they walked down the porch steps, Andrea noticed that part of the frame was already erected.

"Yep. Or most of it, anyway. Sometimes a few men come back the next day to finish the inside or do cleanup."

"How much do they get paid?" Andrea held the platter steady with one hand as she picked up a pickle with the other.

"No one gets paid." Charlotte waved to a couple of women they passed.

"Well that's"—Andrea cleared her throat, careful of her language around her sister—"messed up."

Charlotte shook her head. "No, it's actually really cool. Everyone helps everyone. If someone gets sick, the community pitches in to help with plowing fields, planting gardens, cooking food, or whatever else a family might need. If someone falls upon hard times in some other way, they have the support of the community. And, as in this case, Samuel and Lillian's barn burned down, so everyone is pitching in to help."

"I guess all these people believe all these good deeds will get them into heaven." Andrea wished more than anything that she had that to look forward to. Even if she believed—and she didn't—no way she'd be allowed in.

"Their belief that Jesus died on the cross for all of us and the way that they live their lives as a result of that belief."

Andrea stifled a grunt that threatened to spew as she recalled her and two boys robbing a convenience store when she was fourteen. They'd gotten away with it, even though they shouldn't have. They were young and stupid, not thinking about the security camera. They'd heard later that the camera didn't catch any of their faces. Andrea remembered how hungry she was that day, hoping that she'd go to jail where there would be food and a bed. Instead she lived off the food they'd stolen from the store.

That's all she and her friends had taken—chips, lunch meat, bread, crackers, and whatever else they could fit in their backpacks and carry out.

The next time they'd tried to steal a car, with plans to drive to California. They weren't so lucky that time. But Andrea had been a juvenile at the time, so she'd done some time in a youth detention center before being returned to the streets. As an adult, she'd kept up the same lovely behavior, so, nope. She didn't foresee God opening the pearly gates for her.

"Hey, I'm gonna go look around the property, okay?" Andrea scoped out the house, hoping she could sneak around to the back without anyone noticing.

"You're going to smoke," Charlotte whispered as she set a platter of bread on the table next to the pickle tray Andrea had carried out.

Andrea sighed. "I'm gonna quit. I only smoke one or two a day as it is." Whenever she could scrape together a little cash or Charlotte reluctantly agreed to get her a pack. "I'll be back shortly."

As she shuffled across the yard, she could feel Amish eyes on her, checking her out. But she needed a smoke too badly to care. She rounded the corner to the back of the house, leaned down, and pulled a cigarette out of her sock. When she lifted it up, she noticed an Amish guy on the other side of the septic tank behind the house.

Smiling, Andrea headed his way. "I knew there was bound to be some Amish people who smoked." She took a lighter out of her front pocket, lit her cigarette, inhaled the smooth flavor, then blew it in the guy's face.

He waved a hand in front of his face. "Do you mind? I'm not smoking."

"Oh, great. Even worse." Andrea took another drag, blew a smoke ring, then grinned. "Relieving yourself?"

The Amish kid looked to be eighteen or nineteen. "*Nee*. Just wanted to be alone for a few minutes."

Andrea looked him up and down for a few seconds as she puffed on her cigarette. This kid's hair didn't look like all the others. His blond bangs weren't cropped, he had bags underneath his eyes, and he didn't have the chipper demeanor the others seemed to have.

"What's eating you? You look depressed or something." She flicked an ash in the grass. "Guess I'd be depressed, too, if I had to live the way you people do. What in the world do you do for fun?"

Andrea thought she probably had a few years on this guy, but if he could enlighten her about extracurricular activities, she was all ears.

"I ain't depressed. Just tired."

Andrea waited for a few seconds, until she presumed that's all he was going to offer up. "I'm Charlotte Dolinsky's sister, the only other person here who isn't dressed in funky clothes."

"You're kidding me." He folded his arms across his chest.

"Why, you know my sister?"

"*Ya*, I do."

"What's your name?" Andrea dropped her cigarette and pounded it out with her shoe.

"Jacob."

"Ah . . ." Andrea nodded. "I've heard about you from Charlotte—the prodigal son returned home because your mother is sick." She paused. "I'm sorry about that part, about your mom." She briefly thought about the woman who had raised her, but as a chill ran the length of her spine, she stowed the thought.

"*Danki.*"

Not very talkative. "Okay. Well. Nice to meet you, Jacob." She smiled. She gave a slight wave and started walking along the backside of the house.

She rounded the corner and bumped right into the digger lady. *Edna.*

"*Ach*, I'm sorry." The woman grabbed her chest and smiled. "There's a crowd moving through the living room to the kitchen, so I was going to sneak in the back door to use the facilities. Someone pointed you out to me. You're Charlotte's sister, *ya*? I'm Edna." She extended her hand.

Andrea didn't move, her feet rooting with the grass as her heart pounded in her chest.

A puzzled look on her face, Edna finally lowered her hand to her side when Andrea didn't shake it. Andrea took a step closer to her, then another step, close enough that Edna backed up.

"Don't pretend you don't recognize me. I've caught you twice digging in my sister's yard."

First Edna's neck turned red, then the color rose like hot steam all the way to her forehead. "I—I, um . . . I'm not sure what you mean."

"Lady, I saw you." Andrea smirked.

"I have no idea what you're talking about." Edna turned on her heel and rushed away.

"Oh, I think you do," Andrea said softly.

Twelve

aniel stepped off the bottom rung of the wooden frame, feeling grateful for the beautiful sunshine and cool breeze today. But thoughts of his mother and Charlotte comingled in his mind and left his brain feeling cloudy.

Every time he pictured his mother lying in the hospital bed, so still and lifeless, he said a prayer for the Lord to wake her up. Almost as upsetting was his father's inability to leave the hospital or acknowledge his new daughter.

Then there was Charlotte. A woman who had transformed herself before his eyes, turning from a victim of abuse into someone who spent the bulk of her time caring for others. She'd tended to her own mother despite a horrid past associated with the woman. Charlotte had taken care of Lena in Houston during her chemo treatments. She'd allowed Jacob to stay with her when he'd run away to Houston. Charlotte had given Amos her little dog, Buddy, even though she loved the little fellow probably more than Amos did. And now she was taking care of a sister and niece she'd never known.

Selfishly, Daniel wondered if and when Charlotte was going to factor him into her life. They loved each other. He knew that. She was the woman for him, the person he wanted to be with forever, to have a family with. But each time they headed down a path that seemed more permanent, Charlotte backed off. *What is she so afraid of? Happiness?*

"Daniel, how are you holding up? How is your mother?"

He hadn't seen Edna approaching to his left, but he recognized her scent, a sultry aroma that Daniel had once found intoxicating. "The same." He kept walking, but Edna got in step with him.

"I'm so sorry to hear that." She took in a deep breath. "I think I probably said some things to you that I shouldn't have, and I surely shouldn't have kissed you."

Daniel glanced around, glad to see no one was in listening distance. "*Nee*, you shouldn't have. You know that I love Charlotte."

"I know, I know." She stopped, grabbed his arm. "But she isn't right for you, Daniel. Surely you see that. Even if we can't be together, I want you to be happy, and I don't see how an *Englisch* woman, especially Charlotte, can make you happy."

157

"It's against the odds, but we will make a *gut* life together." *If Charlotte can ever realize that.*

"I meant what I said about leaving John." She started walking again when Daniel did.

"That's your choice, I reckon." No matter the situation, Daniel would hate to see Edna shunned. They walked quietly for a few moments.

"Charlotte's sister is a bizarre woman. I know that the community has accepted Charlotte, even though she isn't one of us." Edna lifted her chin as she pressed her lips together. "But I don't see that happening with her sister. I heard that she's an untruthful person."

Frowning, Daniel glanced at her. "This is the first time most people have met her. How can that rumor already be spreading?" It was a sad fact that gossip circulated in their community the same way as the outside world.

"I don't know. I'm just telling you what I heard. There are reasons for us to stay detached from the *Englisch*. We are unequally yoked with them."

Daniel had been hearing that term his entire life, but the truth was that without the *Englisch* tourism, most of the Amish folks wouldn't be able to make a living. With less farmland and generations piling on top of generations, the need to work outside the home had become practically mandatory.

"We are all people"—he cut his eyes at Edna—"and there is good and bad in every person." It was a statement that would have curled his grandparents' toes, but Daniel's people were changing along with the times. And part of the change was the realization that the Amish had just as many problems as the *Englisch*. Edna and John were proof of that. And so were Annie and Jacob, the star-crossed teenagers who couldn't seem to figure out if they had a future together or not.

But who am I to judge?

⌒

Later that evening Jacob came calling, and while Annie welcomed his unannounced visit, she hadn't been able to get little Grace to stop crying for an hour.

"Let me take her," Aunt Faye said as Annie paced the living room. "You go spend time with your beau, and I'll try to give her a bit more formula." Aunt Faye smelled like mothballs and the liver and onions she'd been cooking all day, but Annie was grateful to have her staying on to help with the baby, and the cooking and cleaning.

"He's not exactly my *beau*." She eased Grace into her aunt's arms as her baby sister cried. "There, there, Gracie."

Aunt Faye cradled the baby in her arms, then started singing to her. Her high-pitched singing voice left much to be desired, so Annie wasn't surprised when Grace started to cry harder.

"Maybe try the formula." Annie forced a smile, then went outside to greet Jacob.

They sat on the porch steps beside each other.

"How's your *mamm*?" Annie squinted against the sun's glare as it met with the horizon.

"How is *your mamm*?" Jacob tipped his hat down a little, also blocking the sun's rays.

"My *mudder* is the same." Annie swallowed back a lump in her throat.

"I hear the baby crying inside." Jacob stared straight ahead as he nervously tapped a foot.

"*Ya*. She's been fussy. *Aenti* Faye is going to try to give her some formula."

"A baby needs a momma." He turned to Annie, his eyes glassy, drooping. "And I don't really think that ever changes. We all need our *mudder*."

Jacob hadn't answered her when she asked how his mother was doing. "Jacob, what is going on?"

He sat quietly, as a muscle in his jaw quivered. "They didn't get it all, the cancer."

Annie brought a hand to her chest. "*Ach*, Jacob. *Nee*. I thought everything was going to be fine after the surgery."

"I think we all did." He paused, scratching his chin. "Everyone but *Mamm*. I felt like she's known all along that the surgery wouldn't be enough."

"Why do you say that?"

Jacob shrugged. "Because she just didn't seem all that surprised when the doctor told us. Hannah took it pretty hard, but *mei daed* actually cried. I don't think I've ever seen him cry before."

"But they'll do more chemotherapy, right? They can get the rest of it, *ya*?"

Jacob shrugged again. "Maybe."

Annie found Jacob's hand and held it tightly. "Why is this happening to both of our *mudders*, at the same time like this?"

"I don't know."

They held hands, watching the sunset, as Annie fought not to question the Lord's will.

"I love you, Annie." Jacob squeezed her hand.

"I love you too, Jacob." She had no idea what the future held, but for now, it seemed like loving each other was the glue keeping them both sane.

"*Mamm* is going to tell Charlotte tomorrow. She takes things real hard. Charlotte's a *gut* Christian and we all love her, but she isn't the best at accepting everything as God's will."

Nor am I, Annie thought, when it came to her mother. Annie had already tried to envision a life without her mom, and the vision never fully developed. Baby Grace needed a mother. God was going to fix this. Mamm *will wake up.*

"*Ya*, Charlotte will take it hard," Annie finally said.

"Do you think she will ever convert and marry Daniel?" Jacob turned to face her, the lines in his forehead deepening. *When did he get those?*

"I hope so. Daniel loves her, and I believe she loves him just as much."

"Now isn't the time for them to be making those kinds of decisions." He shook his head.

"Or"—Annie took a deep breath—"maybe it *is* the right time for them to get married, so they can be there for each other, comforting one another the way husbands and wives do."

Annie recalled the one time she and Jacob had broken the rules, God's rules, and shared in a way that only married people should. They'd sworn not to let it happen again, but right now, Annie could recall the intimacy she'd felt with Jacob, the way they'd seemed as one. What an escape it would be, to fall into his arms and forget about everything for a while.

"But maybe they'd be getting married so they could"—Jacob raised one shoulder, then lowered it—"you know . . . comfort each other."

Annie stayed quiet. She was pretty sure they weren't talking about Daniel and Charlotte anymore. Jacob leaned over and kissed her in a way that would only lead to a place they'd vowed not to visit, but Annie allowed herself to feel all the passion that his lips offered.

"Let's take a walk." Jacob rose, still holding her hand, and guided her to her feet.

"It's almost dark." Annie started down the porch steps with him.

"We won't be gone long."

Annie opened her mouth to protest but didn't.

⌒

Charlotte knocked on Lena and Amos's door ten days after she'd had her surgery. They would just be finishing up with morning devotions since this was an off Sunday for worship service. She'd spoken with Lena several times and visited her twice, but Charlotte hadn't seen her since she'd gotten home from the hospital two days ago.

When Buddy started barking, Charlotte smiled. Giving her precious Chihuahua to Amos might have been the most unselfish thing she'd ever done. Amos had taken to the dog while Charlotte was staying with them, and at the time Jacob had left home. Lena and Amos were both feeling the void. But it warmed her heart when the screen door opened and Buddy ran to her. She scooped him up and scratched behind his ears.

"Hey, Buddy." Charlotte let him give her a big, wet kiss on the cheek before she looked up at Amos. "Am I too early? Hannah left a message for me last night that you and Lena wanted to talk to me. Is everything okay?"

Amos took a step backward, motioning for Charlotte to come in. Lena was still in her nightclothes, covered by her robe, and sitting on the couch. She had a scarf pulled around her head instead of a prayer covering.

"Forgive my disheveled look this morning." Lena touched the top of her head, then folded her hands in her lap. "Are you hungry? Hannah brought over two loaves of fresh bread. I'm still moving slowly."

"You know I'm not going to turn down bread." Charlotte sat on the couch beside Lena. "But first, I want to know what's going on."

Amos shuffled in his socks across the room, opened his bedroom door, and disappeared with Buddy on his heels.

"They didn't get all of the cancer, Charlotte." Lena smiled a little, then reached for Charlotte's hand. "And I need for you to be strong right now."

Charlotte's stomach twisted, like she'd been punched in the gut. "What?"

"*Mei maedel*. The cancer had already spread when they did the mastectomy. The doctors had hoped that wouldn't be the case, but alas . . ." Lena looked down for a few moments before she reconnected with Charlotte's gaze. "All hope is not lost, but it isn't *gut* either."

Charlotte's bottom lip trembled, and she wanted to be strong for Lena, but she couldn't imagine her life without her in it. "Then you fight. You do everything the doctor says. If the chemo makes you sick again, Hannah and I can switch out taking care of you. I'll—I'll cook or have meals brought in or . . ." She took a long, deep breath. "I'll do whatever you need me to. What should I do?" A tear trickled down Charlotte's cheek.

Lena smiled. "Pray."

"Of course. Of course I'll be praying."

"But, my sweet girl, you must also understand that whatever happens is God's will."

Charlotte opened her mouth to speak, but Lena raised a finger to silence her.

"*Nee*, Charlotte. I want you to listen to me. You tend to get angry with God if prayers aren't answered the way you see fit. But that isn't our way, and it shouldn't be your way either."

"This is so messed up," Charlotte said through her tears, knowing she sounded like Andrea. "Just messed up. And there isn't anything you can say that will make me not beg God to heal you completely."

Lena chuckled. "I would never ask you not to pray to God for my well-being, but I will ask you to accept my destiny, either way."

"I can't believe this is happening. I thought for sure you were out of the woods." She searched Lena's eyes. "Did you already know when you went into surgery?" Charlotte recalled Lena's instructions about not keeping her alive on machines.

"No one had told me the cancer was still there. They didn't know. But in my heart, I had a feeling."

Charlotte wiped her eyes. "So, what next? More chemo? Another surgery?"

"*Nee*. My body has put up a *gut* fight, but it's had enough. I am going to try some alternative, holistic healing methods, along with homeopathy. I've joined a group, mostly *Englisch*, who have chosen this route as their treatment."

"No." Charlotte shook her head. "I'm not saying you shouldn't try those things, too, but you need to utilize modern technology, Lena. I feel strongly that—"

"It's not your decision." Lena cut Charlotte off as she raised her chin. "I need you to accept my choice of treatment."

"That's not a treatment. Or it shouldn't be considered as your exclusive treatment. It's not enough." Charlotte's voice hitched as she sniffled. "Please, Lena."

Lena adjusted the scarf on her head, letting go of Charlotte's hand, which felt symbolically awful. "If God chooses to heal me, it won't matter what regimen I choose. I'm putting my faith in Him, and only He knows what is best for me."

Charlotte hung her head as she thought about Daniel's mother being kept alive by machines in the hospital. "I'll respect your wishes, Lena." She straightened and forced a small smile. "But I really need you to be okay."

"I am okay. Hannah and Jacob support my decision, even though I know that, like you, they'd prefer I utilize everything the doctors have to offer." She shook her head. "I'm so tired."

Charlotte glanced around the room and leaned her ear toward the kitchen. All quiet. "Where is Jacob?"

Lena rolled her eyes. "In bed. Apparently, life in the city has left him with some bad habits, like staying up late and sleeping in." She twisted to face Charlotte and flinched. "Amos isn't happy with me. That's why he vanished to the bedroom. He doesn't like to hear that I've chosen not to endure more treatments."

Charlotte fought the urge to try to reason with Lena again, but as she winced again, just from a slight movement, Charlotte suspected maybe Lena had been downplaying her pain. Charlotte recalled the time Lena had spent with her in Houston and the toll the chemotherapy had taken on the woman.

"He loves you. That's why he wants you to fight."

Lena held on to Charlotte's hand again, and she felt infused with strength, if only momentarily.

"I know. But the fight in me is over," Lena said. "God has always been at the helm, and He will guide my way. Now, how about a buttered slice of bread?"

Charlotte had lost her appetite, but she wasn't about to let Lena down. As they made their way to the kitchen, Charlotte asked, "Are you afraid of dying?"

Lena smiled, a genuine, real smile. "*Ach, nee.* Of course not. I will be sad to be separated from Amos, *mei kinner,* and you." She shrugged. "But it's just temporary."

Charlotte nodded. And she thought about Andrea. "My sister doesn't believe in heaven or hell. She believes in God but not an afterlife."

Lena moved slowly as she took a loaf of bread from the stove top to the kitchen table, then she pulled a tub of butter from the refrigerator. She waited until they were both seated and said the blessing. "It's like cake and icing." Lena smiled, even though Charlotte wasn't following.

"One isn't complete without the other. The cake is the foundation for the icing, such as believing in God is the foundation for heaven. Maybe Andrea can only imagine the icing, but she hasn't had a taste of it, to understand and appreciate how it complements the cake."

Lena had a way of turning most conversations into something about food. It was a quirky, loveable trait, but Charlotte was sure Andrea wouldn't accept that explanation about heaven.

"I don't think Andrea would understand that analogy." Charlotte took a big bite of the bread, allowing the melted butter to rest on her tongue before she swallowed. "I'm not even sure I do."

Lena swiped butter onto her own slice of bread. "You must show her heaven, give her a taste of it."

"How can I do that?"

Lena smiled again. "Show her the icing."

"How can I do that? I haven't seen heaven." Charlotte took another bite of warm bread.

"Then how do you know it exists?"

Charlotte stared at Lena, who was still slowly spreading butter on her piece of bread. "Because I just know. I feel it."

Lena laid her knife down and picked up her slice of bread. "Then you must show her how to feel it too."

How could anyone do that? She stared at the woman who had been more of a mother to her than anyone in her life. *What am I going to do without you?*

Thirteen

One thing about the Amish folks—they knew how to cook. Andrea snacked on the last of the cold turkey left over from the day before. Thanksgiving had come and gone without much ado. Charlotte's core group of friends had chosen to celebrate quietly since two of the matriarchs had serious health issues. But her friend Hannah had brought leftovers late yesterday afternoon. Lack of holiday flair might have been a disappointment to some, but Andrea couldn't remember the last time she'd had a true Thanksgiving dinner, complete with turkey, cornbread dressing, and cranberry sauce. Sitting around in sweatpants with her daughter and sister, quietly enjoying the meal in front of a roaring fire, had been heavenly.

She put another log on the fire. It had warmed up to almost fifty, but there was a nip in the air, and something about having a fire made things feel even more homey.

Her phone dinged with Black Friday e-mail sales, and as she finished making two pairs of earrings, she fantasized about what it might be like to sell her jewelry someday.

Charlotte had chosen to go to work on a day that was a holiday for most people, but she'd said that the newspaper had to go to print, holiday or not.

Andrea glanced around the living room. A bit of a mess. Bella's few toys were in the middle of the floor, Andrea's lunch dishes were on the coffee table, and a soiled diaper that needed to be thrown away lay on the floor. Up to now she hadn't felt the need to contribute much. A free place to stay and meals from a sister who owed her something.

But Charlotte had surprised her. Almost everyone in Andrea's life had let her down in one way or another, but Charlotte was housing her and Bella and feeding them. For free.

Charlotte wouldn't be home from work for a couple of hours. A speckled flurry of dust motes floated atop the sun rays that lit the room. Bella was napping since she'd gotten up super early this morning, so Andrea picked up her lunch dishes and carried them to the kitchen, along with the dirty diaper, which she pitched into the trash can. She found a sweeper in the mudroom, along with some other cleaning supplies.

After an hour of sprucing up the place, she wiped her hands on her jeans and inspected her work, proud of the effort. A search in the kitchen led to finding a pound of hamburger meat, some noodles, and a can of cream of mushroom soup. Andrea wasn't much of a cook, but a combo of those three ingredients could make dinner.

She cooked the noodles in a pot on the stove, seared the hamburger meat, then combined both with the soup and set the burner to Warm. Maybe someday she'd make money selling her jewelry and she could buy her sister a stove that actually had an oven. As she inspected her efforts, she heard a car coming up the driveway, and when she peered out the kitchen window, she recognized the vehicle right away. Her heart thumped as she crossed into the living room to the front door.

"Hey," she said through the screen. "You're a sight for sore eyes."

Blake was dressed in a nice pair of khaki slacks and a long sleeve white shirt. "I've missed you." He smiled. "And Bella."

Andrea suspected he might have missed Bella more than her, but she'd missed him too. She pushed the screen door open and stepped aside so he could come in.

"It smells like lemon in here." Blake glanced around the modest living room.

"I've been cleaning"—she folded her arms across her chest—"and cooking." She nodded toward the kitchen.

Blake gasped as he brought a hand to his broad chest. "Be still my heart. Andrea cooks?"

She chuckled. "I didn't say it was chef worthy, but it's a meal."

"Where's Bella?"

"Sleeping on Charlotte's bed." Andrea eyed him up and down. "You've lost weight."

"No job equates to no money, and the food stamps were in your name." Blake shrugged. "But I get by."

Andrea bit her bottom lip and glanced in the direction of the kitchen. "Do you want something to eat?"

"Nah. I just came to check on you and Bella. Things ended kinda . . . badly between us."

Andrea's heart leapt a little. "Yeah, I wish they hadn't gone that way."

Blake grinned, raising an eyebrow. "You did sort of steal my car."

"*Borrowed.*"

"Hey, can I go take a peek at Bella?"

"Yeah, but try not to wake her." She pointed to the closed door that led to her sister's bedroom.

"Thanks." Blake eased the door open and closed it gently behind him.

Andrea sat on the couch. Would she and Blake try to work things out? Part of her wanted to, but as she considered the changes she'd made in her life, she thought better of it. For the first time ever, she felt like she had a family, even if it was a sister she was still getting to know.

After a few minutes, she was hoping Blake hadn't awoken Bella, who napped better at Charlotte's house. She glanced at the time on her phone. Charlotte would be home in about thirty minutes, and Andrea wasn't sure how her sister would feel about Blake being here.

The door to the bedroom opened slowly.

"Still sound asleep?" Andrea smiled, wishing she'd done more with her hair today. *Like washed it.*

"Yeah. I was just watching her sleep." He sighed. "I really do miss you two."

Andrea was tempted to ask him to stay for a little while, maybe even stay for dinner, but Charlotte was usually tired when she got home from work, and Andrea didn't want to mess up the surprise dinner and clean house by adding Blake to the mix. She stood.

"Thanks for stopping by, but we're really okay." She tucked her hair behind her ears, then hung her thumbs in the back pockets of her jeans.

"I was in the neighborhood," he said with a shrug. "Text if you wanna do something sometime."

Andrea nodded. "Will do." *Maybe.*

Charlotte heaved her purse up on her shoulder with two plastic bags of groceries hanging from her wrists. Not much, but it would get them by for a few days until she had time to do normal grocery shopping.

She opened the screen, then the wooden door. Her purse and both bags of groceries slid down to the floor as she breathed in the smell of food. Her gaze darted around her clean living room, then landed on Bella, who appeared to have on clean clothes and a precious little pink bow holding her hair on her head, and a lavender candle flickered on the fireplace mantel. Andrea was sitting by Bella on the floor, grinning.

"Excuse me, ma'am . . . do I have the right house?" Charlotte smiled as she reloaded the two bags of groceries on her arm before tossing her purse on the couch.

Andrea stood and took a bow. "Good evening. Dinner is served."

Charlotte allowed a warm glow to suffuse her senses for a few seconds. There'd been so much unsettling news lately, and her appreciation for her sister's efforts ran deep. Without giving it much thought, she walked to Andrea and pulled her into a one-armed hug as the groceries weighed down her other arm. She kissed her on the cheek. "Thank you."

"It's nothing fancy."

Charlotte bent at the waist and cupped Bella's chin. "And look how pretty you look, baby girl." Then she straightened and turned to Andrea again. "I bet whatever you made is great." She sniffed the air. "Goodness me, I might be in heaven because I think I smell cleaning solution too." She winked at Andrea before she walked to the kitchen and set the bags on the table, which was already set.

Andrea came into the kitchen carrying Bella. "I wanted to do something nice for you. I mean, you . . ." She shrugged. "You've done a lot for me and Bella."

Charlotte lifted the lid from the pot and inhaled. She'd have forced herself to eat what Andrea cooked, even if it was awful, but it smelled wonderful. After she put the lid on the pot, she kissed Bella's cheek, patted Andrea's arm, and started out of the kitchen.

"I need a quick shower before I eat. The regular reporter at the newspaper didn't go in." She scowled. "Guess he missed the memo that said today was a mandatory workday." She shook her head. "Anyway, they asked me to report on an accident. I had to slide on my rear down an embankment to see what was going on, and then a Life Flight helicopter landed and blew dirt all over me. But you and Bella start without me."

"I'll feed Bella and wait for you."

Charlotte was tired, filthy, worried about Lena, and confused about Daniel. But for tonight, she was going to bask in things to be grateful for. Andrea was coming around, and Charlotte was getting to know her sister and her adorable niece. Ethan's small house had become a home for Charlotte's family. *I wish you could be here, Ethan.*

After she'd showered and washed her hair, she threw on a pair of sweatpants and a baggy T-shirt, then wanted to check to see when she'd last written Ethan a letter. It was something her therapist had suggested Charlotte do while she was still living in Houston, but she'd been rather lax about it since she'd moved to Lancaster County. It would be nice to jot down her feelings in the form of a letter to Ethan after dinner, especially since things were going so well with Andrea.

Charlotte opened her bedside drawer and pulled out her journal. She set it on the bed as a reminder for later, but as she started to close the drawer, her heart skipped a beat. She'd cashed her paycheck the day before yesterday and put the envelope inside the drawer, something she'd done for the past month. She was running on cash until all of her outstanding checks cleared, hoping to find out why she was 180 dollars off in her checking account. *I'm sure I put it in there.*

She shuffled through bills, pens, a bottle of lotion, and other odds and ends, until everything was on her bed and the drawer was empty. And no envelope with cash. *No wonder Andrea went to all this trouble.*

Charlotte left her bedroom and crossed through the living room like a speed walker nearing the finish line. "Where's my money, Andrea?" She spoke slow and soft but deliberate since Bella got upset if anyone raised their voice.

"What?" Andrea narrowed her eyebrows. Bella was sitting in a booster chair, courtesy of Dianda from work, nibbling on noodles. "What money?"

Charlotte took a deep breath and released it slowly. She had a little money in her savings account, but that was for emergencies. And it was beside the point. "I can't have you living here if you are going to steal from me. Did you think I wouldn't know?"

"What are you talking about?" Andrea took a step toward Charlotte as she pulled a chain that was tucked into her shirt out for Charlotte to see. "I only borrowed this, your cross. I'm sorry! I didn't know it was worth money. I just—I'm sorry." She reached around to unfasten the clasp. "It was on your nightstand, and I just put it on. I was going to give it back."

Her eyes started to water as her voice got louder. Once it was off, she held it out to Charlotte. "I thought if I wore it just for a day that I might feel something from God."

Charlotte's eyes widened. "You can *have* the necklace. It's the money from my paycheck I'm talking about. It's gone. All of it!" Now, it was Charlotte whose voice was rising.

Andrea took a step backward, enough that her arm touched the hot pot on the stove. Her sister cursed as she grabbed her arm below her elbow, then she cursed again, louder. "I didn't steal your money!" She threw the cross onto the ground. "I borrowed your necklace, and I wasn't going to keep it. But I didn't take any money!"

Charlotte stared at Jesus' likeness staring up at her, and she could almost hear Him whispering, *Love is patient, love is kind . . .*

Bella started to wail, the same way she'd done when she'd first arrived with Andrea weeks ago.

Charlotte took another breath. "Okay, Andrea, just calm down."

Tears poured down her sister's cheeks. "You know,

Sis, you're just like everyone else. I thought you were different, but you're not. Once bad, always bad. And I'm bad!"

Charlotte glanced back and forth between Andrea and Bella, trying to decide who to attend to first, but Andrea started crying hard, threw her hands up in the air, and caught the handle of the pot, sending dinner splattering all over the wooden floors. Bella's wailing was earsplitting, but it was Andrea Charlotte took a step toward.

"Get away from me!" Andrea pointed at Charlotte. "I knew this was a bad idea. Rotten parents, rotten foster parents, and rotten sister. I'm rotten too."

Charlotte's jaw stayed dropped for a few seconds. "I thought you had a great childhood." She edged closer to Bella to pick her up but kept her gaze on Andrea since her sister seemed almost hysterical.

"Don't touch her. She's my baby, and you can't have her. This entire little ploy was probably just so you can take Bella away from me. No one is going to take her from me, not even you!" Andrea jerked Bella out of the booster seat, still screaming, her tiny face beet red as tears streamed down her cheeks. "Don't worry. We're leaving."

"Don't be ridiculous." Charlotte was on Andrea's heels as Bella reached for Charlotte over Andrea's shoulders. "It's almost dark. We'll figure everything out. Maybe I misplaced the money. I'm sorry. Just stay."

Charlotte chased Andrea down the steps and reached for her sister's shirt. "Andrea, stop!"

She kept going, breaking into a slow jog, Bella bouncing on her hip and crying.

"I'm not going to chase you!" Charlotte slammed her hands to her hips.

But that's exactly what Charlotte did. She took off running after them. Andrea was acting like a child, but it was the child on her sister's hip that worried Charlotte the most. "At least leave Bella with me!"

Andrea stopped dead in her tracks and spun around as Bella twisted and cried, trying to wiggle out of her mother's arms. "You. Will. Never. Have. My. Daughter. Do you understand me?"

Charlotte was familiar was hate and the expressions that went along with it, and every bit of that emotion was now leveled at her. So much so that Charlotte started to cry. "If you need some time to yourself, okay, but please leave Bella here."

"You are never going to see us again. Ever! And if you try to follow me, I swear I'll call the police." She pulled her cell phone from her pocket and held it above her head. "I'll call 911 right now and say you're trying to hurt Bella."

Charlotte put both hands to her chest as tears slipped down her cheeks. "Andrea, are you crazy? I would never hurt Bella. I *love* Bella."

Andrea pressed her lips together into a smile that looked anything but happy. "Of course you do. Because *everyone* loves Bella. Everyone always loves Bella." Then she turned around, Bella screaming, still holding her phone in the air. "Do. Not. Follow. Me!"

∽

Daniel lay on his bed. It wasn't even dark yet, but his body seemed to give out before his mind did lately. He stayed busy during the days, which kept his mind occupied, but in the evenings his parents consumed his thoughts. He'd had time to think about Charlotte's opinions. It still seemed wrong to intentionally kill a person, especially a beloved family member, but watching his father deteriorate physically and mentally was causing him to rethink things. Were they interfering with God's plans by allowing machines to keep his mother alive? If that was the case, then weren't they interfering with the Lord's plan every time someone took medication to rid him of a disease? And that thought brought him full circle to Lena. Annie had already told Daniel that Lena's prognosis was grim.

Closing his eyes, Daniel pleaded with the Lord to ease so much of the suffering going on around them, but his cell phone buzzed on the nightstand. *Charlotte.*

"Is it too late for you to come over?" She was crying, and Daniel bolted straight up in bed.

"*Nee.* I can come right now. What's wrong? Are you hurt?" His heart thumped in his chest.

"I'm not physically hurt, but I feel like my insides are

torn to threads—about Lena, and now, Andrea got mad and ran out of the house with Bella. They have no car or place to stay, as far as I know."

Daniel could barely understand her, she was crying so hard.

"Or I can come there, which would be faster."

"*Nee, nee.* It won't take me long to hook up the buggy. I'll leave right away." It didn't sound like Charlotte needed to be driving anywhere.

He dressed quickly, then scurried down the hallway in his socks before bolting down the stairs two at a time. He peeked into the former mudroom, now Aunt Faye's cemetery room. She was humming quietly as she stared at family pictures she'd hung on the wall. A plate of something unidentifiable sat on the hutch, something pickled, but Daniel didn't think it was oysters. He'd learned over the weeks that his aunt would pickle just about anything. Most recently, she'd pickled lemons and carrots. Surprisingly, the carrots were pretty good.

"I'm going to Charlotte's house for a while."

Aunt Faye eased her head around to face him, her eyes wet with moisture, her cheeks flushed. She nodded, then returned her attention to the photos, many of them relatives dressed in Amish clothes.

How did she get the pictures since it wasn't their way to pose for photos? It was an odd room, but it seemed of great importance to her. Daniel remembered a similar room his aunt had at her own home, with a comparable display of photos and memorabilia from those who had gone before her.

Daniel was eager to get to Charlotte's, but he couldn't leave his aunt like this. "Are you okay, *Aenti* Faye?"

The older woman nodded toward her wall of photos, before she looked back at him. "My mind is a blur sometimes, and with age comes forgetfulness." She focused on the wall again. "I make sure to have a picture of everyone I love. Even loved ones who are still in the Old Order have let me photograph them."

A lot of the pictures were the old-timey Polaroid kind. His stomach roiled. "Are you going to be okay if I go to Charlotte's house?" *And where is Annie?* Daniel had passed by his sister's room. The door had been open, and all was dark. But it was still early.

Aunt Faye smiled a little. "Yes, dear. I'll be fine."

Daniel took a step to leave but stopped when his aunt picked up a picture and stared at it. Even in the distance Daniel recognized the photo of his mother, smiling, standing by her garden in a dark blue dress and black apron. Her signature smile crooked up on one side as she held a shovel out.

Aunt Faye brought the photo to her chest. She was already preparing to let go of her niece, to add another photo in her cemetery room. Daniel's heart was heavy, the burdens of life pressing down on him, as he forced himself to think about life without his mother. It was almost unbearable.

Once again, he thought about Charlotte's and his differing opinions when it came to machinery to keep a person alive. But the sound of Charlotte crying resurfaced in his mind, and he picked up the pace.

Fourteen

*S*itting on the porch swing, Annie pried her lips from Jacob's when the front door opened, then she spun to face her brother.

"I'm pretty sure your lack of control has gotten you two in trouble before," Daniel said in a gruff voice. As the sun made its final descent, the propane lamp in the yard lit the porch enough for Annie to see her brother's red face. She was sure her own face was a similar color from embarrassment. "We're not doing anything."

"Keep it that way." Daniel pointed a finger at Jacob before he darted down the steps. "I'm going to Charlotte's for a while." He stopped, turned around. "Go check on *Aenti* Faye in a few minutes."

"*Ya,* okay."

Annie loved her aunt, and she'd check on her later, but right now other thoughts consumed her mind. She recalled the one time she and Jacob had succumbed to their desires. Their sinful act had left Annie thinking she was pregnant. Thankfully, she hadn't been, but keeping their promise not to repeat the act was becoming more and more challenging. They'd almost crossed the line the other night, but they both corralled their actions and emotions and stepped back. Annie knew what these types of kisses could lead to. Even if she wasn't clear what direction their relationship was headed.

Jacob waited until Daniel had hooked the horse to the buggy and was down the road before he started kissing Annie again. She forced herself to back away.

"What are we doing, Jacob?"

He grinned. "Kissing."

She scowled. "I mean about *us*. Both of our mothers are ill. We're using"—she bit her bottom lip—"this, um . . . affection . . . to distract us. I'm not sure that's right."

Jacob had gained back some of the weight he'd lost. He looked healthier, more like the old Jacob she knew and loved, before he'd run away to the *Englisch* world.

He faced forward and leaned his head against the house, stilling the porch swing they were in. "I'm not going back to the *Englisch* world, Annie. That's all behind me."

She wanted to believe him, but Jacob had gone back and forth about his feelings on the subject so many times, she didn't trust his words anymore.

"You don't believe me, do you?" He sighed. "I don't blame you, I reckon."

"I want to believe you, Jacob." Annie took hold of his hand. "I tried to stop loving you when you left, but I guess love isn't something we can control." She closed her eyes, trying to picture her mother standing in the kitchen cooking and not hooked up to machines, lifeless. *What should I do, Mamm?*

"I've always loved you too, Annie." He pulled her to him and kissed her on the mouth, but the moment his breathing became heavier, she backed away.

"I want you to love my heart. You know what will happen if we keep carrying on the way we are. And we promised each other—and God—that we wouldn't fall into temptation again."

"I know." Jacob eased his hand from hers and sighed again.

Annie waited for him to say something to convince her that he loved her for the person she was, not just for the physical part. But he was quiet.

She stayed quiet, too, wondering what their future held. Would it be together or separate?

Charlotte ran across the yard and fell into Daniel's arms the moment he stepped out of the buggy. His strong embrace comforted her, and he would know what to do.

Running his hand the length of her hair, he held her tightly. She forced herself away and swiped at her face. "I'm so worried. She couldn't have gotten that far, but there are acres of farmland I can't drive in. If she doesn't want to be found, she can easily hide."

Daniel tucked her hair behind both ears. "Hopefully she called someone to pick up her and the *boppli*. But maybe we should drive around and look for her."

Charlotte nodded. "Yeah, I think so." They walked toward the house, hand in hand. "I just have to get my purse, phone, and keys. I've tried over and over to call her, but the call goes straight to voice mail." She squeezed Daniel's hand. "If anything happens to them . . ." She'd come to love Bella—and Andrea—despite her sister's shortcomings.

"We will find them."

She called Andrea again as they walked to the truck, but still no answer.

There was a rumble in the distance. Thunder. "Andrea is terrified of lightning and thunder," she said to Daniel as she climbed into the truck.

Please, God . . . please keep them safe.

Andrea crouched inside an Amish barn, no idea where she was, but she'd actually prayed to the God Charlotte loved so much. And behold, there was a basket of apples in the barn. She bit off a chunk and gave it to Bella, afraid her daughter's wailing would wake up the people who lived here.

"I'm so sorry, Bella. I'm so sorry I'm not a better

person, a better mother." She cradled her daughter on her lap as Bella chewed on the slice of apple. "I want to be better," she added in a whisper through her tears.

Bella laid her head against Andrea's chest, still clutching the apple. "Momma."

"Yep, I'm your momma, and I swore I'd be a good mother, not like my own mom who saw fit to give me away." She cringed. Her store-bought parents probably wouldn't have been so bad if Andrea hadn't already been ruined by then. She'd been asking herself if she would have stolen Charlotte's money if she'd known it was there. *Probably.* She'd already been guilty of stealing someone else's money. But wasn't buried money up for grabs to whoever found it?

She was kicking herself for not taking the time to get the money she'd stashed underneath the couch cushions. Five hundred dollars would have gotten her a cheap room for a week and some food.

"I'm sorry, Bella," she whispered again, kissing the toddler on the forehead.

Then she heard it. Thunder. *Oh, God, please . . .*

As tears flooded her eyes, she bowed her head. And she prayed. As best she knew how.

Daniel was quiet as they rode back to Charlotte's house. She was concentrating on keeping Big Red on the road as rain pounded against the old truck.

They'd driven around for an hour, but no sign of Charlotte's sister or her baby. At one point they pulled over and prayed that Andrea and Bella were safe. They'd been torn between continuing to look for the duo and heading home before the weather got even worse. In the end they decided that Andrea was surely smart enough to take shelter.

Lightning bursting, thunder clattering, and rain falling in sheets around them had them both on edge, but when they pulled into Charlotte's driveway, the woman and her baby were curled up in the corner of the porch.

"Oh, thank You, God!" Charlotte jumped from the truck without turning off the engine and sprinted across the yard. She slipped on the porch step and fell before she finally made it to Andrea and Bella.

Daniel turned off the engine and pressed his foot down on the emergency brake, like he'd seen Charlotte do plenty of times. He grabbed the keys and gathered up her purse, stuffing her phone inside, then darted into the weather. By the time he reached the porch, the two women and the baby were inside, all three in a giant hug, crying in the dark.

He reached into his pocket and turned on the small flashlight he'd thought to bring when he left home, then he lit the lanterns on Charlotte's mantel.

"I was so scared. I'm sorry." Andrea clung to Charlotte as she stroked her sister's wet hair.

"I'm sorry too! Thank God you and Bella are okay."

Charlotte had both arms wrapped around mother and daughter. She probably didn't even realize her elbow was bleeding. The baby was wailing, so Daniel eased her from her mother's arms. She tried to resist until Daniel said there were probably cookies in the kitchen.

He headed that way and shone the flashlight around the kitchen, Bella on his hip, eyeing what must have been supper splattered all over the wooden floor. He stepped around the mess until he located a pink container on the counter. Charlotte kept cookies in there, often store-bought, but it didn't matter. And thankfully, two cookies were inside. He offered one to the child, bouncing her gently until she caught her breath and took the treat.

Daniel sat in the chair, Bella on his lap. He looked around the dimly lit room. Maybe he should have seen Charlotte in his mind's eye, since it was her house, but it was his mother he saw. Smiling, cooking, making coffee, preparing a sandwich for his father.

When his eyes became moist, he blinked a few times and refocused on the situation at hand. "Do you want another cookie?"

Bella didn't smile, but she didn't try to bolt from his lap or his arms when he stood to get her another cookie. He set her in a chair, then filled a glass with water. After she'd eaten the cookie, he held the cup for her to take a sip of water, but she gulped the liquid down as if she hadn't had anything to drink in hours. Daniel picked up the pot of food and cleaned the mess as best he could in the nearly dark room.

"She had some water and a couple of cookies," he said as he carried Bella back into the living room. Both women were sitting on the couch, sniffling. Crying, Andrea looked up at him. "I'm sorry, Daniel."

He held up a hand. "*Nee*, no need for an apology to me."

Andrea turned back to Charlotte. "I don't know why it took me so long to figure out that it must have been Blake who took the money."

Charlotte had her arm around Andrea. "It's okay. I'm just glad you and Bella are all right."

Daniel was aware of Charlotte's financial issues. She'd worked hard to build up a small savings, but losing an entire paycheck would be rough for her. After Bella climbed onto her mother's lap, Daniel told the women he was going to leave.

"But the weather is awful." Charlotte stood and walked to him, then touched his arm. "Can't you wait awhile?"

Daniel glanced out the window. "I've been driving a buggy in all types of weather for most of my life. I'll be fine." He smiled. "And it sounds like the rain is letting up."

Charlotte walked with him onto the front porch. She wrapped her arms around his waist. "Thank you a thousand times for coming over and going with me."

He hugged her back, cupping her head in one hand. "I'm glad everyone is okay." She eased away and looked into his eyes. With Charlotte, it always seemed she was searching. Searching for peace. Searching for happiness. *Lost relatives.* And now, searching his thoughts.

"I love you." She said the words with a finality that made his stomach flip.

"I love you too." He waited for her to drop a bomb on him, but she just smiled.

"I can loan you the money that was stolen." He kissed her on the forehead.

"Thank you, but I'll be okay."

Now Daniel tried to decipher Charlotte's thoughts, but the woman was a mystery sometimes. "*Ach*, well, I'm here if you need anything."

She leaned up and kissed him on the mouth, lingering for longer than usual before she said, "Thank you."

"I want you to know . . ." Daniel coughed a little, hoping he could complete the rest of his sentence without tears accumulating again. "I'm thinking about what you said, about *mei mamm* and the machines keeping her alive."

"I probably overstepped, Daniel." She shook her head. "It's a personal decision, and my beliefs don't have to be your beliefs."

He nodded. "I know. But it's heavy on my heart, and I'm thinking about it."

She cupped his face with her hand. "I know."

"Although . . . it is *mei daed*'s decision to make."

"Of course."

Daniel kissed her again before he ran across the yard to his buggy.

⌒

Charlotte closed the front door and went back to the couch where Andrea and Bella were sitting.

"Are you going to marry him?" Andrea bounced Bella on her knee.

"Well, that's the big question, I guess." Every time she talked herself out of a future with Daniel, the other Charlotte who lived in her head talked her back into seeing it as an option. "I love him," she added in a whisper.

"So, what are you waiting for?"

Charlotte leaned back against the couch and sighed. "It's a lot to think about."

They were quiet for a while.

"I'll get your money back from Blake."

Charlotte shook her head. "No. Let it go. We can't prove it, and I don't want to draw attention to us. The Amish don't really like police snooping around or outsiders in their business. And even though I'm not Amish, my house is right in the thick of their district. And they are my friends."

Andrea hung her head. "I can't believe Blake did this. I really didn't think he was like that."

"Maybe he needs it more than we do." Charlotte shrugged.

"Does it matter if he needs it more? It wasn't his to take."

Charlotte looked at Bella, sitting quietly on Andrea's

lap, her eyelids heavy. Then she locked eyes with her sister. "Tonight, when you and Bella left, I . . ." She took a deep breath, blinking back tears. "I realized how much you both mean to me. But I would never try to take Bella from you. I really do want us to be a family."

"I know I'm not the best mother. I didn't have good role models."

"But you can be different than our mother." She recalled Andrea's outburst about not having a good childhood with her adoptive parents. "And different from whoever raised you. I see how much you love Bella."

Charlotte heard the words slip from her mouth, almost as if she were talking to herself. *Why can't I be a good mother if I believe that?*

Andrea kissed Bella on the cheek. The tired baby had fallen asleep before they'd even had a chance to clean her up or feed her something besides cookies.

"I'm so sorry about everything. About Blake. About running out and the things I said." Another tear slipped down Andrea's cheek.

Charlotte stared at her only remaining sibling. "We are going to be okay. I suspect you have issues to work through, the same way I did." She offered up a weak smile. "I'm still working through some of them, but overall I've become a much stronger person, a better person. I give that credit to God." She shook her head. "I wish I had an oven."

"Um, that was rather random. But yeah, kinda limits you as to what you can cook without an oven."

"If I had an oven, I would make Lena's bread recipe. I used to make it in Houston, but my bread never turned out as good as hers." Her thoughts drifted to her surrogate mother as sadness wrapped around her. "But today, if I had an oven, I'd make something else."

"What?" Andrea leaned back against the couch, Bella still sleeping against her.

Charlotte smiled. "I'd make a cake. With icing."

Andrea ran her tongue along her top lip. "Yum. I love cake. And no cake should be without icing."

Charlotte stared at her sister. "How right you are."

But Charlotte didn't have a clue how to offer up Lena's cake analogy about God and the afterlife in a way that it would make sense to her sister.

Andrea thought about the five hundred dollars that was directly underneath the cushion where Charlotte was sitting. Most likely, Charlotte wouldn't keep the money if Andrea told her where it came from. She'd return it to the Amish woman, Edna. And Edna Glick didn't sound very deserving. *But it's evidently her money.*

Maybe Blake did need the money more than Andrea or Charlotte, but Andrea was pretty sure she needed the five hundred dollars more than the Amish woman. *So why do I feel so crummy?*

Maybe she could tell Charlotte she found the money?

As she looked at her newly found sister's face, streaked with dried tears and dots of mascara under her eyes, she fought not to start crying again. Charlotte really cared for Bella and her, and Andrea realized she really cared for Charlotte too. That was something she hadn't foreseen.

Andrea put her hand on the couch, resting along the seam where the cushions met. With one swoop she could reach underneath where Charlotte was sitting and pull out five hundred dollars. *Or not.*

Fifteen

Saturday morning Daniel stood next to Annie in their mother's hospital room, watching the rise and fall of *Mamm*'s chest. The smells of the hospital: ammonia, disinfectant, and sometimes coffee brewing had become all too familiar.

"That person doesn't even look like *Mamm*." Annie spoke in a whisper, her bottom lip trembling.

Their father had taken to watching television in the hospital room, and at the moment he was focused on a cowboy movie. How much money did it cost to keep her alive this way? Not that it should matter, but he had the thought anyway. Everyone in their community contributed to a fund for health care, but several unplanned medical emergencies could deplete the account quickly.

Did Lena's decision not to pursue traditional methods of treatment have anything to do with money? Maybe she was worried about drawing from the fund because of Daniel's mother's condition.

"*Daed*, have they said anything else to you about *Mamm*?" He didn't think his father would be allowed to stay in the hospital room forever, but as Daniel eyed the blankets and pillows on the foldout chair and the empty bags of chips nearby, maybe he could.

His father didn't pull his attention from the television as he shook his head.

Daniel took a deep breath. His father's obvious loss of weight made him appear older than he actually was, and his failure to groom himself was getting worse each day. His gray-and-white-speckled beard looked like birds could be living in it, and his blue shirt was wrinkled like he'd slept in it, which he probably had.

"We're going to get a soda." Daniel cleared his throat. "Do you want anything?"

Their father shook his head again before Daniel led Annie out into the hallway.

"We have to do something," Daniel said once outside the door. "He hasn't left this room, he hasn't held his daughter, and I'm wondering how often he is bathing."

Annie pushed back wisps of brown hair that had fallen from her *kapp*. "I know. But you know how he is. He isn't going to listen to us." She touched Daniel's arm. "Do you think we're doing the wrong thing by not unplugging those machines? I used to not think so, Daniel, but now I'm wondering." She blinked a few times. "I don't think *Mamm* is going to wake up. I wish she could tell us what to do."

Daniel rubbed his chin. "Stay here with *Daed* for a little while. See if you can get him to eat something other than chips. I'll have the driver take me to run an errand, then we'll come back to get you."

"Where are you going?"

"To the one person who might be able to help us work our way through this."

⁓

Andrea typed a text to Blake. *You are a horrible person. A thief. And* . . .

She deleted the text for the third time, Charlotte's words ringing in her head. As much as she wanted to please her sister, she was having a hard time not calling out Blake for what he'd done. Charlotte was running errands this morning, and the temptation to blast Blake kept coming and going.

Andrea glanced at Bella. All clean, with a full tummy, and playing with the toys Charlotte had brought home for her. Then she looked at the jewelry she'd made today. Six pairs of earrings, two necklaces, and a bracelet. Charlotte had commented on all the pieces, saying what she loved about each one. Andrea had felt like crying as she swelled with joy. Someone cared about her enough to see the person she wanted to be.

She set to making more jewelry. If Charlotte really thought the pieces might make some money, then Andrea was going to work hard to save enough money to pay her back the cash Blake had stolen. Maybe she'd sell enough jewelry to buy Charlotte an oven, so she could bake her bread and cake.

Her heart warmed at the thought of doing something for her sister, which surprised and elated her. But niggling in her mind was something beneath the couch cushions that Andrea would have to take care of somehow. She hadn't touched the five hundred dollars, but it gave her a sense of peace that it was there. *Or a false sense of peace?*

She glanced around the room. How much would it cost to have electricity put in the house? Too tall an order, she decided. Besides, Charlotte didn't seem interested in having power. She was more like her Amish friends than she'd admit, and Andrea didn't mean just living without power.

Daniel knocked on the front door of the King homestead. Amos answered the door holding Buddy.

"*Wie bischt*, Amos." Daniel shook the older man's hand. "I was wondering if I could visit with Lena."

"Is it an urgent matter?" Amos set Buddy on the floor but didn't invite Daniel in.

"Um . . ." To Daniel it was urgent, but he wasn't sure

how to answer. "If she's not well, I can come back another time."

Amos nodded. "Maybe another time—"

"Step aside, Amos, and let the man in." Lena came around the corner in a wheelchair, which Daniel wasn't expecting. "I'm perfectly capable of having visitors, even in this mobile chair." She smiled. "Come on in here." She motioned with her hand, and Amos stepped aside so Daniel could go inside.

"Let's sit in the kitchen. I've got bread cooling on the rack and hot coffee that's freshly percolated." Lena rolled herself toward the kitchen, and Daniel followed behind her, unsure if he should offer to push her or not.

"I'll be reading in the bedroom." Amos gave a quick wave before he headed off in the opposite direction with Buddy.

"Sit, sit." Lena motioned toward the table, then she stood and pulled two cups from the cupboard and filled them with coffee. Daniel took both cups of coffee, set them on the table, then sat down. Lena settled back into her wheelchair and joined him at the table. "I get tired easily. We had this mobile chair delivered yesterday, but I don't use it all the time." She pointed at the wheel of the chair, then she sighed, smiling again. Lena smiled a lot. Even now. "So, how is your *mudder*?"

Daniel took off his hat, got up, and hung it on the hook by the kitchen door. "Sorry. I forgot about *mei* hat." He cleared his throat. "*Mamm* is the same."

"I'm sorry, *sohn*. We pray for her daily, for God to take her home or for Him to open her eyes."

"I pray for that too." He scratched the side of his face, wishing he'd thought out what he was going to say.

Lena took a sip of her coffee and set her cup on the table. "Daniel, I've known you since you were born. But I can't think of one time that you've come calling just to chat. So, child, what is on your mind?"

He took a deep breath and blew it out slowly, but the words weren't coming.

"Let me see if I can help you with this." Lena tapped a finger to her chin. "I imagine that by now the hospital is putting a little pressure on your family, hoping you'll soon make a decision about your mother's condition. I saw other families dealing with such a situation while I was at the hospital in Houston having chemotherapy. Once a person was no longer considered curable, they were ready to make the bed available to someone who was. And now you're here, wondering what I would do if I were in your mother's situation. Am I right?"

"Charlotte told me about the paper you asked her to sign. I hope that's okay." Daniel hoped he wasn't betraying a confidence, but he was desperate to understand Lena's mind-set.

She nodded. "It's a personal decision, Daniel."

"That's what everyone keeps saying, but the one person who can and should make that choice isn't able to." He paused, diverting his eyes from hers. "*Daed* is opposed to taking *Mamm* off the machines. Annie and I were, too, in the beginning. But now we are watching both of our parents turning into people we don't recognize." Daniel fought the twitch in his jaw. "*Daed* hasn't even held baby Grace."

"*Ach*, sweet boy. I see the pain in your eyes, and I feel it in your heart." Lena reached over and put her hand on his. "But I can't make this decision for you."

"I know." He scratched the side of his face again. Lena removed her hand when he made the movement. "But I want you to tell me what you would do if you were in my mother's situation."

"You are trying to trick me into making a choice for you." Lena winked at him. "But I'll bite." She stared at him long and hard, the way a mother does with a child, and Daniel could almost feel his mother in the room with them. "I don't want to be kept alive by machines. And I've given strict instructions related to that. I don't feel it's a decision that Amos could make. He'd keep me alive forever, even if"—she paused and took a deep breath—"even if . . . I was already gone."

"I went to the library. I did the research. People in a coma can wake up weeks, months, or even years later. Aren't we killing her by taking the machines away, depriving her of any opportunity to live out her years, to see her new baby daughter?" Daniel swiped at one of his eyes, fearful of the emotion that was building, not wanting to cry in front of Lena. "I don't know if we are interfering with God's will by keeping her alive with all this technology. Maybe God wants us to let her go home. I didn't expect this to go on so long."

"All I can do is to answer your question honestly, about my own wishes. But I'm not saying that is what Eve would want. Only your family can make the decision." Lena's eyes watered up when a tear slipped down Daniel's cheek.

"I'm sorry," he said in a whisper as he brushed it away.

"Don't be. God's will is being done at this very moment, just by you being here. And He will continue to walk beside you until you are sure about what to do."

"Even if Annie and I were able to come to terms with disabling the machines, our father would never do that." Daniel shook his head. "He won't even leave the hospital."

Lena took another sip of coffee. "We love our children in a way that we'd give our lives for them, unconditionally. But we know they will eventually go off to live their own lives." She smiled. "But a marriage is for life, and when one spouse goes home before the other, I suspect that person thinks he will never be whole again. So I understand your father's way of thinking. And my husband's way of thinking. But I'm ready to go home when the Lord calls me, and I don't want any such technology keeping me away from the kingdom and my Father."

Daniel stared at Lena, his mouth opening a little. The woman was practically glowing when she talked about going home.

"Continue to pray about it, Daniel. The answer will come on God's time frame. Not ours."

He knew she was right, but his heart was in his throat, and he had no words.

"Would you like for us to pray together now?" Lena's soft, comforting voice caused his eyes to well up again, and he nodded.

⌒⌒

Charlotte parked Big Red, then shuffled through the grass in her front yard, one hand over her stomach. She wasn't sure if it was the Chinese food she'd treated herself to while running errands or a bug, but she hoped the nausea subsided soon.

"You're early," Andrea said from the couch. Beads, hooks, pliers, and other jewelry-making paraphernalia were scattered all over the coffee table, but the house still had a lemony scent, and Bella was happily stacking blocks in the corner.

"My stomach is acting up." She sat beside her sister, longing to scoop Bella into her arms but not wanting to get the baby sick if Charlotte had a bug. "Wow, Andrea, you've made some beautiful pieces."

Andrea's face lit up. "I'm sorry you're sick, but I'm bursting at the seams to tell you something!"

Charlotte fought the urge to hurl, taking in a deep

breath. "Yeah, what's that?" She forced a smile, not wanting to deflate her sister's excitement.

"Remember how you said I might be able to sell some of my jewelry?"

Charlotte nodded.

"I contacted some local boutiques and sent pictures on my phone. Two of them are willing to take some bracelets and earrings on consignment." Andrea almost squealed at the end. "I might make some money doing this, and I love it."

"That is great, Andrea."

Her sister's expression fell. "Do you want me to make you some soup or something? You look awful."

Charlotte half smiled. "Gee. Thanks." She shook her head. "I appreciate the offer, but I think I just want to lie down."

"Okay." Andrea picked up the pliers and two small green beads. "Maybe if you feel better, we can take some of my jewelry to those shops." She shrugged, smiling. "But if not, that's okay too."

Charlotte was proud of the efforts Andrea was making, but she also suspected her sister had a touch of cabin fever. "Do you know how to drive a stick shift?"

"Yeah. I learned how to drive in a little Toyota pickup, and it was a standard."

Charlotte reached into her purse and pulled out the keys. "It's a beautiful afternoon if you want to take a drive and deliver some of your jewelry. You could leave Bella here, but I'm not sure that's a good idea. I don't want to get her sick."

Andrea's eyes widened. "You'd let me drive your truck?"

Despite her queasy tummy, Charlotte laughed. "It's not exactly a Cadillac. And Dianda from work gave me a car seat the other day. Her kids have outgrown it. It's in the truck." She paused, recalling their recent episode. "You won't go far, right?"

Andrea shook her head. "No. And thank you so much. I bet Bella'd like to get out for a while too. Maybe we'll stop at the park or something."

Charlotte tossed her the keys. "Just be careful."

Andrea ran to Bella and picked her up, scooping up her Hello Kitty purse too. "Want to go see if we can sell some of Momma's jewelry?"

Seeing Andrea so happy and excited warmed Charlotte's heart, but her stomach wasn't in compliance with the rest of her. She wanted to lie down.

"The gears are tricky so don't worry if you kill it once or twice. Just go slow," she said as Andrea loaded up the diaper bag. "And there's a new package of diapers in the laundry room. They were on sale at Walmart, so I grabbed some."

"Thank you." Andrea slung the bag up on her shoulder, then switched Bella to her other hip before she started toward the door.

"Wait." Charlotte snatched up the pack of cigarettes

and lighter her sister kept on the mantel, then started toward Andrea. "You forgot these." She hated that Andrea smoked, but at least her sister had never bickered about smoking outside.

"Oh." Andrea smiled. "I haven't had one in three days. Maybe just leave them there a few more days, just to be sure I don't, um . . . relapse."

"Deal." Charlotte smiled back at her and waited on the porch until Andrea had Big Red out of the driveway, wishing she wasn't feeling so badly so she could have kept Bella. But after a dose of Pepto-Bismol, Charlotte found her way to bed, curled up with a hand across her stomach, and hoped the sick feeling would go away soon.

And she said a quick prayer that Andrea and Bella would be safe. Charlotte felt like she was raising two children, but maybe giving Andrea some freedoms would help her to feel good about herself. Charlotte had certainly had lots of help from her Amish friends, and she was happy to pay it forward.

Annie sat in a chair next to her mother's bed reading the *Die Botschaft* she'd brought from home, while her father watched another cowboys and Indians movie on television. Glancing at the clock on the wall, she hoped Daniel would be back soon. Annie missed baby Grace when she was away from her for too long. Aunt Faye was capable and good with Grace, but Annie was the one who felt like she'd bonded with the baby the most.

"*Daed.*" Annie waited for her father to turn her way, and he scowled a bit, as if interrupting his television show irritated him. "Maybe I should bring Grace to the hospital for you to hold her." She'd asked him before, but she hadn't given up hope.

"*Nee*, a hospital is no place for a *boppli.*" He turned his attention back to the television.

Annie closed the newspaper and folded her hands atop it. "Why don't you let me stay here with *Mamm* while you go home and get cleaned up? *Aenti* Faye will try to feed you, but Daniel and I keep back-up food in the basement too." Annie had brought pickled oysters like her father had requested, but after no one ate them, one of the nurses asked if she could remove them. Her father had reluctantly agreed.

"I do just fine using the bathroom here to bathe." *Daed* ran his fingers through his beard, and Annie wondered if that was to ensure nothing was living in it.

She crossed one leg over the other, kicking it into motion, but after a few seconds, she crossed the other leg and kicked even harder. Then she slammed both feet to the ground. She was close to telling her father how she felt, but a sideways scowl from him quieted her.

Annie had never been one to back talk. Her parents wouldn't have allowed it. And as much as she wanted to yell and scream at her father, she still respected him too much to do so. She tried to imagine what it would be like to be married to a person for as long as her parents had been married, over thirty years. It seemed like a lifetime to Annie.

She loved Jacob, and he'd repeatedly said how much he loved her and wanted a life together. But Jacob's passionate kisses and roaming hands had made her question exactly which part of Annie he loved the most. *Can I trust him not to leave me again?*

She picked up the newspaper, even though she couldn't focus on the happenings in other districts, which she usually loved to read. *Where are you, Daniel?*

Another twenty minutes went by, along with more shooting on the television, before the hospital door swung open. Aunt Faye burst into the room like an angered bull, her mouth scrolled into a frown, red lipstick badly applied, and strands of gray hair falling from a bun on the top of her head. As usual, she smelled a bit like mothballs and oysters, but a floral fragrance also comingled with the scent that made Annie's stomach churn.

"Faye, what are you doing here?" *Daed* turned the television off and stood.

Annie stood too. "And where's Gracie?" She brought a hand to her chest.

Faye slammed her hands to her hips. "Grace is fine. She's with Daniel at home. And I've got a driver waiting to take you and your father home. I'm taking the next shift here at the hospital."

Annie held her breath. To her knowledge their father hadn't gone any farther than the vending machine downstairs in weeks.

"Woman, are you out of your mind? Eve is *mei fraa*, and you will not come in here and dictate to me what I will or will not do." *Daed*'s face was beet red as a muscle flicked in his jaw.

Aunt Faye turned to Annie, smiled sweetly, and blinked. "Hon, you go on out in the hall now. Your father will join you in a minute."

Annie's feet were rooted to the floor as *Daed* clenched his fists at his sides.

"Go along with you, now." Aunt Faye swooshed her arms at Annie like she was herding deer out of a garden.

"Annie, take your aunt home!" *Daed* walked to the side of the hospital bed and laid a hand on Annie's mother. "Both of you. Leave us be."

Aunt Faye inched closer to the other side of the bed, opposite Annie's father, and she also laid a hand on *Mamm*.

"Leave, Annie. Wait in the hallway." Aunt Faye didn't turn around when she spoke, and Annie was sure she'd never heard her great-aunt speak with such a growling authority.

Annie forced herself to step outside.

"Close the door, dear," Aunt Faye said, still not turning around.

Annie did as she was told. Her aunt was quirky, everyone knew that, but she was also almost always cheerful, even when she was trying to be stern. Rarely were her feathers ruffled. Annie stood perfectly still, recalling the time Aunt Faye chased Daniel with a baseball bat. But she could also remember her father chasing Daniel with a large switch after he'd taken on a green-broke horse that he wasn't supposed to ride.

She thought about a movie she'd seen with Jacob a long time ago, the only one she'd ever seen during her *rumschpringe*. At the end of the show, the main character had said, *"Only one of us is going to come out alive."* That movie line was echoing in her mind.

Sixteen

Andrea set Bella in the high chair at the café and then placed the bowl of chocolate cake and ice cream down for them to share. It felt good to have a little money to spend on her daughter. Bella had eaten almost an entire grilled cheese sandwich, so Andrea was happy to share a dessert with her.

The café had a Christmas tree in the corner, and Bing Crosby's rendition of "It's Beginning to Look a Lot Like Christmas" played in the background. Even at lunchtime, the smell of the morning's breakfast offerings still lingered in the air.

Bella had a ring of chocolate around her mouth, and Andrea cautiously chose to submerse herself in joy. *Today is a good day.*

"What a beautiful little girl." An older woman slowed her steps near them.

And for the second time recently, Andrea was proud—about her life, the changes she was making, and of the beautiful little munchkin beside her. "Thank you so much."

The lady waved at Bella before she walked on to her table.

What had started out as a way to live off of her sister had turned into something Andrea couldn't have predicted. Two boutiques had taken some of her jewelry on consignment, but another shop paid her outright for eight pairs of earrings, over a hundred dollars. Maybe she'd buy Bella a pair of new shoes at Walmart on her way back home.

Home. It felt good.

But as she fed Bella another bite of dessert, Blake's thievery was under her skin in a big way. He had a lot of nerve coming into her sister's house, going through the drawers, and leaving with the cash Charlotte had.

Andrea straightened and stopped chewing. Was she any different? *Yes,* she decided. She'd dug up money that belonged to a woman who had probably played a part in her brother's death. And the money wasn't even on Edna's property. *Hmm . . . does that make it Charlotte's money?*

Her sister clearly had no idea why anyone would be digging on the property, and Andrea had opted not to tell Charlotte that the digger was Edna. Would Edna be back, digging again when they weren't around? Andrea doubted it, now that Edna knew Andrea was on to her. *Guess it depends on how badly she wants the money.*

Andrea let Bella finish up the ice cream with her hands in the bowl while Andrea pulled out her cell phone and typed.

You stole Charlotte's money. We're pressing charges, and you are going straight to jail, you piece of scum.

Her finger hovered over the Send button for a few seconds before she deleted the text. Maybe she would give Charlotte the five hundred dollars from the metal box, and when Andrea had sold enough jewelry, she'd pay back the rest that Blake stole. She liked this new person she was becoming. It was confusing since she'd been told she was bad her entire life. But something was changing, and it was because of Charlotte.

Andrea picked up a napkin, dipped it in water, then wiped the chocolate ring from Bella's face. Sighing, she shook her head. "Bella, I have to fess up about the money, don't I? I have to tell Charlotte I took it, right? That I dug it up?"

"More." Smiling, Bella dipped a finger into the bowl and pulled back a small piece of cake.

Andrea leaned back in the chair, not sure she completely liked this new person. Five hundred dollars would buy a lot of stuff.

She started texting again, if for no other reason than she felt conflicted and confused.

You're going to jail for stealing Charlotte's money. We are pressing charges, you scumbag.

She deleted the text, again, and spent the next few

minutes wondering how to handle the five hundred dollars, wondering if she was any better than Blake. But her finger got itchy, and she pounded out another text message to Blake, worse than all the others put together. And she hit Send.

$\sim$

Charlotte woke up that afternoon feeling better. And hungry. She shuffled across the living room in her socks toward the kitchen, opened a can of chicken noodle soup, and heated it on the stove top.

She'd almost finished the entire bowlful when she heard the grinding of gears and crunching of gravel that could only mean Big Red and its occupants were returning. Charlotte breathed a huge sigh of relief that they were home.

"Look, look, look!" Andrea walked into the kitchen toting four plastic bags from Walmart. "I got food, and I got Bella some new shoes. One of the shop owners paid me a little over a hundred dollars upfront! Two others took my jewelry on consignment."

Bella ran to Charlotte, lifting her arms, so Charlotte heaved her into her lap, throwing any sickness bug to the wind. She smothered Bella in kisses. "I missed you." Then she looked up at Andrea. "That is fantastic."

Charlotte gave Bella a final kiss before she put her down, then stood to help her sister unload the bags. "Wow.

This is a ton of stuff for a hundred dollars." She eyed the five-pound package of hamburger meat, three packages of chicken, and salad fixings. There was also baby food, crackers, chips, sodas, a tub of butter, a gallon of milk, two boxes of cookies, and other things that had never seen the inside of Charlotte's fridge—like a gallon of chocolate milk and a huge box of kiddie drinks, the type with the little straws in them.

"Oh, I know how to budget shop." Andrea stashed the lettuce, tomatoes, onions, and cucumbers in the vegetable crisper.

"Andrea, you didn't have to do this. I have some money in savings. I would have made sure we ate." Charlotte put the chocolate milk in the fridge.

"I know. But we live here and I should contribute." Andrea smiled as she pulled a bag of Hershey's bars from one of the bags.

Charlotte had known this was a permanent arrangement long before Andrea just admitted to it, but she'd seen some significant changes in her sister, and that made her heart smile.

Daniel looked out the front window while Annie paced the living room holding the baby. His sister had ended up coming home alone while Aunt Faye stayed at the hospital to continue her chat with their father.

Daniel recognized the blue van, driven by the same *Englisch* man who had brought Annie home earlier. Inside was either *Daed* or Aunt Faye.

"This is not going to be a *gut* night." Annie shook her head as she gently rocked Grace. "If it's *Daed*, he's going to be fit to be tied." She stopped in the middle of the room. "And if it's *Aenti* Faye . . . *ach*, well . . . she's going to be fit to be tied too."

Daniel had his money on Aunt Faye, so his heart raced when he saw their father step out of the car.

Annie gasped when she joined Daniel at the window. "I think this would be a *gut* time to go bathe Gracie."

"*Nee, nee.* Don't go yet. See if *Daed* even looks at the baby. Maybe he will feel different about things once he's in his own surroundings."

"That can come in time, Daniel. It's a big enough step for *Daed* to be home, even if it's just for one night."

Their father slowed his step when he got to the porch, and for a second Daniel thought he might race back to the van. But *Daed* latched on to the handrail and swung his right leg up on the step, then his left, catering to his bad knee. He pushed the door open, and Daniel didn't think he'd seen a more pitiful sight: an untamed beard, salt-and-pepper hair that was much too long, pale sunken cheeks, dark circles underneath tired eyes, and the same wrinkled clothes he'd had on earlier in the day. *He looks broken.*

"Can I prepare you a meal, *Daed*?" Annie held her position with the baby across the living room, and Daniel was glad. Pushing Grace on their father might not fare well right now after all. "Or maybe some *kaffi?*"

"*Nee*, but *danki.*" *Daed* shuffled across the floor, his shoulders slumped as if he carried the weight of the world on him. He didn't even look at Annie. Or the baby.

Daniel held his position near Annie, but he glanced at Grace, now sleeping soundly. *How could a man not want to see his own child?* But he decided to heed Annie's advice and not say anything about the baby. "*Daed*, how long will *Aenti* Faye be at the hospital?"

Their father stopped in the middle of the room, ran his hand through his beard, and locked eyes with Daniel. "Three days." He spoke with a calm, almost eerie voice that Daniel might not have recognized if he didn't see the man standing right in front of him.

Daniel looked at the baby again, then back at his father. "Okay. *Gut* to have you home for a few days." He forced a smile.

"You know . . ." *Daed* ran his hand the length of his beard again. "I think your *mamm* moved her foot today."

"Really?" Annie's face lit up, but Daniel had read that such an action could just be a reflex.

Their father nodded. "Soon, she will be back to us." He started to limp toward his bedroom.

"*Daed!*" Annie scurried toward him.

Don't do it, Annie. Daniel braced himself.

"Don't you want to see Grace? Maybe hold her?" Annie offered the baby, swaddled in a white blanket, to their father, as if she were holding a bag of flour out to him.

219

Daniel rubbed his chin as he held his breath. His eyes widened when their father stepped closer to Annie, and a fury flamed in his eyes that caused Daniel to take an instinctive step in their direction.

Daed's bottom lip trembled as he stared at the child, and just when Daniel feared the older man was going to knock the baby from Annie's arms, or something even worse, their father's eyes filled with tears before he vanished into his bedroom.

Annie eased Grace back to her chest, holding her tightly, as her eyes began to water. "What are we going to do, Daniel?" She shifted her gaze to the baby, kissing her repeatedly on the face.

"I don't know." He gently took Grace from Annie, comforted by the baby's powdery smell, easy breaths, and simplicity of a life so young.

Following a rough week at work, Charlotte was looking forward to spending some time with Lena on this beautiful Saturday morning. It was a nippy forty-three degrees when she pulled Big Red out of the driveway.

Andrea had been busy making earrings. Dianda from work had gifted Andrea with more beads and accessories left over from her own attempts at making jewelry awhile back. Charlotte offered to take Bella with her to see Amos and Lena, and Andrea had happily agreed. Seeing the changes in Andrea had been like watching a caterpillar blossom into a butterfly. Charlotte wished Ethan were around to witness the transformation of the sister he'd never known.

Amos answered the door, holding Buddy, and a few minutes later, Charlotte was sitting at the kitchen table with Bella in her lap. Lena came into the room in a wheelchair. It was unsettling to see her this way, but Charlotte had already heard that Lena was becoming less and less mobile. Her normally rosy cheeks were void of color, strands of gray hair had escaped the confines of the brown scarf on her head, and her hands were trembling.

"I don't feel as bad as I look," Lena said in a soft voice, lacking the jolly tone that was part of her nature.

"You don't look that bad." It was a small lie, something Charlotte had sworn off long ago, but she didn't have the heart to agree with Lena. *Forgive me, Lord.*

"Hello, Bella." Lena pointed to a tray in the middle of the table. "Can she have a cookie?"

Charlotte nodded as she took a cookie and handed it to Bella, kissing her on the cheek before she looked back at Lena. "This sweet girl is a cookie monster. She loves cookies, all kinds."

"You're a natural with *kinner.*" Lena smiled. "But I'm not surprised."

Charlotte bit her bottom lip as she stroked Bella's hair. "I—I don't really think I'd be a *gut* mother. I mean, look at my history."

Lena stared at Charlotte for a few seconds. "Your

history doesn't have to dictate whether or not you're capable of being a *gut* mother. If anything, your upbringing has shown you the things that can go wrong in a family. You'll work hard to bring your *kinner* up the right way, with love, compassion, and nurturing care. All qualities that come easily to you." Lena's eyes brightened. "I'm not supposed to tell, but I can't stand it. I need to tell someone . . ." She took a deep breath. "Hannah is pregnant."

Charlotte stifled a squeal. "That is wonderful!" Bella jumped when Charlotte's voice rose in volume. "Now, there is someone who will be a *gut* mother."

"*Ya*, she will be." Lena squinted, studying Charlotte. "You don't even realize that you have adopted some of our dialect. This isn't the first time I've heard you pronounce *gut* in *Deitsch*. When are you going to marry Daniel and let God bless your relationship with lots of *kinner*? I know you were taking the baptismal classes after church awhile back. Are you still doing that?"

"I took the required amount right after I moved here, even though I was undecided about what I was going to do."

Lena winked at Charlotte, a bit of the joyous Lena visible for a few brief seconds. "Daniel is a wonderful man."

"He is." Charlotte reached for one of the cookies and avoided Lena's gaze, not wanting to say anything to upset her. But Charlotte still remained unsure about a lifelong commitment to Daniel, and to the Amish life. "I would have to be baptized before we could take our relationship to the next step."

Lena tucked a few strands of hair underneath her scarf, slowly, as if buying time to think. "Do you want to convert, Charlotte? We think of you as one of us, but the bishop is not going to let this go on forever."

"I know. He said something to Daniel a month or so ago, but it was right when Andrea had found me, right after my mother's funeral, so I think the bishop agreed to give us some time."

"Bishop Miller is a *gut* man too. Young, but fair. Talk to him if you have qualms about baptism that you aren't comfortable sharing with Daniel or me."

"I share everything with you, Lena. I'm just . . . scared."

"Scared of what?"

Charlotte looked past Lena out the window and into a yard that was losing its luster in preparation for winter. "Failure," she said in a whisper.

"We all fail, dear. But with baptism, you get a clean slate, and Jesus already paid for our sins, so His arms are wide open to lift us when we fall, to set us on the right path again. Not trying to live the way the Lord intended us to, now that's failure."

Charlotte let Lena's words soak in. She nodded, then kissed Bella on the cheek. Her niece smiled, part of the cookie still in her mouth. "This little angel has certainly been a welcome surprise."

"God wants to give you joy. Let Him." Lena smiled.

Charlotte wondered if Lena would live long enough to meet Hannah's child—her grandchild—or would

Hannah's baby never know this amazing woman? As she turned the thought over in her mind, she also mulled over her own situation, wondering if Lena was right, if Charlotte could be a good mother. Charlotte had certainly preached to Andrea about them both not being products of their childhoods. If it rang true for Andrea, then maybe it should for Charlotte too.

"I have a date tonight with Daniel. He made a really big deal about it. I'm picking him up in my truck, and he's taking me to a fancy Italian place in Lancaster City, and I'm just wondering if—"

Lena brought her palms together and clapped lightly. "You think he's going to propose!"

Charlotte felt her cheeks flush as she lifted one shoulder and dropped it. "Maybe."

"And . . . ?"

Giggling, Bella clapped her hands together, mimicking Lena, even though she didn't know what they were talking about, but it made Charlotte smile. Then she stared at Lena. How long would her mother here on earth be with them? "And . . . maybe."

That's the best Charlotte could do right now.

Daniel had just finished bathing when his cell phone rang in his bedroom. After rushing down the hall in a towel, he slid into his bedroom and answered it.

"Daniel Byler?"

"*Ya.*" His heart sunk. The last time the hospital had called, it was to tell them that his mother was in a coma. "What is it?"

"It's about"—the woman paused—"it's about your aunt."

"*Aenti* Faye? What about her?"

"She is singing. Actually, it's more like yodeling. We've asked her repeatedly to quiet down, but she tells us her tactics are necessary to wake up Mrs. Byler." The woman huffed in exasperation. "Mr. Byler, we have rules in the hospital, especially in a wing where patients are critically ill." She sighed. "And something doesn't smell right in that room. I'm not going to say that your father didn't need to go home to do a little grooming, but there is a rank smell in there, like mothballs and something pickled."

Daniel put a hand over his mouth to keep from laughing.

"And that's not all. In addition to your aunt's yodeling and unusual smells, she has the television loud enough for people down the hall to hear it. That is, when she's not singing or yodeling, of course."

Daniel chuckled. "Sorry. I know *Aenti* Faye is, um . . . what's the word?"

"I think *eccentric* might be the word you're looking for, but we need her to leave or to adhere to hospital policy. We tried to call your father, but there isn't an answer."

"He's resting, I think, but I'll talk to *Aenti* Faye tomorrow."

The nurse thanked him before they hung up, then Daniel hurried to get into his clothes, which Annie had ironed for him. Bless his sister. She had a full plate, especially without Aunt Faye at home. Daniel smiled as he pictured his aunt yodeling in the hospital. No one he knew yodeled, but he'd heard it told that in some Amish districts, yodeling was a fun pastime still practiced by the elders. Maybe in Aunt Faye's Amish days, they'd yodeled. Who knew with her, though.

"Who was on the phone?" Annie peeked her head into his room. "Was it the hospital?"

"*Ya*, but everything is okay." Daniel chuckled. "I guess. There seems to be a problem with the way Aunt Faye smells and she's yodeling in *Mamm*'s hospital room."

"Aw." Annie grinned, but her eyes got moist. "She's trying to wake up *Mamm*. I wonder if *Mamm* can hear her."

Daniel had read as much as he could about comas. "Sometimes, I think people like *Mamm* hear a little, but I don't really think the thought stays with them."

"*Ach*, if anyone can stir up *Mamm*'s thoughts or wake her up, it's *Aenti* Faye." Annie left, smiling.

Daniel prayed for his mother to wake up, the way he did a dozen times a day. Then he grabbed his hat and headed downstairs to watch for Charlotte to arrive. He wanted to make this a great evening for her.

Seventeen

Charlotte sat across the table from Daniel, a white linen atop the small square table, with a tea light flickering between them. In the dimly lit room, soft music played seductively in the background as the aroma of sun-roasted tomatoes teased her palate for the meal that was to come.

Daniel had never looked more handsome. His dark hair was freshly cut, his bangs high above his eyebrows, a look Charlotte had grown to love. His gray eyes sung to hers in the ambience of the quiet restaurant. Tonight was the night.

"You look beautiful," he said as he gazed into her eyes.

Charlotte had chosen black slacks, a dark blue blouse, and her black furry coat. Simple yet elegant, she hoped. She'd curled her wet hair with foam curlers earlier in the day, letting it dry into a slight wave that fell almost to her waist. She'd left her house feeling good about Andrea and Bella. They'd all been sleeping in Charlotte's bed each night, Bella in the middle of the two women. When Charlotte left, they were both tucked in, even though it wasn't dark yet. Bella's eyelids had been heavy, and Andrea had been working on a necklace she was making.

"Thank you," she said to Daniel. "You clean up well yourself." Smiling, she'd been thinking about this night since she'd left Lena. Seeing Lena in the wheelchair had left Charlotte with the realization that life was short. Being around Bella had made her feel like she could truly be a good mother. She was ready. When Daniel asked her to marry him, she was going to say yes.

"I know you like Italian food. I've only been here once before, a long time ago. But it was really *gut*." Daniel glanced around the room before he looked back at Charlotte.

She wasn't exactly clear about Amish protocol when proposing, but she suspected that Daniel would meet her somewhere in the middle, a proposal that was both Amish and *Englisch* in nature. Would he drop to one knee, which would surely draw attention to himself?

It didn't matter. Charlotte loved him, and the Plain People were her family. She couldn't imagine being anywhere else. *Buttered bread for life.* Only thing was, she would have to give up Big Red and driving. But learning to maneuver a horse and buggy could be exciting.

She was still concerned about failure, but something Lena had said resonated with Charlotte in a big way. *"Not trying to live the way the Lord intended us to, now that's failure."*

They fell into an easy conversation about Andrea and Bella, and then Daniel told Charlotte about his Aunt Faye's yodeling at the hospital. As they both laughed, ordered, and enjoyed each other's company, Charlotte waited. And waited. And before she knew it, they'd finished off a three-course meal and Daniel was paying the bill.

Maybe he was going to wait until she dropped him off at his house to propose? It seemed like he would have asked her to marry him at the restaurant.

It was a quiet ride home with occasional chatter about their jobs. Daniel commented on how great the food was, and he told Charlotte again how beautiful she looked. At his house, Daniel leaned over to her and kissed her in a way that made Charlotte long to be his wife, then he said good night and she thanked him again for dinner—or supper—as the Amish called the last meal of the day.

Charlotte had been the one calling the shots in the relationship for so long that despair fell over her all of a sudden. She'd made up her mind that she wanted a life with Daniel, and not only did he not propose, but he didn't mention anything about marriage or even hint at a future together.

Andrea was standing on the other side of the front door when Charlotte got home and entered the living room.

"Well, did he propose? Was there a ring? Did you set a date?" Andrea grinned, clapping her hands softly.

"No. He didn't."

Andrea's expression fell as she lowered her arms to her sides. "Um. Okay. How was the food?"

Charlotte gave her sister a thin-lipped smile. "Great. The food was great."

⁓

Annie closed the door behind Daniel Sunday morning, wishing him well at the hospital. Normally, Sunday was reserved for relaxation and devotions, even on Sundays when there wasn't a worship service, but Annie didn't think the hospital staff cared much about that. They just wanted Aunt Faye to stop the racket, and they'd called Daniel's phone again early this morning.

Today was a scheduled church service, but both Annie and Daniel had chosen not to attend. He needed to handle Aunt Faye, and Annie couldn't drive the buggy and keep Grace warm during the commute, and it didn't appear their father had plans to go anywhere.

"*Aenti* Faye is just trying to wake up your *mamm*," Annie whispered to Grace as she held the baby close, feeding her a bottle of formula. She smiled thinking about Aunt Faye going to such extreme measures.

Annie and Daniel had eaten breakfast before Daniel left, but their father hadn't come out of the bedroom yet. Would their lives ever be normal again? If her mother never woke up, she feared that they would feel the void forever. And Annie worried that her father wouldn't survive the grief.

Shouldn't Daed *be comforting his* kinner *at a time like this, or does role reversal begin when a person reaches adulthood?* Annie wasn't sure. She still felt like a kid most days, not the eighteen-year-old woman she'd become.

She held Gracie close, then prayed for all of them.

⌒

Daniel stopped at the nurse's station on the wing where his mother's room was.

"Thank goodness you're here," the nurse named Wanda said as she stood between two other women. "That woman is driving us crazy, and every time we ask her to be quiet, she threatens to use a baseball bat on us." Wanda threw up her hands. "We haven't seen a baseball bat, but who knows? If you hadn't shown up, we were going to have security escort her out." She shook her head. "We'd hate to do that, considering the state your mother is in and the grief you must be feeling, but we have to think about the needs of our other patients too."

"*Ya,* I understand."

He eased the door to his mother's room open. All was quiet, just the sounds of the air machine keeping his mother alive, the beeps on the monitors . . . and Aunt Faye's raspy snoring from the lounging chair. The lingering smell of pickled oysters hung in the air.

Daniel walked to the side of his mother's bed, then leaned down and kissed her on the cheek. This was the first time he'd been alone with her. Almost alone, just Aunt Faye in dreamland nearby.

"I love you, *Mamm*," he whispered. "And we miss you." He found her hand and put it in his. He stayed standing, holding his mother's hand, until Aunt Faye awakened.

"What are you doing here so early?" Aunt Faye's gray hair was a balled-up mess on top of her head, and her eyes were dark and puffy. It looked like she'd been crying.

"I came to relieve you. Annie needs you at home, to help with the *boppli* and *Daed*." Daniel and Annie had agreed this was the best way to handle their aunt.

"Is your father giving you children trouble already?" Aunt Faye sat on the edge of the chair, pushing hair from her face. "I thought I made it clear to him how things were going to be."

Daniel held his tongue, opting not to tell his aunt that she was being thrown out. "It's just a lot for Annie, that's all. And I think you'd be a bigger help to her than me. I don't have any jobs scheduled for a few days, so I can sit with *Mamm*."

"Well, of course I'll be a bigger help to Annie than you will." Aunt Faye grunted. "Women invariably take up the slack when a man becomes too emotionally disabled to go on. It's what's expected of us, and we deliver." She cut her eyes at Daniel. "And men don't." She pointed a long, crooked finger at him. "And you don't just *sit* here with your *mamm*. You need to talk to her. Sing to her, if you can carry a tune. I realize most folks can't sing the way I can, but you can at least try."

Daniel nodded. Despite leaving the Old Order, being shunned, and her husband dying, Aunt Faye still loved her niece very much. But as Daniel looked at the person who used to be his mother, shriveling into a lifeless form he didn't recognize, he again wondered if they were doing the right thing by allowing this to go on.

"I'm taking my pickled oysters with me, the ones left in my little ice chest." Aunt Faye pointed to a small red cooler nearby. "Every time I take some out and put them on a plate, they vanish." She shook her head as more hair toppled from the loose bun on her head. "If those nurses would just ask politely, I would make them their own batch, but they are a catty bunch out there." She nodded toward the door. "They're constantly complaining about something."

Daniel knew the nurses disposed of the oysters when the smell became too rank. He suspected the vanishing oysters went missing while Aunt Faye was snoring. She stood and brushed wrinkles from her light green dress. Her clothing was Mennonite, so her dresses were adorned with little flowers or other patterns. And she wasn't bothered if she didn't have her head covered.

"I'll go tend to your father, sister, and baby Grace." Aunt Faye scowled. "And you *try* to make good use of the time you're here." His aunt rolled her eyes before she left the room.

Daniel hoped she'd walk quietly by the nurse's station without causing a ruckus. He cringed when he heard Aunt Faye out in the hallway. Yodeling.

Andrea sat perfectly still on the couch, unsure how to react to Blake's text. Her ex-boyfriend often fooled people into thinking he was someone he wasn't. He had a steadiness about him that would imply he rarely got ruffled. And he was handsome in a cowboy sort of way, with a gentle smile that lent him an air of trustworthiness. Blake was confident and friendly, but he had some anger issues that rose to the surface from time to time. *But would he really hurt Bella or me?*

She reread the text for the tenth time.

> I'm warning you, Andrea. If you get me in trouble with the police, you'll be sorry.

After staring at his text for a while, she reread the one she'd sent him.

> You stole Charlotte's money, you scumbag. We are reporting you to the police, and I hope you rot in jail. I knew you were nothing but trash. You might fool some people, but you don't fool me. Don't come around me or my family again.

Andrea tapped a finger to her chin as she contemplated a reply. Finally she sent him a return text.

Are you threatening me?

She waited.

Not a threat, babe. A promise.

A shiver ran the length of Andrea's spine. Whether or not Blake was capable of violence, she couldn't risk it because of Bella. She chose not to reply, but after about ten minutes, she got another text.

Meet me tomorrow afternoon outside the Amish Market at three o'clock. And bring Bella. I miss her.

Andrea stared at the text, then she looked at Bella playing with two toy cars on the floor. No more texting with Blake. Andrea was just going to put her past behind her.

She picked up her box of beads and matched up three pink ones to make into a necklace, but her phone buzzed beside her.

And you better be there.

Andrea shivered as she thought about whether or not to tell Charlotte about this. Charlotte didn't want her to try to get the money back. She said to leave it alone. *But I didn't.*

Charlotte stopped in town after church service. She needed milk and cream cheese for a holiday recipe she wanted to try out later. Maybe she could snap out of the funk she had settled into. Even a good night's sleep hadn't diminished the disappointment she felt about Daniel not proposing.

When she got home and opened the front door, Bella was crying, Andrea had her face in her hands on the couch, and the fire had died out.

"What's wrong?" Charlotte put her purse and grocery bag on the coffee table when Bella ran to her, arms stretched above her head. She scooped her niece into her arms.

"Nothing's wrong. Bella is just fussy, and I've got a headache."

"Sweet girl, you're okay." Charlotte bounced Bella on her hip until she calmed down. "Mommy just has a headache."

Andrea's bottom lip trembled, though, and Charlotte suspected more was going on. "Are you sure that's all, just a headache?"

"It's not *just* a headache. It hurts."

"There's aspirin in the bathroom. Did you take some?" Charlotte sat in the rocking chair, Bella in her lap, and kicked the chair into motion.

"No. I'll go get some." Andrea huffed as she stood, then shuffled toward the bathroom.

Charlotte stopped rocking when Andrea's text beeped with a new message. Instinctively, Charlotte looked that way, and she could see the message from where she was sitting.

I'm not kidding, Andrea. You better be at the Amish Market at three o'clock tomorrow . . . or else.

Charlotte hadn't realized her sister and Blake were still communicating.

"I took two ibuprofen," Andrea said as she walked back into the living room. "Do you think that's enough?"

"Um . . . yeah. Probably so." Charlotte nodded toward the phone. "You have a text." She narrowed her eyebrows, frowning. "And I saw it. What does 'or else' mean?"

Andrea grunted as she rolled her eyes. "Really? You read my text message?"

"Your phone is sitting in plain view. What does that mean, Andrea?" Charlotte's heart raced as she clung to Bella. Something in her gut told her trouble was brewing.

"Nothing. It's just Blake being a jerk. No worries, okay?"

Too late. Charlotte was already concerned. But, for now, she'd let it go.

Daniel sat in a chair beside his mother, praying silently for God to interject wisdom and guidance into a situation

Daniel and his family didn't know how to handle. More and more, he thought they were doing his mother an injustice by not letting her go home to be with the Lord. Lena's words stayed on Daniel's mind, how she wouldn't want to be kept alive in this way.

"*Mamm*, what should we do?" Daniel leaned closer to her. "We want to do the right thing."

Did it even matter? Ultimately, it was their father's decision, and he was having no part of unhooking her from these machines.

Each day felt like a new day of mourning, grieving a life still on earth, but one that was gone just the same.

As the familiar churning started up in his stomach, Daniel switched gears, turning his thoughts to Charlotte, how beautiful she'd looked the night before. He'd wanted nothing more than to drop to one knee, to beg her to stay with him for a lifetime, and to be the mother of his children. But Charlotte continued to have a lot on her plate, and so did Daniel. They could both find comfort in each other, handling things together, but he wanted to tread softly. Charlotte had come a long way. But the woman Daniel loved still hadn't committed to converting to the Amish way of life.

He wished he could talk to his mother.

Closing his eyes, he allowed himself to rest his head against the back of the chair, his breathing in rhythm with the beeping machines and bursts of air from the ventilator.

He looked up when he heard his name. "*Wie bischt,*

Jacob." Daniel stifled a yawn. He hadn't gotten much sleep last night. "What brings you here this afternoon?" His heart skipped a beat. "Is Lena okay?"

"*Ya, ya. Mamm* is doing *gut* today. Annie told me you were here, and I wanted to talk to you about something."

"Okay." Daniel stayed seated and motioned to the other chair.

Jacob sat and heaved a sigh. "Do you think people can change?"

Daniel was sure this was going to be about Jacob wanting to reunite with Annie, citing himself as a changed man. "*Ya*, I think so."

The lines on young Jacob's forehead wrinkled as he scratched his chin. "I think I've changed. I don't feel the need to leave here, to leave our people. I want to make a home in Lancaster County, like all the generations before me." He searched Daniel's eyes. "A home with Annie."

Frowning, Daniel sighed also. "Jacob, you've gone back and forth so many times about this, it makes a person wonder if you have a clue what you want. Have you told Annie this?"

"I haven't formally asked her to marry me, but I want to prove myself to her by getting baptized soon. I had the baptismal classes a long time ago, and I spoke with the bishop about it. He said even though it's the holidays and not the normal time for baptisms, he would make an exception."

Daniel felt one of the many loads he was carrying

lighten a little. Although he figured the bishop's expedience was probably out of fear that young Jacob would change his mind again. "I think that's a fine idea, if you're sure about it."

"I'm sure," Jacob responded without the hesitation Daniel had expected.

Jacob had left to seek out the world and apparently decided it wasn't for him. But throughout it all, Daniel still thought of Jacob as a good person, no matter his wishy-washy ways when it came to leaving or staying in their district.

Jacob hung his head. "And there's something else. I wasn't completely honest about my job." He kept his eyes down. "*Ya*, I worked for a pharmaceutical company, but the medications weren't the kind that save lives, like I'd thought at first. I was more of what the *Englisch* call a 'drug runner,' someone who delivers illegal medications to people that will pay a lot of money for them. And I wasn't very good at it. The Big Rabbit"—Jacob looked up—"that's the man in charge—he fired me. He said I looked nervous all the time. I wasn't nervous in the beginning, but that's before I knew what I was delivering."

He paused as his bottom lip trembled. "I ain't proud of what I've done. I'm just trying to be honest. I did some bad stuff. It's behind me, and I want to be baptized and marry Annie. I'm going to tell her everything so there are no secrets between us. I'm a changed man. I've seen the outside world, and I know for sure that I don't want any part of it."

"I hope you mean that, because I don't think Annie's heart can go another round with you, Jacob. Even now, I'm not sure she'll believe you."

"And that's something I may have to work on. But I just wanted you to know my intentions."

"I appreciate that." Daniel wondered if maybe Jacob should have had this conversation with *Daed*, but this was probably better under the circumstances.

Jacob stood and walked closer to the hospital bed. "I'm real sorry about Eve. We pray for her every day, the same way we pray for the Lord to heal *Mamm*."

"*Danki*. We pray for Lena too."

Daniel waited until Jacob was gone before he picked up his cell phone to call Charlotte. He got her voice mail. Again. She had left him a message earlier and told him about a meeting that Andrea had tomorrow morning with her ex-boyfriend, the man Daniel had met at Janell's funeral, Blake. Charlotte said she was worried about Andrea going, based on a text message she'd seen.

Daniel called a couple hours later and there was still no answer. He couldn't in good conscience leave his mother. He'd just have to keep trying to reach Charlotte.

Eighteen

Andrea walked with Charlotte to the front door, holding Bella.

"I'm relieved you're not going to meet Blake today," Charlotte said. "The tone of his text message makes me nervous." She'd allowed herself an extra thirty minutes to stop at Walmart to get more minutes on her phone before going to work.

Andrea shrugged. "I'd like to think I've outgrown Blake. I shouldn't have texted him, but . . ."

"No, you shouldn't have. But just let it go." Charlotte heaved her purse up on her shoulder. "Sometimes, it's better that way."

"See, you're like them." Andrea smiled, bouncing Bella on her hip.

"Like who?" She pushed the screen door open but paused and waited for Andrea to answer.

"Like the Amish. I bet there was a time in your life when you would have wanted revenge or justice if someone stole something from you. But now, you're passive, like the Amish."

Charlotte smiled a little. "I guess so, but I'm surprised you knew that. I didn't think you knew much about the Amish."

"I didn't. But I've been Googling stuff about them since you're going to be one of them."

"I'm not joining a cult or a dystopian universe. I'm accepting a religion with ideals I believe in."

Andrea twisted her mouth back and forth. "Hmm, I just wonder, though . . . would you be thinking about joining their group if you didn't want to marry Daniel?"

Charlotte looked over her shoulder past Andrea, at the clock on the mantel. She needed to get going, but this was an important question that deserved an honest answer. "I don't know."

Andrea grinned. "I figured you would say yes, but I would have known you were lying."

Charlotte's stomach roiled like she'd been sucker punched. "I didn't say I wouldn't convert. I said I didn't know."

"Same thing."

Charlotte kissed Bella on the cheek, wished them both a good day, then headed to Big Red, her heart heavy. How would she really know that baptism into the faith wasn't strictly motivated by her relationship with Daniel? And if it were, was that such a bad thing?

Driving to work, she started to wonder if she could get

off early today. There was only one person she could think to talk to, someone who could help her with this dilemma.

⌒

Three o'clock came and went, and Andrea breathed a sigh of relief that she hadn't gotten a text message from Blake. As she lay Bella on the bed for her nap, she thought about the life she was leaving behind: dishonest people like Blake, abusive folks like her adoptive parents, and a bunch of druggies with no life purpose.

I'm going to be different.

She went to the kitchen, opened the refrigerator, and pulled out the gallon of chocolate milk. As she took a glass from the cabinet, she heard horse hooves crunching dry gravel as someone came up the driveway. Andrea quickly poured a glass of milk and put the container back. She was headed to the front door, but when she saw her visitor, she ducked into the mudroom out of sight.

Edna Glick marched across the yard toting a basket draped over one arm.

Andrea cringed. She'd confronted Edna, and she wasn't in the mood to face the woman head-on today.

Edna knocked several times. She had to know Charlotte was at work. Big Red wasn't in the driveway, and Charlotte worked at her office most days. *Then why the visit? Edna's way of making peace with me?*

When Andrea heard footsteps descending down the

porch steps, she tiptoed into the living room, staying clear of the window, until she was close enough to pull back the closed blind and peek out with one eye. She eased out of view when Edna started to look around the yard, but then took another peek.

Edna walked to her buggy, stashed the basket, and returned to the yard with a shovel.

This time, Andrea was going to let her carry out the task.

A few minutes later, Edna pulled out the metal box and brought it to her chest. The woman's shoulders gently rose and fell. Edna was crying.

Andrea hadn't known Ethan. But he was her brother. What did he see in Edna besides a pretty face?

Andrea opened the wooden door, then the screen. Edna jumped and ran to her buggy.

"Don't run away this time! I know it's you, Edna, so you might as well stop."

Edna untethered her horse, the box under one arm. "I'm not stealing anything," she said as Andrea got within hearing range.

"I didn't say you were." Andrea stopped a few feet from her. Would the woman open the box now or wait until she got home?

"I—I buried something here a long time ago, and now I need it." Edna swiped at her eyes, glanced at Andrea once, then gave the horse a pat on the nose before she walked to the driver's side of the buggy.

"You had a relationship with Ethan." Andrea folded her arms across her chest as Edna lifted herself into the seat. "Charlotte told me."

"I'm sure she did." Edna sniffled. "And you can think whatever you want to about me. I don't care." She started to cry.

Andrea knew that feeling, the place in a person's psyche where darkness loomed, drawing you in like an old friend with bad intentions. Edna wasn't Charlotte's favorite person. Edna might have played a role in Ethan's death. Edna had hidden money on Ethan's property. *Why?*

"Well, my sister certainly doesn't care for you." Andrea held her position in the grass next to the buggy.

"*Ya*, I'm aware of that."

"Maybe it's because you keep hitting on her boyfriend, or maybe it's because you broke our brother's heart before he killed himself." Andrea shrugged. "Sounds like enough for me not to like you either. And that means that whatever you found on this property isn't yours."

"It's mine if I put it here!" Edna's eyes blazed red and wide, like the poster child for "Amish Gone Wild."

"Settle down, Sista." Andrea frowned. "I thought you Amish people were reserved and passive."

"I won't be Amish for long." Edna's eyes had melded back to tears, the rage seemingly induced by temporary panic. "And you can tell Charlotte I won't be bothering her and Daniel anymore either. I'm leaving this place!"

Good riddance, perhaps? Andrea chewed on her lip, a

thought niggling at her. "You're leaving the church to go be something else, like Lutheran or something?"

Edna didn't even try to stop the tears streaming down her face. "*Ya*, whatever you want to think."

"Um, where are you going?"

"Somewhere there isn't any pain."

Andrea sighed, wishing she had a cigarette. But it had been over a week since she'd had one, and she was proud of that fact. "Like where?"

"What does it matter to you?" Edna picked up a pair of black sunglasses from the buggy seat and slipped them on.

"Maybe you shouldn't drive your buggy so upset." An odd feeling swirled in the pit of Andrea's stomach.

"Don't bother trying to pretend you care about my well-being."

"Maybe I do, maybe I don't. What's the five hundred dollars for?"

Edna cried harder as she quickly reached for the box and worked hard to pry it open with her short fingernails.

"It's all there. Five hundred dollars." Andrea had put the money back the day she'd bought groceries. And she'd felt good about spending her own money on the groceries.

"It's to pay a debt I owe. I want to leave this world debt free in hopes that God will have mercy on my soul."

Attention seeker? Or a cry for help? Edna could have already pulled away in the buggy. Andrea thought about Ethan, deciding she wasn't willing to risk it.

"Edna, whatever is going on, I'm sure it's nothing that can't be fixed." Andrea had been preached to by the choir plenty of times. She wasn't sure she'd ever been the preacher.

Edna shook her head so hard that her prayer covering fell to one side. It wasn't tied—none of the women tied the things—so it was easy for her to yank it off.

Andrea wasn't sure what the purpose of the head covering was, but it seemed symbolic that Edna would rip hers off like that.

"It can't be fixed. *I* can't be fixed." Edna covered her face with her hands. "I've made bad choices repeatedly, done things that are wrong in God's eyes." Still crying, she took her hands from her face and tossed her sunglasses on the seat as her lip trembled. "John never touches me!" Her voice rose as her eyes took on the wild look again.

She held her palms up and looked up at the top of her buggy. "Why, Lord? All I've ever wanted was to be loved and to have a child. And I end up with a man who wants nothing to do with me physically." She dropped her gaze and turned to Andrea. "This is what I get. I'm being punished! God is denying me happiness now."

"Um . . . I'll be the first to say I'm not up to speed on religion, particularly yours, but I'm not sure that's how it works." Andrea shrugged. "Something about forgiveness of sins and all that."

"Do you know what my biggest regret is?"

Andrea couldn't imagine. Edna sounded like she had a bucketful, so Andrea just shrugged again.

"I can't be here anymore. I just can't. And what if my actions keep me from heaven? I won't see my parents who have passed, or my cousins whom I loved, or even Ethan. I'll burn in hell, I fear."

"I don't think you have to worry about that. Really."

"How can you say that?" Edna shook her head until most of her hair landed past her shoulders. "Hell for eternity."

"Well, good grief, if you believe that, why kill yourself?" Andrea figured she might as well play along. Even if there wasn't a heaven or hell, this crazy gal believed there was.

Edna put both her hands against her chest as she cried. "Because I can't breathe anymore. And I'm tired of trying. Too much pain."

Andrea sighed. *God, if You're listening, I could use a little help right now.* The last thing she needed was Edna's suicide on her conscience. Andrea had enough regrets without adding that to the mix.

"Okay, so your husband doesn't want to have sex." Andrea tucked her hair behind her ears, then scratched her forehead. "Most guys around our age have a healthy appetite when it comes to that. Maybe there is something wrong with him, you know . . . physically. And maybe it embarrasses him, if that's the case."

Edna blew her nose in a handkerchief, then sniffled again as she blushed. "Then maybe his distance isn't all my fault."

Maybe he isn't attracted to you. Andrea doubted that

was it. Edna was pretty. *Maybe he just doesn't love you any-more.* Whatever the case was, Andrea didn't feel the need to pour salt in Edna's open wounds. Edna's husband could be keeping his distance for all kinds of reasons. Right now, Andrea wanted Edna to calm down and readjust her thinking.

"Correct. It takes two to tango, so whatever is going on isn't exclusively your fault." Andrea gave a taut nod. She waited for Edna to bid her farewell and to scurry along, no longer feeling the need to off herself, but Edna just stared at her.

"What made you hide the money here?" Andrea scratched her head. "Wouldn't it have been easier to stash it at your house?"

Edna lowered her eyes for a few moments before she looked back at Andrea. "I used to come here sometimes after Ethan died. It was a quiet place to think. I saved money I made at the market selling potholders, cookbooks, and other handmade items. I wasn't happy with John, and I felt like I needed some emergency money." She shrugged, sighing. "One day I brought the money with me, and this seemed a safe place to hide it. I couldn't foresee Charlotte actually coming to Lancaster County."

Andrea nodded, then looked over her shoulder. "I need to check on my baby. Um . . . do you want to come in?"

Edna peered past Andrea, the lines on her forehead wrinkling. "I haven't been in that house since . . . since before Ethan died." She bit her lip for a few moments. "And

I'm not sure Charlotte would appreciate me going inside since she doesn't care for me." She rolled her swollen eyes. "Not that I blame her. I don't really care for me either."

"It's fine to come in." Andrea figured she'd take one for the team by letting Edna come in. "Come on. Really, it's fine."

Edna slowly slipped out of the buggy. A wad of used tissues fell in the grass. After she picked them up, she walked with Andrea to the house. As soon as they were in the living room, Andrea looked at the clock. Four thirty. She'd have to scoot Edna out in about thirty minutes, before Charlotte got home in an hour or so.

"What lovely jewels." Edna leaned down over the coffee table eyeing several of Andrea's projects.

"Thanks. Have a seat. I just want to check on my daughter." Andrea eased the bedroom door open. Bella was still sleeping, pillows propped up around her.

When Andrea returned to the living room, Edna was standing in the middle of the room looking around. "It feels odd to be here." She offered a weak smile to Andrea. "Did you know your *bruder* at all?"

"No, I didn't. We were separated when I was a baby."

"Ethan was full of goodness. And, despite our differences, it seems as though Charlotte is a good person too." She smiled again. "Like you."

Andrea was trying to be a good person, but hearing someone acknowledge it caused her to swallow back a lump in her throat.

"I'm sure you wish you'd known him. But you'll meet him someday."

Andrea rolled her eyes. "I don't see how."

"Heaven, of course."

Andrea sat down while Edna stayed put in the middle of the living room. "Forgive me for saying this, but a few minutes ago you were ready to end it all, believing that you might not go to heaven if you did so. If heaven is so great, why would you risk not going there by killing yourself?"

Aha! Maybe attention seeker, after all.

Edna's eyes filled with tears. "I'm so embarrassed about my outburst. You don't even know me. I just get confused."

I might know you better than you think.

"Sometimes, when I can't breathe, I really do just want the pain to stop. But then . . . I do have thoughts of heaven. Today, you helped me to think about my actions, and I'm grateful to you for that."

Andrea wished that she could close her eyes, open them, and believe in an afterlife that so many others believed in. She'd just spent a chunk of time convincing Edna to stick around in this life, to avoid possibly being denied access into the next life—the life Andrea didn't believe in. *The craziness of it all.*

Charlotte had done a lousy job of trying to convince her there was a heaven. Maybe this Amish woman had something new to offer. "I don't believe in heaven. Or hell." She raised an eyebrow, challenging Edna to make a case for the afterlife she longed for.

Edna's jaw fell. "How can you say that? Do you believe in God?"

Andrea nodded. "Yeah, I do. I think someone is responsible for all this"—she waved a hand around the room—"and I've had great success with prayers at certain times in my life." *Like when I was hiding from my adoptive father in a closet.*

"Great *success*?" Edna slid into the rocking chair. "Does that mean your prayers were answered?"

"Yeah. Sometimes."

Edna scowled. "How can you believe in our Father but not believe in heaven? It's like . . . cake and icing."

These women must have gone to the same Bible study or something. "I don't understand what that means, cake and icing."

Edna smiled a little. "At another confusing time in my life, many years ago, a woman highly regarded in our community explained heaven to me in a way I could understand. I'll do my best to explain it to you." She took in a breath. "The cake is the foundation for the icing, such as believing in God is the essence of heaven. Once you've experienced even a little taste of heaven, you appreciate how it complements the cake. A slice of heaven on earth."

"Not everyone likes icing." Andrea pressed her mouth into a thin-lipped smile.

"True. But even if you put icing on a cake, try it, and decide you don't like it and scrape it off, the taste lingers, even if you can't see it. Once you know in your heart that there is a heaven, you have that to savor and draw on."

"I need tangible evidence there is a heaven. What if a bunch of people got together to write the Bible and the entire thing is fictional?"

Edna smiled. "What if they did? I don't believe that, but heaven is a place we can visit while here on earth, a place as real and tangible as the chair I'm sitting in."

You'll have to do better than that. Andrea raised an eyebrow again.

"Imagine perfect love. Unselfish, pure love. Picture yourself inside a bubble of love, a place where no harm can come to you."

That would be awesome, if it was possible . . .

"Take yourself to that place. Like the icing, it's always available to us, whether we accept it or not. And through forgiveness of our sins, we are cleansed in God's perfect love."

"Well, beam me up, Scotty. It sounds great." Andrea folded her hands in her lap and leaned into the couch. "Where does the tangible part come in? Because if heaven is so great, I'd like to see it for myself. And I don't mean I'm ready to die. You said it's real and tangible. So show me."

Edna smiled. "I can't show you my heaven, any more than you can show me yours. You must feel it, know it to be true, without a shadow of a doubt. It takes *faith*." Edna stood, clasping her hands in front of her. "I see now that today was not about me. It was God's will that we have this conversation. For you."

Andrea stood also, more confused than ever. "So, I just try to feel God's love, and He will show me a slice of heaven, like the cake with the icing I don't like?"

Edna took a few steps toward Andrea and winked. "You just haven't found the right icing."

Andrea's heart pounded in her chest as her temples throbbed. "How do I do that?"

"It's your journey, Andrea. You might have to sample a lot of varieties that you don't find tasty, but when you are on the right path, the right icing will become very appealing and latch on to you with a wonderful vengeance." Pressing her palms together, she said, "Now, I must go." She took another step and hugged Andrea. *"Danki."*

Andrea didn't move as Edna left the room, closing the door behind her. She was pretty sure she'd never look at cake and icing in the same way. And she thought about what Charlotte had said about Blake maybe needing the money more than they did. It sounded like Edna needed the five hundred dollars more than Andrea. She was glad she put the money back in the metal box.

As she opened the bedroom door, Bella was sitting amid the pillows smiling. There hadn't been any of her wake-up noises. No whining or tears. Just love in its purest form staring back at her. Andrea closed her eyes for a moment as she stood at the threshold, a divider between two rooms. She could step forward toward the love or step backward, knowing what was behind her but allowing it to pull her in anyway. Never before had putting one foot in front of the other seemed so important.

She took the step with her eyes closed. A baby step. Toward the love. Knowing there would be a learning curve, like a baby learning to walk, falling often. But Andrea was going to keep getting up.

As she eased her eyes open, everything looked different. Brighter. Hopeful. And her heart sang in a way she'd never heard before. Or maybe she hadn't been tuned in prior to this moment. Perhaps this was her first melodious glance at what heaven would be like.

She ran to Bella, picked her up, and clung to her with all the love a mother had for a child. Then she went back to the living room, facing forward this time. She could travel from one room to the next without taking a step backward. She could see what was ahead of her, not behind her. Smiling, she liked what she saw.

As a tear trickled down her cheek, Andrea stood at the window, watching Edna leave. Edna never looked back. Andrea wasn't going to either.

But then she saw a car turning into the driveway. A car she recognized. If ever there were a time for prayer, it was now.

Nineteen

Charlotte started Big Red, then called Daniel. She listened as he told her about a conversation he'd had with Jacob. When he was done, she said, "It sounds like Jacob is turning over a new leaf. Andrea has also made a lot of positive changes in her life. She's still rough around the edges, but at her core, she's a good person. It really doesn't matter how messed up our childhoods were. It's how we handle our pasts that will determine our futures."

"Wow. This is a new twist on the Charlotte Dolinsky I know. If I'm not mistaken, that sounds like a cup half full, not half empty."

Charlotte smiled. "I feel good. I think God has put Andrea and Bella in my life for a reason, and I think I'm ready to take a big step forward." *Hint, hint.* Daniel didn't bite. Instead he was quiet. "Um, how's your mother? Any change?"

"*Nee.* The same. *Daed* will be back at the hospital in a couple of days. I have no idea what *Aenti* Faye said to get him to go home, but he needed a proper shower and something besides potato chips to eat. Charlotte . . ."

"Yeah, I'm here."

"I've been thinking about what you said, about *Mamm* not really living, all hooked up to machines. But I don't think my father is ever going to agree to letting *Mamm* go, even if Annie and I decide it's the best thing to do." He paused, and Charlotte had heard the shakiness in his voice. "It would be hard not to have our mother here. Even though we are adults, and . . ." His voice faded away.

"I know. And I'm so sorry this is happening." Charlotte fought the tinge of guilt swirling around inside. How could she be thinking about marriage when Daniel was in the throes of this horrible situation with his mother?

"*Ya.* It's awful."

They were quiet, but as Charlotte pulled into Bishop Miller's driveway, she ended the call, telling Daniel she was running errands on her way home from work.

She knocked on the front door of the bishop's modest farmhouse. For a man with such power, she supposed she'd expected something a bit fancier, even though fancy was something her Amish friends tried to avoid. The small house was painted white with black trim around the windows. It wasn't nearly as big as the Byler or King residences, which had been in their families for generations. Based on the structure of this small house, it looked newer than those.

"Charlotte." The bishop extended his hand to her. "What brings you calling at this hour?"

"Oops. I'm sorry. This is the supper hour, and I should have waited until a bit later. But I was on my way home from work, and . . ." She sighed. "I can come back another time."

"*Nee, nee.* We just finished a fine meal of roasted chicken and dressing." He smiled as he stepped aside for her to enter the living room. She could hear a woman and children's voices coming from the kitchen. "Are you hungry?"

She was, but her stomach churned too much for food. "I'm okay. Please finish your meal. I'm happy to wait on the porch if you'd have time to speak with me afterward."

"Let me just go let Marianne know we have a guest." He walked away. Bishop Miller probably had two decades on Charlotte, a man in his mid to late forties, but that seemed young to be a bishop.

Charlotte looked around the modest living room. There wasn't a Christmas tree, but groups of wrapped gifts were placed in various piles in the room. A vine of holly ran along the fireplace mantel, along with three red candles in holders. It was festive, but not overtly so.

The bishop returned moments later. "Let's chat on the porch, if you don't think it will be too cold. The *kinner* are having cake, and the noise coming from the kitchen may be distracting."

Charlotte pulled her jacket snug. It was probably in the forties, but a cloudless sky and bright sun gave the illusion it was much warmer. She followed him onto the porch, and they each sat in a white wicker chair, a small table in between them.

"I'm glad you've come for a visit, Charlotte. I've been expecting you or Daniel. But I know the Bylers are consumed by the situation with Eve."

"Yes, Daniel said just earlier that things are the same." Charlotte wanted to get right to the point. "Of course, you know that Daniel and I have been dating. And now I'm considering baptism into the faith, but I'm worried if I'm doing it for the right reasons."

Bishop Miller ran his hand the length of his beard. "I appreciate your honesty. You are concerned that you seek baptism just so you can have a life with Daniel, *ya*?"

Charlotte lowered her gaze. "Exactly." She looked back at him. "Actually, that's part of my concern, but that's not all."

"Talk freely. And maybe we can work through this together." Bishop Miller crossed one leg over the other, then took off his straw hat and set it on the small table.

Charlotte took a deep breath. "I love Daniel. And the people here are like my family. But I'm not sure that's a good enough reason to convert to the faith."

"I agree." Bishop Miller offered a slight smile.

Charlotte was caught a little off guard. Maybe she'd assumed that Bishop Miller would be more enthusiastic about someone wanting to join the community.

"I feel like I should be asking myself what the other reasons are, but what if I'm just seeing things the way I want to see them, as justification to convert and be with Daniel?"

"That's a possibility."

Ouch. The man wasn't going to make this easy.

"Charlotte, do you love the Lord and believe that Jesus Christ died on the cross to free us from sin?"

"I absolutely do."

"Are you prepared to give up all things prideful, to honor and respect our ways?"

She swallowed hard. "Yes. And I already live in a house without electricity and gave up makeup and my hair dryer a long time ago."

The bishop smiled, and Charlotte felt herself flush. "That sounded silly, I know. But I've already thought about some of those things. I'd have to give up my truck and driving, and I'm prepared to do that. And I know I would be expected to dress appropriately."

Bishop Miller stared at her for a while. "*Ya*, this is all true. But these things you speak of are what is seen on the outside. It is what's inside that must drive this decision, an honest and pure admission to live according to our *Ordnung*." He raised a bushy eyebrow. "Do you know what the *Ordnung* is?"

Charlotte nodded. "The accepted ways of the Amish, and most of you know the rules by heart."

"Do you know the rules?" He grinned a little.

"I think I know most of them, but I would work hard to be proficient."

Bishop Miller looped his thumbs beneath his suspenders. "I know that you attended the baptismal meetings awhile back to help you make a decision about this important possibility. You would be expected to know *Deutsch* or, at the least, have a strong desire to learn our dialect."

She nodded. But none of this was at the core of what she needed to know. "I'm afraid."

The bishop's eyebrows drew into a frown. "Of the commitment you'd need to make to achieve these goals?"

She shook her head. "Partly, but I'm also afraid of . . . failure. I'm afraid of letting God down."

"You *will* let God down, repeatedly. It's called sin."

Charlotte folded her clammy hands in her lap, twisting them as her thoughts swirled and collided. "I'm also afraid of letting Daniel down."

The bishop smiled. "You *will* let Daniel down. It's called marriage."

Charlotte managed a half smile, but this wasn't going how she expected.

"There is not a person in our community who has not failed God in some way, myself included. In 1 Peter 3:21, it is explained in this way, 'The like figure whereunto even baptism doth also now save us (not the putting away of the filth of the flesh, but the answer of a good conscience toward God,) by the resurrection of Jesus Christ.' Charlotte, baptism saves us through an inward cleaning. If you live in good conscience, God takes away the sins of our past, present, and future. His Son gifted this to us."

Charlotte smiled.

"You already knew all of this." Bishop Miller put his hat back on his head. "You just needed to hear me say it. And you are here seeking permission for baptism so you can begin a life with Daniel. And as for your question as to whether or not you are doing this for the right reasons, only God can see your heart, Charlotte." He paused. "And even if you aren't 100 percent sure of such a conviction, you wouldn't be the first person to join our faith with doubts. But the Lord has a way of guiding us onto the right path, even if the steps we take are based on free will. If it is your path to stay in our community, the steps will feel natural and be taken with ease."

Charlotte stood when the bishop did, and she extended her hand to him. "*Danki*, Bishop Miller."

He smiled. "You are most welcome."

Charlotte walked with a bounce in her step, got into Big Red, and hurried toward home. She'd rather be going straight to Daniel's house to tell him that she'd chosen baptism, but his heart was so heavy right now about his mother, she chose to tell Andrea first.

But when she pulled into the driveway and opened the door of the truck, she heard Bella screaming before she even killed the engine. Almost forgetting to press the brake on the floorboard, she ran across the yard to the opened front door, then gasped when she walked inside the house.

Andrea was pacing with Bella on her hip. Her sister's yellow T-shirt was speckled with blood, which looked like it had come from a cut on Andrea's nose, and a few dots of red were also on Bella's white shirt. Andrea had a black eye that was swollen shut.

"Don't talk or get near us." Crying, Andrea kept Charlotte at an arm's length as she held her palm toward her. "We will be out of here right away."

Charlotte gently slapped Andrea's hand out of the way and moved closer, inspecting her sister's eye and nose as Bella screamed and clawed to go to Charlotte. Andrea finally handed the baby over, and after a quick inspection of Bella, Charlotte was relieved that she seemed fine.

"No one is going anywhere, Andrea. Stop thinking I'm going to throw you out all the time." She kissed Bella on the cheek. "You're okay, sweet girl." Then she turned to Andrea. "What happened?"

"Blake happened. When I didn't show up, he came here. I told him I was done with him and to leave or I'd call the police. Thank God Bella was napping and our conversation took place out on the porch." Andrea swiped at her runny nose with her hand. "And I know this isn't the kind of life you signed on for, so if you'll just give us some time to find a place to go—"

"Andrea, stop it." Charlotte snuggled Bella who laid

her head on Charlotte's shoulder. "I'm not throwing you out, but this doesn't have to be your life either."

Charlotte sat on the couch with Bella and patted the seat cushion until her sister finally joined her.

"I shouldn't have texted him, but I was so mad." Andrea covered her eyes with her hands and cried. Bella jumped from Charlotte's lap to her mother's, wrapping tiny arms around Andrea's neck.

"No, you shouldn't have. But it's over. Let it go. Just be done with that part of your life." Charlotte clenched her fists at her sides. A large part of her wanted to find Blake and punch him in the face for doing this. But if she was really going to live the ways of the Amish, a more passive behavior was expected. And no good would come from confronting Blake.

Andrea kissed Bella on the cheek, leaving a trace of blood on the baby's face. She shook her head. "That's not how it works. I mean, do you really think we can shed our pasts to live normal lives?"

Charlotte pushed back hair from her sister's face. "Yes, I do. We are not products of a past environment. We've talked about this. We are who we choose to be. Just don't look back. Move forward. One baby step at a time."

"Edna was here today."

Charlotte's eyes widened. "Uh, that was random. But, why?"

"Can I just say it's a long story, but it ended with a

great tale about cake and icing?" Andrea tried to smile but flinched as she brought a hand to her eye.

Charlotte recalled Lena's cake-and-icing analogy about life on earth and heaven. "If it's the same story I've been told, it's a good one." Charlotte wished she'd been the one to tell it to her sister.

Andrea nodded. "Yeah, it is." She stared at Charlotte. "Do you think God sends unexpected people into our lives to help us see things more clearly?"

"Yes, I do."

"I know you don't like Edna, but she's kinda messed up. I'm thinking maybe I will ask her to go to lunch or something. Is that okay?"

Charlotte shrugged but then smiled. "It's fine. This might be your first baby step."

"I had a taste of icing earlier today, and it felt so awesome." She pointed to her eye. "Then this happened and reminded me that I'm still the same Andrea." Her voice cracked. "And I don't want to be her anymore."

Charlotte cupped her sister's cheek. "I want you to be exactly who you are." She grinned. "With maybe just a few tiny improvements."

Andrea tried to smile again. "I want a fresh start. I want a clean slate. But I don't know how to erase my past."

"I understand. I really do. But God forgives us the moment we ask Him to. That's something I struggled with for a long time. Just ask, and you are forgiven."

Andrea stared at Charlotte for a long while, her black eye twitching. "Have you always been religious like this?"

Charlotte chuckled. "No. And I'm still on the journey. But my steps are larger and more confident as I navigate my path. The light is easier to see when you step away from the darkness."

Andrea touched her eye. "I don't want the darkness anymore."

"Then baby steps it is." Charlotte squeezed Andrea's hand before she kissed her sister gently on the cheek, then she kissed Bella. "We are a family. We will just keep picking each other up when we fall. Now, let's get you girls cleaned up." She pointed at Andrea as she stood. "No more communication with Blake, right?"

Andrea nodded as she stood with Bella. "I promise."

They walked toward the kitchen. "I have some news to share."

Andrea grunted. "I hope it's good news, 'cause it's been a weird day."

"Yes, it's good news." Charlotte smiled, eager to tell Daniel later about her decision to be baptized.

After she'd talked to Andrea for a while, Charlotte tried to call Daniel. Even as she stared at her phone, Charlotte had to admit that she would be glad to keep it after she converted. The more she thought about this life change, the more she wanted to talk to Daniel about it. She tried to call several more times, but there was no answer.

Daniel sat in the living room he'd grown up in, a house filled with love, fellowship, obedience, and devotion to the Lord. Precious memories were held within these walls, but a dark cloud hung thick in the room as his family gathered. Daniel and Annie sat on the couch while Aunt Faye and their father sat in the rocking chairs on the other side of the room. It was a forced meeting that Aunt Faye had demanded, and it was the first time that no one was at the hospital with their mother. It was also the first time their father had come out of the bedroom for longer than five minutes, and Daniel was pretty sure that was his aunt's doing also.

"I've called this meeting because Eve would want me to. And we all know what it's about." Aunt Faye glared at *Daed*, a stubborn man who ruled his household with a mostly fair mix of discipline and love. But he was broken, slumped over in the chair, and seemingly without energy to even argue with Aunt Faye.

"It's time, Lucas." Aunt Faye sat taller, her eyes filled with tears. "And I respect your role as head of this household, but your children are adults, and they should have a say in this matter."

Daniel felt like a hand had closed around his throat. Annie gently rocked Gracie on the couch next to him. Their father continued not to take notice of the baby, and more and more Annie had assumed the parental role. Daniel was proud of her for that. She'd been through her fair share of heartache, yet she made sure that the baby's needs were met, including a healthy dose of cuddling and love.

Daniel glanced at his father, his elbows on his knees and his forehead in his hands.

"Let us pray." Aunt Faye bowed her head, and so did Annie and Daniel. *Daed* didn't move, his head still low.

After they'd prayed silently, Daniel tried to clear his throat, but it was hard to breathe as he fought to hold back tears. He couldn't get any words to come.

"I've consulted with the bishop," Aunt Faye said.

This seemed odd to Daniel since his aunt had been shunned years ago and the rule was that after a person was shunned, the Amish were no longer permitted to speak with them. But exceptions had been made, and Daniel wasn't sure whether to credit that to Bishop Miller exclusively or to the overall changing ways that were being forced on them by the *Englisch*.

"And Bishop Miller has said that only God can decide if a person lives or dies." Aunt Faye's voice was shaky. "And Lucas, our beloved Eve isn't living. It is an injustice to leave her in this state where she is left somewhere in between life and death. And it seems only fair to take a vote on this matter."

Prior to now, his father would have bucked up, told everyone the decisions made in this house were his alone, and most likely stomped a foot—or possibly thrown

Aunt Faye out. But *Daed* didn't move or speak, his focus on the wood floor beneath his feet.

Even though Daniel's thoughts had shifted and he felt like his mother was already gone, he wasn't sure he could be a part of unplugging her life support, now that they were down to an actual decision-making process.

"I vote to disable the machines." Aunt Faye raised her chin, and Daniel held his breath, waiting for *Daed* to tell his aunt that she wasn't included in the voting, but he remained still and silent. "Annie? Daniel?"

Annie started to cry and reached for Daniel's hand, and as his own tears formed, he found himself unable to commit either, so he remained silent.

"Sweet children . . ." Aunt Faye spoke softly as a tear rolled down her cheek. "Follow your heart and think hard about what your mother would want."

Daed bolted up from the chair and the two women and Daniel jumped. "We will have the doctors disable the machines." His voice was gravelly and his chin trembled as he spoke. "There will be no more discussion. We will go to the hospital this morning." He left the room, went to his bedroom, and slammed the door.

Aunt Faye dabbed at her eyes with a tissue. "And so it shall be." She walked up the stairs, leaving Daniel and Annie alone. Annie sobbed quietly.

Daniel appreciated and respected the fact that their father had come through in the end. He wasn't going to make his children vote on whether or not to end their mother's life.

Daniel had already decided that he couldn't do it. And he suspected Annie felt the same way, even if it was the right thing to do. Knowing the right decision didn't always mean being strong enough to make it. The weight on Daniel's shoulders lifted, but as the load settled into his chest, a new form of grief tightened the muscles around his heart.

Charlotte was concerned about leaving Andrea and Bella alone this morning, but Andrea had assured her that Blake wouldn't be coming back. Charlotte took the day off work today. It was a slow time during the holidays, and she was eager to tell Daniel that she was choosing to be baptized the Sunday after next. Bishop Miller had told her that there was already another baptism scheduled for that day, and Charlotte could be a part of those proceedings.

Excitement and nervousness left her feeling light-headed. She'd gone by the Byler's place, but no one was home. Charlotte had called Daniel's cell phone this morning, but still no answer. Annie also wasn't answering her phone. Maybe Lucas had finally put an end to the cell phone privileges. Daniel said his father threatened all the time to ban the phones.

Next stop, the hospital. If Daniel wasn't there, surely Annie or their father would know where he was. She parked Big Red and found her way to Eve's room. The door was closed, so she knocked.

No one answered, but she heard muffled cries from inside. She knocked again, and Annie answered, her face red and streaked with tears. "Come in, Charlotte," she said softly.

Charlotte stepped into the room as a flat, green line ran across Eve's monitor, and it became obvious why Daniel, Annie, their father, and their aunt were gathered around Eve's bed, along with a doctor and a nurse.

"I'm so sorry," Charlotte said in a whisper. "I'll go." She turned to leave, but Annie grabbed her hand.

"*Nee*, you're family." Annie held tightly to Charlotte's hand, but when Charlotte locked eyes with Daniel, she could feel the daggers he threw her way. He was crying, but an anger was etched into his features that she'd never seen before.

"I think I should go."

"*Nee*. It's fine, and—"

"Let her go, Annie." Daniel's voice was stern and louder than Charlotte would have expected.

Lucas Byler was standing perfectly still, looking at his wife as if there weren't anyone else in the room, no conversation, no one but the woman he'd loved for decades. Charlotte's heart was broken for all of them. But, selfishly, she felt her own heart breaking as well—about Daniel.

"Go, Charlotte," Daniel repeated again.

She pulled her hand from Annie's. "I'm sorry," she said again. Then she ran out of the room, down the hall, and to her truck.

Grief made people react in different and sometimes strange ways, but there was no mistaking the look in Daniel's eyes when he told her to leave. And Charlotte didn't think he meant for her to just leave the room. His words felt much more substantial than that.

Twenty

Three days later, Daniel and Annie stood in the living room greeting visitors who stopped by to pay their respects and to view the body, as was customary. Annie clung to Gracie, occasionally allowing a guest to hold the baby for a short time.

Daniel had talked to Charlotte on the phone, but he hadn't seen her since his mother passed from this life to the next. He didn't really want to see anyone, even the woman he loved. Resentment threatened to take over where grief had settled in, and anger was replacing hurt. He'd been taught to accept God's will, not to question it. But the constant pain in his heart had left him feeling cheated.

Unlike his father, who still wouldn't have anything to do with Gracie, Daniel's emotions were closer to his sister's when it came to the baby, relishing a new life. He prayed daily that *Daed* would bond with the baby and not see the child as the reason their mother was no longer alive.

He'd treated Charlotte badly at the hospital, but she'd risen above it and not mentioned anything about it on the phone, only saying how sorry she was and that she was available to Daniel and his family for whatever they might need. He needed his mother back, and that was something no one could provide. And in his grief, he was sure that no one knew the dejection etched into his soul.

"Jacob and his family are here." Annie left Daniel and maneuvered around the bishop and a few of the elders standing nearby, until she was standing by the front door. Jacob and Amos lifted Lena's wheelchair up the porch steps as Hannah and Isaac trailed them.

Hugs and condolences followed. Lena and Hannah both brought containers of food, which Hannah stashed in the kitchen after they'd spoken to the bishop, Daniel's father, and a few others. Where was Charlotte? Maybe she wasn't coming. He was torn between clinging to her and distancing himself, and the latter had won out. It wasn't Charlotte's fault that his mother was no longer with them, but he didn't feel like he had the strength for Charlotte right now. She rarely took control of her own destiny, but right now, Daniel needed her to stand on her own while he worked through his feelings.

"*Wie bischt*, Daniel." Edna and John came into the living room holding hands, which was uncustomary and particularly unusual for Edna and her husband.

"*Danki* for coming." Daniel was tired of thanking people. He didn't care about the food everyone was talking about in the kitchen. And if one more person said his mother looked peaceful, he might snap. He just wanted this day to be over. And tomorrow was the funeral.

Edna hugged him at the exact moment Charlotte came into the room, waiting her turn to speak to Daniel, as if they were merely two people who cared for each other, not a couple who had made memories together and talked of a future. But Charlotte had veered away from that conversation so many times, Daniel was tired of bringing it up.

She said hello to Edna and John, and even smiled while doing so, which irritated Daniel even more since Charlotte couldn't stand Edna.

"*Danki* for coming," Daniel said to Charlotte.

"Of course." Her eyebrows drew inward as if she was confused by the formality. "How are you holding up?"

Daniel had asked Charlotte the same question the day of her mother's funeral, so it didn't stand to reason that her question should embitter. "*Gut*. I'm fine."

She nodded. "Andrea wanted to come to pay her respects, but Bella was running a low fever. I didn't think it would be *gut* for her to be around Grace."

Daniel caught her use of the *Deutsch* but didn't acknowledge it. He wanted to pull her into his arms and hold on to her for life. But losing her scared him more than having her, and he was sure his heart couldn't risk another onslaught of grief.

Charlotte wasn't sure why Daniel had distanced himself so much, but she was going to respect his need for privacy during this difficult time. She would have thought he might have leaned on her a little, the way she'd leaned on him so many times. Maybe it was different with a man. Perhaps he was trying to stay strong. He excused himself to greet other guests.

Edna cozied up to Charlotte, which, prior to a few days ago, would have made her cringe. But Andrea had eventually shared her entire conversation with Edna and Edna's desperateness the day she visited. Charlotte was trying to see her in a new light. She doubted they would ever be great friends, but she sympathized with the woman. And for whatever reason, God had chosen Edna to enlighten Andrea about a life after this one. For that, Charlotte was grateful.

Charlotte's thoughts traveled to her baptism a week from Sunday. She hadn't mentioned it to Daniel, as badly as she'd wanted to. It seemed that her baptism should be a time of celebration, and this wasn't the right time to rejoice in her decision.

She scanned the room and found Amos leaning over Lena's wheelchair talking to her. Whatever he said to her caused her to smile, and Charlotte was sure Lena was the strongest person she'd ever known. She tried to imagine what it would be like to lose Lena, and she knew Daniel's pain had to be overwhelming. Then she saw Lucas standing off by himself, his expression void of emotion as he held his position away from small groups that had gathered.

She moved to his side. "I'm sorry, Lucas." Charlotte touched his arm, then eased her hand to her side. Daniel's father nodded but otherwise kept his eyes down. "If there is anything I can do, please let me know."

Lucas nodded again but didn't make eye contact.

As Charlotte looked around again, she recognized most of the people in the room, a community she'd come to love and would soon be a part of. When she felt eyes on her, she turned to her left and found Daniel's gaze. But he quickly looked away. Wondering what she'd done, she started to walk his way, but Hannah eased her hand underneath Charlotte's elbow and steered her in another direction until they stopped on the other side of the room.

"Congratulations on the baby." Charlotte hugged Hannah. "I'm so happy for you and Isaac."

Hannah smiled. "*Danki*. We are excited."

Charlotte had only told Andrea about her plans to be baptized, and while it might not be the right time to tell Daniel, she was bursting to tell someone. "I have some exciting news too."

Grinning, Hannah raised her eyebrows. "I'd love to hear."

"I'm going to get baptized, here, in this community."

Hannah lifted up on her toes as she let out a small gasp. "Charlotte, I'm so happy for you." She playfully rolled her eyes. "But I knew you would. You're family. And then you and Daniel can get married."

Charlotte looked toward where Daniel had been standing, but he was gone. "Well, I hope so."

"What's wrong?" Hannah inched a little closer, an ear peeled.

Charlotte shrugged. "I'm not sure. I mean, I know he is grieving, but he seems angry at me for something, and I'm not sure what. I haven't pushed him on it, considering the circumstances."

"I agree." Hannah folded her hands in front of her. "He needs time to grieve. And men can be funny about these things. It must be a lot of pressure to pretend to be strong when you are hurting so much. Maybe he just needs some time. What did he say about your upcoming baptism? I'm sure he was happy to hear that news."

Charlotte bit her bottom lip, then cringed a little. "I haven't told him yet. I guess . . . I guess I want him to be happy about it and celebrate with me."

"In some ways it is a celebration." Hannah glanced at Eve's coffin, open halfway with a sheet covering her. For those who wanted a viewing, a family member lifted the sheet. Charlotte hadn't ventured that way yet. "She's finally home."

"I know. But those closest to her will feel the loss for a long time." Charlotte recalled her own mother's funeral not so long ago, but there was an equal amount of sadness and relief in Janell's passing. This was different for Daniel.

And Annie and Lucas. Also heartbreaking because of baby Grace.

"Eve is wearing her wedding clothes. Did you know that? It's tradition." Hannah stared at the coffin in the distance.

Charlotte nodded. "*Ya*, I did."

Hannah grinned. "Speaking a little *Deutsch*, are you?"

Amid the sadness, Charlotte welcomed the light moment and smiled, then she caught sight of Jacob holding Grace. "Look." She nodded toward Annie and Jacob both huddled on the couch with the baby. "He looks like a natural. Do you think Jacob and Annie will try to make a go of it again?"

"*Ya*, I think so. They are together a lot, and Jacob seems more grounded and ready to stay in our community. Whatever happened during his time in the *Englisch* world, it seems to have calmed his restless soul."

"I hope so."

Annie smiled as Grace cooed and stretched her tiny arms above her head. "Isn't she beautiful?"

Jacob ran a finger along Grace's cheek, bringing forth a smile. "*Ya*, she really is. Has your father come around?"

Annie swallowed back a lump forming in her throat. "*Nee*. Every time I ask him if he'd like to hold the baby, he has an excuse. It breaks my heart. And it would break *Mamm*'s too."

"Do you think he blames the *boppli* for your *mudder's* passing?"

Annie sighed but smiled again when Grace did. "Maybe when he looks at Grace it reminds him of why *Mamm* died." She shrugged. "I don't know, but this sweet girl is so easy to love and cherish."

Jacob scrunched up his nose. "What's that smell?"

Annie shook her head. "*Ach*. Don't you recognize it? *Aenti* Faye must have heated up her pickled oysters. They are awful enough cold, but when she heats them up, the smell is enough to make your stomach curdle like bad cheese. But I don't know what we would have done without *Aenti* Faye. Her cooking has been challenging, but in a weird way, she's kind of been the glue that's held us together. And she's the only one who can get *Daed* to do anything."

"Do you think she'll stay on now? Since your *mamm* . . ." His voice trailed off along with his eyes, until they both met gazes with her father, who hadn't moved from his spot in the corner, except to occasionally nod to a visitor.

"I don't know."

Jacob found Annie's hand and squeezed. "I love you."

She smiled. "I love you too, Jacob."

Jacob was different in a lot of ways, quieter and a bit more subdued. But all the things she loved about him were the same. He was tender and kind, a hard worker, and as of his recent return home, more mature. He'd already told her he was getting baptized a week from Sunday, but Annie hadn't committed to marrying him. She wanted him to take this step on his own, a true commitment to the church. Then they would decide if they were ready to commit to each other.

"I miss *Mamm* so much." Annie blinked back tears. "And this little bundle of joy is never going to know how wonderful her *mudder* was."

"We will make sure Grace knows about her mother. We'll tell stories and share memories about your *mamm*."

Annie smiled. His choice of words wasn't lost on her. *We.* As she gazed into Jacob's eyes, she thought about everything they'd been through together, and deep in her heart, she knew they were going to be okay, no matter what life threw their way.

Andrea dabbed concealer underneath her eye, enough that the makeup almost completely masked the yellowish-purple bruise underneath. She wasn't going anywhere, but she didn't like Bella to see it. Her daughter would point and say, "Boo-boo."

Blake had texted and apologized, saying that he'd just panicked about Andrea possibly involving the police.

She wasn't sure how to forgive him, so she just ignored his texts, like she and Charlotte had discussed. Her sister gave her hope that she could be a better person, a better mother. And Edna had surprised her with a story about cake and icing that had also left Andrea feeling hopeful.

"This is a new life for us, Bella. And things are going to be different."

Andrea closed the compact and threw it back in her purse, along with the concealer. She'd gotten used to sitting on the couch to apply any makeup, since the window was behind her and shed some light. Then she pulled out a tray of beads for a necklace she was working on. She slid alternating pink and white balls down the string.

"Your aunt is going to be an Amish person," she said to Bella as her daughter chewed on the strap of Andrea's purse. She eased the strap out of Bella's mouth and replaced it with a teething ring. "No makeup, no music, she'll wear Amish clothes, and . . . and no *driving*." She glanced at Bella. "How are we going to get around?"

Bella chomped on the rubber toy, and Andrea suspected Bella had another tooth coming in.

After she finished the necklace, she tied off the end and set it alongside four others she'd made. One of the boutiques she'd taken jewelry to had sold out and requested more earrings. Andrea was happy to oblige. It wasn't a lot of money, but you couldn't put a price tag on self-worth. In most ways Andrea was the richest she'd ever been. Wealthy with an abundance of love. For the first time. Thanks to her sister.

She was going to do something extra special for Charlotte.

Twenty-One

Charlotte rode with Hannah and Isaac to Eve's funeral the next morning. A cold front had blown in overnight and dropped the temperatures to almost freezing. Isaac had a portable heater in his buggy, and, thankfully, most buggies had windshields. Charlotte's teeth still chattered as they made their way to the cemetery amid a long line of buggies.

The procession to the cemetery followed a ceremony held at the Byler's home. Charlotte had been to Amish funerals before, so she wasn't surprised that no one eulogized Eve, and there weren't any flowers or music. The service had focused on the world yet to come, and the bishop also referenced the story of creation several times. Like the funerals outside of the Amish community, it was a somber occasion with almost everyone dressed in black clothing.

"I'm sorry your parents weren't able to come today." Charlotte leaned over the seat in front of her so Hannah could hear her, and also so she could warm her face closer to the battery-operated heater.

"*Mamm* has her *gut* days and her bad days." Hannah looked over her shoulder at Charlotte. "Today isn't a *gut* day, and *Daed* felt like he needed to be home with her. They were both sorry to miss Eve's service, but they were glad they were able to visit the family in their home yesterday."

Charlotte nodded and snuggled into her coat as she leaned back against the seat. Hannah's heart was heavy about her mother. Charlotte could hear the pain in her voice. When the time came, Charlotte had to be strong for Hannah and her family; Lena would want that. But that didn't mean she would quit praying for Lena's complete healing.

She wanted to be someone Daniel could lean on today, but the distance between them had never seemed greater than yesterday during the viewing. He'd used a formality with her that was unfamiliar and avoided being around her for any length of time.

Eve's death had seemed to draw Jacob and Annie closer. Jacob had stayed by Annie's side, both of them tending to Grace, and Annie smiled often despite the circumstances. Maybe Annie just coped differently than her brother. Or maybe Daniel had changed his mind about wanting to be with Charlotte. But was it fair to judge any relationship at a time when grief was immeasurable?

She chose to put her swirling thoughts to rest for today. She was going to pay her respects to Eve and support the family as best she could. As they rounded the corner to the Amish cemetery, Charlotte glimpsed the hearse, a boxlike enclosed carriage, leading the procession. Daniel's family would be following right behind it, and if the long line of buggies were traveling for an event other than a funeral, it would be a majestic sight. There was a thunderous *clip-clop* that sounded like an army of soldiers, the smell of manure wafting in the breeze. Charlotte estimated over a hundred buggies traveling to Eve's final resting place.

Daniel drove his buggy and carted Jacob and Annie with him, along with Gracie. They followed his father, whose only passenger was Aunt Faye. Daniel didn't think he'd ever know what Aunt Faye had said to *Daed* that day to get him to leave the hospital, but she continued to be the only person he listened to.

Annie cried softly in the backseat, where she had the baby wrapped up like an Eskimo. Jacob sat in the front seat with Daniel.

"Why didn't you ask Charlotte to ride with us?" Jacob rubbed his gloved hands together as he blew out puffs of cold air.

Daniel turned up the small heater and shrugged. "She's not family."

"Neither am I." Jacob raised an eyebrow beneath freshly cut bangs.

"Well, you probably will be soon enough." Daniel twisted his mouth into a grin that probably looked sour, but Annie and Jacob had gone back and forth so many times before, who knew what would ultimately happen?

"What about you and Charlotte?" Jacob turned to face him. "She's getting baptized the same day I am."

Daniel stiffened as he accidently pulled back on the reins, causing the horse to buck up on his hind legs for a couple of seconds. "Whoa, fellow."

"I didn't know Charlotte was getting baptized, especially not so soon." Annie sniffled, then cleared her throat. "I'm guessing Daniel didn't know either."

"*Nee*, I didn't." Why hadn't Charlotte told him? Then again, he hadn't given her much opportunity.

"What is going on with you and Charlotte, Daniel?" Annie's voice had a demanding tone, and he wasn't in the mood to answer to his little sister. But he reined in his anger. Annie was hurting just as much as he was.

"I don't know." He made the statement strong and firm, hoping to end the discussion, which wasn't always possible with Annie, but his sister stayed quiet.

⁓

Annie held Gracie close to her chest with her coat wrapped around the baby. She'd considered hiring a friend, an

Englisch girl she knew, to keep Grace today since it had turned cooler, but someday when her baby sister was older, Annie would be able to tell her that she attended the funeral of the most wonderful woman who ever lived. The ceremony at the cemetery wouldn't last long. Although this day would be etched into Annie's mind forever. How was her family ever going to feel normal again?

Her father remained quiet and detached, but somewhere along the line Daniel joined him in a grief that seemed specific to the two of them. Annie's heart was breaking, but she didn't feel the need to abandon those she loved. And she was grateful to Jacob more than ever for being emotionally supportive and attentive to her and Gracie.

It angered her that her father and brother felt that it was acceptable to just check out. Life would go on, and it would be painful for all of them, but Annie wanted her mother to look down from heaven and see that her family was intact and handling their grief in a way that God would approve of.

As the buggies parked in a long line side by side, drivers hurried to tether their horses on the hitching posts, and tearful attendants shivered as they made their way to a grave already dug and waiting. Annie kept Grace close to her as Jacob kept an arm around her, guiding her to the area. Charlotte stood with Hannah and Isaac. Hannah's chin trembled as she fought not to cry, but Charlotte was sobbing.

Annie wanted to go to Charlotte, but her place was with her family right now, so she followed Daniel, her father, and Aunt Faye to the gravesite. *Daed* sobbed openly, which only made Annie cry even more. She'd never seen him in such pain, and it was a hurt that seemed to latch on to him in a way that Annie feared he would never be the same. Her people were taught that this was a somber time, but it was also to be cherished as a loved one finally went home. She glanced toward Charlotte again, happy to see that Hannah had her arm around her.

Charlotte feared death. And the fact that it scared her bothered her even more. If she was as strong in her faith as she thought, then why the apprehension? It was a question that had bounced around in her mind recently, adding to her confusion about baptism.

She glanced around at the people present to say a final good-bye to Eve. They were her friends, and—she squeezed Hannah's hand—if she left the community, she would be heartbroken. But it was more than that. This was where she'd found her faith and accepted God into her life. She couldn't imagine being anywhere else, but in her vision of life here, Daniel had been in that picture. Now she wasn't sure.

Bishop Miller read a hymn. Charlotte already knew there wouldn't be any singing. And after a few words

were said, everyone bowed their heads to say the Lord's
Prayer silently.

She looked up and caught Daniel staring at her, but
he quickly looked away. *What is going on with him?* She
wasn't going to judge or speculate at a time when his grief
was so intense, but it didn't stop her heart from hurting,
and she missed his nurturing ways. Maybe she'd relied
on him too heavily in the past. Did he want her to be
more independent? Why now?

As the service came to a close, no one lingered around
the gravesite. The pallbearers would stay until the casket
was lowered, and then they would fill the grave.

Charlotte felt a hand on her arm, and she turned to see
Annie with the baby. "I'm so sorry, Annie." She hugged
her friend, then snuck a peek at Grace, who was mostly
wrapped inside Annie's coat. "She's just beautiful."

"*Danki.* She's such a *gut* baby. She only cries if she's
hungry, wet, or tired." Annie smiled. "I love her so much.
Mamm would have loved her too." Her eyes began to water,
but she sniffled and regained composure. "Charlotte, I
don't know what's wrong with my *bruder.* He seems to
have slipped into a dark place and is acting like my *daed.*
But please don't give up on him. He might just need some
time."

Charlotte dabbed at her eyes. "I don't know if I made
him mad, but he won't really talk to me."

"I know. And I don't understand him. But none of us
are in our right minds now." She looked toward her left

at the line of people making their way back to the buggies. "I should go."

Charlotte took a deep breath. "Can you tell Daniel
that I love him?"

Annie smiled, nodding. "*Ya*, I will." She leaned in for
a hug, then Charlotte found Hannah and Isaac.

As they walked back to Isaac's buggy, Charlotte
searched for Daniel. When she finally found him, he had
his head down and was walking fast.

He didn't even speak to me.

Andrea played patty-cake with Bella for what seemed
like the hundredth time that day. But once her daughter had learned how to play the game, she couldn't seem
to get enough of it, and Andrea loved to hear her giggle
when they slapped hands and Andrea sang.

"Your aunt Charlotte is home." Andrea set Bella on
the floor and went to the door. Charlotte staggered up the
stairs like she was drunk. Andrea doubted that was the
case, but she opened the door and waited.

Charlotte's eyes were red and swollen. *Of course.* She'd
been at a funeral. But something else was wrong. Her
sister was crying in a weird way, like an injured animal,
sobbing like she was defeated and slumped over as she
held the handrail and pulled herself onto the porch. When
she looked at Andrea, she stood perfectly still except her

shoulders moved up and down as she cried, tears streaming down her red face as she blew out bursts of cold air.

"Charlotte?"

She didn't move, so Andrea walked closer. She put an arm around her. "Let's get in the house where it's warm. I kept the fire going and I'll get you some hot tea or make some coffee."

Andrea got her inside the house and helped her out of her coat. Charlotte usually beelined for Bella, but she just shuffled to her bedroom and closed the door. Bella looked at Andrea, then at the closed bedroom door. Even Bella seemed confused as she twirled a sliver of blonde hair in her fingers. Andrea laid with Bella on the couch for a nap. Then she tapped on Charlotte's door. When she didn't answer, Andrea opened the door.

Her sister was curled in a ball and lying perfectly still on her side. Her eyebrows were drawn in, her lips in a frown, as if she couldn't rid herself of the pain even while sleeping. Charlotte had said she wasn't particularly close to Eve, so Andrea assumed there was more to her sister's emotional state than just the funeral. Most likely it was the distance Charlotte mentioned between her and Daniel.

Bella would sleep for at least an hour. Andrea eased onto the bed, curled up beside her sister, and draped her arm across her. "I love you."

Charlotte's hand moved, and she reached up and touched Andrea's arm. "I love you too," she said in a whisper.

Andrea lay there with her until Charlotte was lightly snoring.

$\backsim$

Thursday morning Annie was cleaning the breakfast dishes when she heard racket coming from the living room. Drying her hands on her apron, she walked that way. Aunt Faye had packed her suitcases and had them at the bottom of the stairs.

"You're *leaving*?" Annie's voice probably sounded as panicked as she felt. Her father and Daniel did nothing but lounge around like lizards on a rock, neither of them making much effort to do much of anything since the funeral. Aunt Faye was the only one who kept the tiniest sense of normality alive. Annie shook her head, blinking. Who would have ever thought that Aunt Faye would represent normal in any sense of the word?

"Yep. I've been called away." Aunt Faye straightened her stance as she raised her chin. "Your cousin Mae needs my help." She tapped a finger to her chin as she clicked her tongue against the roof of her mouth. "Actually, she's not your cousin. Well, maybe twice removed. Either way, Mae broke her leg, and she has four young children she needs help with. So I'm leaving." She rolled her eyes. "Just call me Mary Poppins!"

Was there really another relative? It didn't matter. "It's almost Christmas. And . . . and what about Gracie?" *And what about the lounging lizards who have gone back to bed after breakfast?* Christmas was going to be hard enough without *Mamm.* Would Annie prepare a Christmas meal? What would she do about her father and Daniel?

Aunt Faye had a bright red scarf draped over her arm. She put it around her neck, then walked to the rack by the front door and retrieved her coat. After slipping it on, she walked back to Annie and touched her on the arm. "You are going to be just fine. I was willing to stay on when we thought this was a temporary situation." She blinked teary eyes a few times. "But now you must adjust to a new situation and work toward making things feel normal again."

"It's never going to be normal again." Annie hung her head, but Aunt Faye cupped her chin, forcing Annie's gaze to hers.

"It might not seem like it now, but life will go on, and there will be a new normal for all of you. Your *mamm* would want that."

Annie folded her arms across her chest. "What about *Daed*—and Daniel? *Mei bruder* seems to have fallen into his own dark hole."

Aunt Faye sighed. "For two strong and capable men, they have withered into puny little slugs. People grieve, and they have a right to do so." Aunt Faye started buttoning up her coat. "But they cannot do so in a way that affects the livelihood of others, especially you and Gracie." She pointed an index finger at Annie. "So it is up to you to make them behave."

Annie's eyes widened. "Are we talking about the same Lucas Byler? Because I doubt I can force *mei daed* to do much of anything. And Daniel has always bossed me around, so I'm doubtful my older *bruder* will listen much to me either."

"Annie, child . . ." Aunt Faye smiled. "I've watched you over the past weeks, the way you have nurtured Gracie, the way you've stayed calm and levelheaded, and the way you have made calculated decisions about you and Jacob. You aren't the love-struck teenager you used to be. You have matured into a beautiful young woman." She kissed Annie on the cheek, followed by a hug. "Keep God close at hand always."

Her aunt pointed upstairs. "I've already said my good-byes to Gracie before she lay down for her nap. Daniel was sleeping just now, so I let him be." She pointed toward the kitchen. "There are pickled oysters in the refrigerator. I regret not having shared my recipe with you before I leave, but that's the way it goes."

She turned toward the front door, carrying two suit-cases. Annie followed her to the door.

"Your father knows I'm leaving today, but since he is sleeping, I'll let him be as well."

"This is awful," Annie blurted out as she shook her head.

Aunt Faye smiled. "Only if you allow it to be." She stomped a foot. "Take control of these men, Annie Byler!"

Annie put on her coat, then picked up the third

suitcase and followed her aunt to the car. After the bags were loaded, Aunt Faye gave her a final hug. "You will be fine, dear." She spun on her heel and waved over her shoulder. "I am in high demand, and I can't be everywhere at once."

Annie didn't move as her aunt started up the old station wagon and pulled out of the driveway. She recalled her aunt's response to Annie when she said this was awful.

"Only if you allow it to be."

Twenty-Two

Charlotte left work early on Friday. In two days her life would be changing in a big way, a decision that had been brewing for a long time. As she pulled Big Red out onto the highway, her mind filled with excitement and trepidation. Sunday she would renounce the devil and commit her life to Christ—both of which she'd already done anyway. But she would be adding acceptance of the *Ordnung* to the commitment she'd be making.

She wouldn't be permitted to cut her long hair, no matter how unruly it became. Her clothes would go to Andrea, and anything left over would be donated. She would put Big Red for sale, and with the money she would purchase a buggy and a horse. As she tightened her grip around the steering wheel, she wished she could just park her beloved truck on her property to have nearby. It was silly, her attachment to Big Red, but it was more than a mode of transportation to her.

Her cell phone would be for emergencies, according to Amish standards, but it was a widely abused privilege. Hannah had already given her dresses, aprons, and *kapps*. Charlotte had purchased short black socks and black leather shoes. She supposed giving up electricity, and everything that went along with it, might have proved a difficult adjustment, but Charlotte had already been living without those amenities.

But in all of her imaginings of her big day, Daniel had been with her, proud that she had taken this step through prayer and devotion, the first in a series of strides for them to have a life together. And now, she hadn't even spoken to him since the funeral. She'd texted him and tried to call once, but no response.

Had he turned his phone off or just turned off any feelings for her? If so, how could a person do that, just shut off love?

She turned onto his street, her truck not even warm inside yet as she blew out clouds of cold air. Bundling up with a scarf and hat, she jogged to the front door and knocked.

Annie opened the door holding Grace. Her prayer covering was lopsided, her black apron covered in something white—flour, perhaps—and she was barefoot. She had dark circles underneath her eyes.

"Aren't your feet cold?" Charlotte stepped into the living room. Her Amish friends were known to have immaculate houses, and the Bylers' house had been no exception. Until now.

"*Ya, ya.* I need to go put some socks on, at least." Annie glanced around the room. There were glasses, empty potato chip bags, and a bag of Almond Joy candy bars on the coffee table. On the couch were newspapers, a paper plate, and a pair of shoes. "Forgive the way our home looks."

"Here, here." Charlotte held out her arms to take the baby. "Get some socks on, then we'll talk."

Annie handed over baby Grace. "If you're looking for Daniel, he's upstairs . . ." Scowling, she clenched her fists. ". . . upstairs *sleeping.*"

"At four in the afternoon?" Charlotte raised an eyebrow as disappointment swept through her.

"*Ach,* trust me, there is no schedule around here. People eat when they want, leave their mess everywhere, and rarely do anything more productive than take a bath! And even that doesn't happen on a daily basis."

Charlotte rocked Grace in her arms as she took another look around the living room. "Where's Faye?"

"She left. And she took any order she'd established with her!" Annie shook her head. "I'll be right back."

Charlotte lay Grace in the bouncy seat on the floor, then tossed a log on the fire, since it was mostly just glowing embers. She took off her coat, then warmed her hands as small flames caught onto the wood. Once she could feel her fingers, she coddled the baby in her arms again.

"Annie, I'm happy to help you clean up, or anything else you need help with," Charlotte said as Annie walked back into the room with shoes and socks on, and she'd straightened her *kapp* and brushed the flour from her apron.

"I appreciate that, Charlotte, but then what? You have a life and can't be expected to come over here every day to help. Nor would I ever ask that of you, or anyone." Annie stepped closer to Charlotte. "These boys are out of control."

Charlotte fought a grin since it seemed such an *Englisch* thing for Annie to say.

"But I know that's not why you came by, to hear me moaning." She smiled. "Sunday is the big day, *ya?*"

Charlotte nodded and smiled back at her, even though a part of her wanted to cry. She'd been nervous and anxious to talk to Daniel.

"I'll go get Daniel." Annie turned to head back to the stairs.

"No. I mean *nee*. Don't do that. I don't want you to wake him up." Charlotte brought the baby up to her shoulder, rubbing her back.

"Are you sure?" Annie held her position at the base of the stairs.

"*Ya*, I'm sure."

Annie smiled. "The *Deutsch* suits you well."

Charlotte felt her face flush. "I still have a lot to learn."

Annie walked back to her as Charlotte brought Grace from her shoulder and back into her arms. "She's a beauty, isn't she?" Annie asked.

"She is precious." Charlotte handed the baby to Annie, sensing she was ready to have her in her arms again.

"I'd be happy to go throw a glass of cold water on Daniel, if you'd like." She smiled and winked at Charlotte.

"*Nee, nee.* Let's not do that."

Annie sat on the couch, motioning for Charlotte to do the same. In a whisper, she said, "*Mei daed* is in his bedroom. I don't think he's sleeping, and I hear shooting and yelling coming from in there." Her eyes widened as she leaned closer to Charlotte. "I think he is watching cowboy and Indian movies on his phone."

"Really?" Charlotte frowned. "But he's been the one who disliked cell phones. I actually thought maybe he'd banned everyone in the house from using them." She shrugged as she cast her eyes downward. "I haven't heard from Daniel, so I didn't know if maybe that was why."

Annie's gaze darted to her cell phone on the coffee table, partially covered by a paper plate. "*Nee,* there's been no banning of the phone." She raised her eyes to Charlotte. "I wondered if Daniel had talked to you . . ."

"*Nee,* I haven't heard from him." The Pennsylvania *Deutsch* slid off of her tongue easily.

Annie laid the baby on her lap facing her as she shook her head. "Everyone is entitled to grieve. Sometimes I cry myself to sleep at night, missing *Mamm* so badly that I feel sick to my stomach. But I'm raising a baby on my own, and I don't have the luxury to become a potato chip–eating lounge lizard who sleeps and watches cowboy and Indian movies. Something will have to change in this house." She sighed and looked around at the mess.

"But let's talk about you and Daniel. Did something happen between the two of you?"

"Not that I know of. I mean, he was pushing me for a commitment a few weeks ago, and I told him I needed more time. For me, it's not just being with Daniel, but it's also a huge commitment to God." Charlotte shrugged. "He let the subject drop, then we had a lovely dinner out one night." She paused. "I actually thought he might propose that night, but he didn't even mention us being together. And I'd already made up my mind that I was going to say yes. But I figured he had a lot on his plate, with your mother and everything. Then he just got quiet when she passed."

Charlotte hung her head again for a few seconds. "I thought he must need time to himself, but then at the funeral . . . he wouldn't even look at me." She swiped at a tear. "And he isn't returning my texts and hasn't called."

"I want to smack him." Annie growled. "I want to smack him and *mei daed* too."

Charlotte raised her chin and sniffled. "I love Daniel. But even if we aren't going to be together, I am getting baptized as planned. This has been a decision that's been percolating for a long time, but it's a biggy and I had to be sure. And I am."

A broad smile filled Annie's face. "I am so happy for you, Charlotte. And Jacob will be right there with you, also professing his promise to Christ through baptism."

Charlotte smiled. "I'm happy for Jacob. Do you think you and Jacob will get married soon after he's baptized?"

Annie nodded. "*Ya*, I think so. There were times when I wasn't sure, but we've both been through a lot, and I'd like to think we have matured and are capable of making *gut* decisions, choices that will affect the rest of our lives." Annie stood. "I best get this little one a bottle and down for a nap."

Charlotte had kept Annie away from her chores for long enough. She hadn't even taken her coat off. She stood and hugged Annie, then kissed her on the cheek. "Your *mamm* would be proud of you, the way you have taken care of Grace and are running the household."

Annie grunted. "*Danki* about the *boppli*, but I doubt *Mamm* would be happy about the state of this house."

"Baby steps," Charlotte said as she moved toward the door. "And will you tell Daniel I stopped by?"

Annie nodded. "Are you sure you don't want me to go throw a glass of water on him?"

"*Nee, nee.*" Charlotte forced a smile before she left, then hurried to her truck.

Saturday morning Andrea left Bella with Charlotte, then took her truck to the boutiques where she had her jewelry for sale. Two hours later, she had 215 dollars. She'd earned it doing something she loved, and she owed her new life to her sister. She counted out a hundred dollars and stashed it in her purse's side pocket so she could make a stop later. After visiting the last boutique on the outskirts of town, she was walking to the truck when a buggy pulled into the parking lot.

"Whoa, whoa." Edna slowed her horse to a stop. "I thought that might be you in Charlotte's truck. I wasn't sure if she still had the truck since she's getting baptized tomorrow."

Andrea walked closer to the buggy. "I think she's going to sell the truck to get a horse and buggy." She put a hand to her forehead to block the sun as her teeth chattered. "How are you?"

Edna smiled. "Much better. I talked to John. I told him everything." She locked eyes with Andrea. *"Everything."*

Andrea cringed, unsure if that was the right thing to do. What exactly did *everything* mean?

"I—I also spoke to him about how much I thought we both wanted *kinner*, and that I was depressed that we weren't trying for children." Edna lowered her gaze. "It took awhile, but he eventually opened up to me. We are planning to see a doctor soon since John feels there might . . ." Edna cleared her throat as she looked up at Andrea again. "He feels there might be a problem. John wants *kinner* just as much as I do, and once everything was out in the open, we seemed to have found each other again. Things aren't perfect, and some of what I told John was hard for him to hear. But I think we can make things right."

"That's great, Edna." Andrea smiled. "I hope it all works out."

"It's because of you. You talked candidly to me, made me think about things and have the courage to have a hard talk with *mei* husband. *Danki* for that."

"I didn't really do anything."

Edna pulled her coat snug. "I'm not going to Charlotte's and Jacob's baptism tomorrow. I hope that one day things will be different for Charlotte and me, but for tomorrow, I think it best if I not go."

Andrea wasn't going to argue the point and just nodded.

"But I hope God sheds blessings on the day."

"I'm sure Charlotte and Jacob both appreciate those sentiments. I'm kind of looking forward to seeing a real-live Amish baptism." Andrea chuckled.

"It's very special," Edna said, a twinkle in her eye. "I must go. God's blessings on you too, Andrea."

"Um, wait. Where are you off to?"

"Just on my way home after delivering baked goods to Widow Hostetler. Why?"

Andrea recalled Edna's story about cake and icing. "Do you maybe want to get some coffee or something? I mean"—she dropped her gaze and held up a palm—"it's perfectly fine if you don't because I know your people aren't really supposed to hang out with us."

Edna laughed. "I'm afraid our people are dependent

on your people for tourism and a host of other things. We are all just people, loving the Lord and trying to find our way in this world. I'd love to have some coffee. The shop nearby has holiday flavors this time of year."

"Wanna hop in Big Red? It might be warmer." Andrea pointed to the truck.

"There's nowhere to hitch my horse here, and he needs to keep moving in this cold weather, or at least be sheltered from the cold. I have a portable heater if you don't mind riding with me, and there is a coffee shop once we get on the main road. There is a covered area there where I can pull in, a place my horse will be protected from the wind and cold."

"Sure." Andrea walked around to the other side of the buggy and got in. "This is my first time to ride in a buggy."

Edna laughed again, which was really nice to hear after seeing her so distraught not long ago. "Well, you better hold on then because I'm quite the buggy driver." She clicked her tongue and the horse took off into a fast trot.

"Well, now. This is cool." Andrea put her palms against the dashboard as she bounced up and down more than she thought she would. "Guess I need to get used to this since it will be Charlotte's new mode of transportation. And hey, do you mind if we make a stop on the way? I need to drop some money off to someone."

"*Ya*, that's fine."

Andrea settled in for the ride, a smile on her face she couldn't hold in.

Sunday morning Annie sat on the couch wearing a freshly pressed maroon dress and black apron. Gracie had been fed, released a hardy burp, and was wearing a fresh diaper. Annie had built up the fire into a roaring blaze, and she'd had a big bowl of cereal, along with half of an apple. Now, tapping her foot against the wood floor, she waited for the lizards to awaken. She'd made plenty of racket in the kitchen.

"I don't smell bacon," Daniel said as he hit the bottom stair, rubbing his eyes and yawning.

"I didn't prepare breakfast." Annie lifted her chin and pressed her lips together, gently rocking the baby.

Moments later her father emerged from his bedroom, and he shuffled in his slacks, T-shirt, and socks across the living room toward the kitchen. He returned right away.

"There's no *kaffi* made." His bushy eyebrows drew into a frown. "And where is breakfast?"

Annie set Grace in the bouncy seat, tucked a blanket in around her, then kissed her on the cheek. "Grace has eaten and she has a fresh diaper." Annie walked to the rack by the front door. She put on her big black bonnet and coat. "She will need another bottle around ten. And please remember to burp her if you don't want her to spit up on you."

"Have you fallen ill?" Her father took a couple of steps into the living room. "Is that why you haven't made breakfast?"

"*Nee*, I am not ill. I am tired of you two acting like you are the only ones who are grieving. I am tired of you eating potato chips, living like lizards, sleeping half the day . . ." She glared at Daniel, then glowered at her father. "And not being mindful of this beautiful new life we should be celebrating."

"Lizards?" Daniel scratched his head and yawned again.

"Shame on both of you. Charlotte and Jacob are getting baptized today, two people who we love very much. It's been a long time coming for both of them following many hardships. You should both be attending."

Both men stared at Annie with their mouths hanging open. They'd both told her the night before that they would not be going to the baptisms today. Annie had fumed about it until she'd eventually fallen asleep.

"Will you be making our meal before you go?" *Daed* ran his hand along his beard, his nose scrunched up and his eyebrows drawn inward.

"*Nee*. I will not." Annie picked up her purse.

"You aren't taking the baby?" Daniel took a few steps into the living room.

"*Nee*. I'm not going to take Gracie out in the cold when there are two perfectly *gut* babysitters right here. I have already hitched the horse, and I don't know when I'll be back." She marched to the door.

"*Dochder*, you cannot speak to me in this way," her father bellowed.

Something in Annie snapped. When she turned

around to face her father and brother, she could almost feel smoke rising from the top of her head. "*Ya*, I can! I am not a child, so don't talk to me as if I am. I am the only one rearing this beautiful baby. I clean for you, cook for you, mend your clothes, gather the eggs, and brush down the horses. I'm tired!" She pulled open the front door and turned around. "Might I suggest that both of you bathe? And there will not be another meal cooked in this house until you both straighten up yourselves and your mess."

Her father's eyes blazed as he opened his mouth, but Annie cut him off. "*Nee, Daed*. Don't you say anything. I love you, but this must end." She glanced at Gracie as her eyes filled with tears. "*Mamm* is gone. She's not coming back. She's gone home. And now we have a new member of our family who you won't have anything to do with. Gracie is not responsible for *Mamm*'s death. If you are harboring such thoughts, then you need to sweep them under a rug for good!" She pointed her finger at him. "Shame on you!"

Then she locked eyes with Daniel. "It's bad enough you are not attending Jacob's baptism because I'm going to marry him. But how can you not attend Charlotte's? She loves you, Daniel. I don't know what your reasons are for treating her so badly lately, but you are being cruel by not going." Annie started to cry as she slammed the door behind her.

Daniel called her name, but she kept going.

Twenty-Three

Bishop Miller and his wife offered to have the worship service at their home since it would be a small gathering. Charlotte was dressed in a dark green dress, white apron, and her hair atop her head was covered by a *kapp*. As she looked down at her black socks and black leather shoes, she fought the urge to cry happy tears. She'd come a long way, and she was ready to commit herself to the *Ordnung*.

Jacob looked handsome in a black pair of slacks and long-sleeved blue shirt, wearing shiny black shoes and a black felt hat. Annie stood near him, glowing. Amos was standing behind Lena's wheelchair as Lena softly wept. Hannah and Isaac were standing beside Amos. They'd waited a long time to see Jacob get baptized.

Charlotte kept glancing at the door, hoping and praying that Daniel would show up, even if it was just to be present for Jacob's sake. Annie was planning to marry Jacob, and Daniel's family had known Jacob his entire life.

But Charlotte chose to focus on the good things in her life today. She smiled at Andrea, who was holding Bella. *Thank You, God, for gifting me with family.*

⌒

Daniel had never heard Annie stand up to their father in that way, and he waited for *Daed* to go into a rage after Annie left. But he sat in the rocking chair, perfectly still and silent. Daniel sat on the couch near the baby seat where Gracie was sleeping soundly. He didn't know what to say. His sister was right about their father.

"Your sister is right," *Daed* said.

Danki, *Lord for allowing* mei *father to see the error of his ways about the* boppli.

Daniel nodded.

"You should be at that baptism."

Daniel sat taller and started to speak, but his father cleared his throat and went on. "Charlotte has done many *gut* things for Annie and Jacob, taken them in like family when they were confused and lost. I was slow to accept her, but her goodness shines brightly." He scratched his head. "Why, exactly, are you not going?"

Daniel wanted to redirect the conversation to his father's inability to bond with his new daughter, but *Daed* wasn't likely to move to another subject until this question had been satisfied. But Daniel didn't feel like explaining himself. Then he might have to take action, and he'd rather lie around eating potato chips and sleeping. At least until he was able to drift to sleep without crying, his mother's face the last thing he saw each night.

He'd have to explain to his father that Charlotte had spent a long time postponing a commitment, and how he feared she wouldn't go through with the baptism today. Which meant she wouldn't be able to marry him. He couldn't take another hurt piled on top of his grief. "I don't know," he finally said.

His father sat quietly, running his hand the length of his beard over and over again. Hopefully, *Daed* was now thinking about his own actions.

"I do not know how to cook. Do you?" Frowning, he turned to Daniel.

"*Nee.*" Cooking wasn't high on Daniel's priority list right now, but not eating did cause a shiver to run up his spine. But only for a moment.

He began to picture Charlotte, dressed in Amish clothing for the first time, preparing to commit herself to the church for the rest of her life. As Daniel thought about everything she had been through to reach this point, his heart beat faster. *How can I miss this? I love her.*

But what if she didn't go through with it? What if she wasn't even there right now? Should Daniel go for Jacob and Annie, no matter what? Despite the lad's waywardness at times, Jacob was a good lad and seemed to have put his worldly ways behind him.

Daniel thought about the life he'd longed for with Charlotte. And now she was taking the first step toward that dream. Was she doing it just for him? If he wasn't there, would she change her mind and not choose baptism? That seemed like reason enough not to go.

His heart slammed into the wall of his chest. This was what he'd wanted—for Charlotte to commit to God and to him. She'd always said he gave her strength and confidence, and he wasn't there now to provide that.

He bolted upstairs and minutes later he returned, hoping his father would have ventured over to Gracie, or at least paid the tiniest bit of attention to her.

"You're right. I should be there. And I'm going!" He darted toward the door.

"Wait, wait, wait!" His father quickly closed the distance between them. "You can't leave the baby. I don't know how to tend to a child." Scowling, he glanced at Grace, then back at Daniel.

"Annie was right about you too, *Daed*." Daniel stared at his father. "Grace didn't cause *Mamm* to die. She is a beautiful little person, and she's your *dochder*. Go to her."

His father's bottom lip twitched, and Daniel wasn't sure if he was going to yell or cry. Daniel didn't wait to find out.

As he readied the horse for travel, he prayed that his

father would take this opportunity to get to know his daughter.

$\sim$

Charlotte tried to corral the bursts of adrenaline coursing through her veins as butterflies fluttered in her stomach. The deacon had arrived a few minutes late, so they were starting a few minutes after eight o'clock. Charlotte had thanked the bishop and his wife for working in the baptisms before Christmas, instead of making Jacob and Charlotte wait until the spring. Charlotte suspected that Lena might be part of the reason the bishop had bent the rules.

Charlotte was grateful to the bishop—and God—for Lena's presence. Lena had stood by their son as he tried to find his way in the world, but she'd wanted him baptized into the faith. And now it was finally happening.

As everyone took their places, their attention was drawn to the window. In the distance, a buggy sped up the driveway. Charlotte dared to pray that it might be Daniel, and when Annie let out a slight gasp, smiling, Charlotte's hope soared as Daniel came into view. Everyone waited quietly until he was at the front door. As he stepped over the threshold, he blew cold air into the room, his teeth chattering.

"Sorry I'm late." He smiled at Charlotte, and she forced herself not to break out in tears. She glanced around the room at all the happy faces, but Annie and Jacob exchanged glances, their disappointment also reflected in their expressions. They were surely hoping that Lucas would be here too.

Annie edged her way to where Daniel was standing. "You left Grace with *Daed*?" she asked in a whisper loud enough that everyone in the room heard her.

"*Ya*. It is too cold for the *boppli*."

Annie stared at Daniel before she finally stepped back to her place.

Jacob and Charlotte kneeled before the bishop and deacons. Her life here flashed in her mind's eye like a photo collage of pictures that had finally come together and made sense. She'd arrived in Lancaster County seeking answers to Ethan's death. Her knowledge of the Plain People had been limited and inaccurate. But what had started as a divide-and-conquer mission had morphed into a beautiful path of discovery she never could have foreseen. And for the first time in her life, a sense of peace washed over her as she committed her life to God and the church.

Andrea smiled as she bounced Bella on her hip. Lena wiped her eyes. Daniel blinked a lot, surely wishing his mother were present to witness this blessed event.

The deacon poured water through the bishop's hands and onto Charlotte's and Jacob's heads. Afterward Bishop Miller awarded Jacob with a holy kiss on the forehead as the bishop's wife did the same with Charlotte.

Lost in the moment, Charlotte cried softly, thankfully,

and with renewed hope and faith. A lot of hugs and blessings followed the ceremony, but Charlotte's gaze kept drifting to Daniel.

"The weather prediction is not *gut* for later in the day. As much as I would like for you all to stay and celebrate this blessed occasion, I feel it best for everyone to get safely home," Bishop Miller said.

Charlotte found Daniel's eyes again and smiled.

Annie had never been more grateful for impending bad weather, an excuse to hurry home and check on the baby.

"I hope Gracie is okay," she said to Daniel, followed by a sigh. "I'm happy you came, but I'm disappointed that *Daed* didn't see Jacob and Charlotte getting baptized."

"Give *Daed* and the *boppli* this time together." Daniel leaned down to Annie's ear as the bishop's wife hugged Charlotte. "I need you to do me a favor. Can you follow me in your buggy to Charlotte's house?"

Annie opened her mouth to decline but thought better of it since Charlotte's house was on the way home. She wouldn't lose much time. She nodded. What was Daniel up to? Whatever it was, she silently thanked God that her brother seemed to have come around.

Jacob sidled up to Annie and squeezed her hand. She wanted to jump into his arms, but that would be inappropriate, so she just held tightly to his hand.

"I want a life with you, Annie. I've never been so sure of anything before." Jacob's eyes locked with hers, and Annie was sure her future was with him.

"I want that, too, Jacob, and I'm so happy you've taken this step toward that." She cupped his cheek in her hand. "I've got to follow Daniel to Charlotte's house. I'm not sure why, but then I'll hurry home to make sure Gracie is okay. I can come by later, though."

Jacob shook his head. "*Nee*, stay at home. I will come there if the weather looks better by tonight, or I will see you tomorrow." He blinked a few times. "And I will see you every day after that for the rest of my life."

Annie threw caution to the wind and hugged Jacob. "I love you with all my heart."

"And I love you."

Annie eased away. "I've got to find Daniel."

Jacob nodded.

It saddened Annie to have such worries about her own father tending to his daughter.

Daniel had plans to do something he'd dreamed of for a long time. He'd even planned for it to some extent. But then grief and fear had overwhelmed him, to a point that he'd almost missed Charlotte's baptism—something he would have regretted for the rest of his life.

"Annie and I would like to stop by your house on the

way home, if that's okay," he said to Charlotte as they said their good-byes to the others. "I won't be able to stay long because Annie is anxious to get home, but I have a gift for you."

Charlotte had been crying on and off since the beginning of the ceremony, overwhelmed with emotions Daniel understood. Committing to the church was a blessing not to be taken lightly, and Charlotte had done so even though she was unsure where her relationship with Daniel stood.

"I'd like that." She smiled through her tears. "I've missed you."

Daniel waited until they were out on the porch before he hugged Charlotte. The others hurried to their buggies, Andrea started the truck to let it warm up, and Amos bundled Lena up with a blanket before he and Jacob carried the wheelchair down the porch steps.

"I'm sorry," he whispered as he clung to her tightly. "I want you with me for the rest of time, but for now, ride in the truck with Andrea and Bella so you'll be warm." He grinned. "You'll be the passenger now."

Charlotte sniffled, but another smile stretched across her face as she eased out of his arms.

"You look beautiful," he said with a hitch in his voice. "That green dress and *kapp* suits you perfectly."

A minute later Daniel followed Big Red the short distance to Charlotte's house, with Annie following behind in her buggy. Once there, he stepped out of the buggy with his cold hands in the pockets of his coat as it started to drizzle, rain that would soon turn to ice.

He waited for Andrea to take Bella out of the car seat, then he carried her inside the house, telling Annie he would be with her shortly. His sister was antsy. Daniel was too.

Once in the living room, the remnants of a fire glowed, but a chill wafted through the room, so Daniel set Bella down and added a log.

"We'll let you two chat." Andrea scooped up Bella and started toward the bedroom.

"*Nee*, that's okay, Andrea. I must go. Annie is going to take me home." Daniel winked at Charlotte. "But we will talk later. Possibly tomorrow, depending on the weather."

Andrea nodded, but she still walked into the bedroom and closed the door.

"I'm so sorry. I'm so, so sorry, and—"

Charlotte put a finger to his lips, shushing him. "You're here now, and that's what matters."

"I want to stay. But Annie and I are both worried about Gracie. *Daed* still hasn't had anything to do with the *boppli*, and we are concerned about his being alone with her. I'm going to ride with Annie in her buggy."

"I understand." Charlotte nodded. "But why are you leaving your buggy here?"

Daniel smiled. He'd waited a long time to tell her. "Because it's your horse and buggy now. I'll put the horse under the old lean-to on the back of the property and make sure he has water. I'll bring hay tomorrow after the weather clears, but he will be okay for tonight. I fed him heartily this morning." He paused, smiling. "The lean-to needs to be replaced with a barn, so, once the weather allows, the community will come together to build you a proper barn."

Charlotte's eyebrows rose. "What?"

Daniel chuckled. "Maybe don't go anywhere until after the weather has cleared and I've shown you how to handle the animal. I've had another horse and buggy on order for a while. But my buggy is worn in, along with my gentle horse, and it will be easier for you to handle."

Charlotte jumped in Daniel's arms and smothered him with kisses. "This is happening, isn't it?"

He laughed. "*Ya*, it is." He kissed her one last time. "I will see you tomorrow." He cupped both of her cheeks. "I love you so much."

"I love you too."

After he'd tended to the horse, Daniel got in Annie's buggy, and they hurried off. Charlotte opened the bedroom door.

"Are you two back in the saddle again?" Andrea smiled as Bella played with a faceless doll on the bed next to her, one of the toys Dianda had sent over and symbolic to Charlotte at this moment.

"I do believe we are."

"Excellent!" Andrea clapped. "Because I have a surprise for you."

Charlotte brought a hand to her heart. "So many surprises today! Daniel just gave me his horse and buggy. It's real." A tear slipped down her cheek. "I'm Amish."

Andrea's eyes filled also. "I'm so happy for you." She shook her head, grinning. "I don't think I could do it." She laughed, dabbing at her eyes. "But if it works for you, then I'm happy."

Charlotte reached into the pocket of her black apron and pulled out the keys to Big Red. "I won't be needing these anymore." She tossed the keys to her sister, whose eyes rounded like saucers.

Andrea jumped off the bed, jumped up and down, and squealed. "I get the truck?"

"*Ya*, of course." Relief swept over her that the truck would remain in the family.

Andrea ran to Charlotte and threw her arms around her neck as Bella clapped. "Thank you, thank you, thank you."

"Well, you need wheels to deliver jewelry and pick up your money."

Andrea pulled away and gasped. "Speaking of. Come see your surprise!" She picked up Bella and led Charlotte across the living room to the kitchen. "I've been making payments on it."

A shiny white oven was in the place of her old stove top, and it was attached to a propane tank.

"I hope you don't mind, but I had to get rid of the cabinet underneath the stove top to make room for the oven." Andrea glowed, and Charlotte didn't think she had any more tears, but one slipped down her face anyway.

"You did this? But how . . . ?"

Andrea rolled her eyes as a hand landed on her hip. "Well, okay, I didn't do everything by myself. I bought the oven, but Edna's husband, John, installed it this morning. He helped me put it in Big Red and everything." She raised a hand, palm facing Charlotte. "But I paid for it." She frowned, but then grinned a little. "Well, I paid for most of it. Edna threw in some money she'd stumbled upon, deciding this was as good a use for it as anything."

"Edna?" Charlotte was too overwhelmed to speculate why Edna had done such a thing, but as she eyed her new oven, she dabbed at her eyes. "I can't believe this."

"I'll explain about Edna another time." Andrea stared at Charlotte for a long time. "What you've done for me and Bella"—Andrea blinked back tears—"I can't even really ever repay you. I hope you like the oven. And"—she bit her bottom lip—"I hope you will give Edna a chance too."

Andrea sniffled, then clapped her hands. "But for now, let's try it out!" She set Bella on the floor, walked to Charlotte's pantry, and returned with a chocolate cake mix and a white cake mix. "I wasn't sure if you liked chocolate or white cake." She set them on the table, went back to the pantry, and filled her arms with tubs of icing. "And I thought we'd choose the right icing together."

Charlotte brought a hand to her mouth to keep from sobbing openly as a river of tears poured down her face. "That sounds perfect."

Annie sprinted through the yard and pulled the front door open. Her father was sitting on the couch holding Gracie, his eyes bright as he gave the baby a bottle.

"I don't believe I've ever done this," he said, smiling. "But I found the formula and warmed it in a pan of hot water. She's a hungry girl." He refocused on Gracie as Annie hurried to his side, needing to see for herself that the baby was okay. She brought a hand to her chest and smiled.

"Hello, Baby Gracie." *Meet your* daed. She put a hand on the baby, then looked up at her father.

"She has her *mudder*'s eyes," he said softly as he kept his eye on his younger daughter. Eyes filled with emotions that Annie suspected he hadn't allowed himself to feel prior to now.

Daniel walked in a few minutes later, after tending to the horse in preparation for a freeze overnight. He strode across the living room, then squatted beside Annie and their father.

"She looks happy in your arms." Daniel smiled.

Daed glanced back and forth between Annie and Daniel. "I am sorry. I just couldn't . . ." His voice cracked as he tried to express his feelings. "I just . . ."

"It doesn't matter, *Daed*." Annie placed her hand on top of his as his shoulders shook slightly. "We are a family, and *Mamm* is looking down from heaven smiling."

Annie wasn't sure if life could get any more perfect, but then Daniel shared his hopes for Charlotte and him, and Annie bowed her head in prayer.

Charlotte, Andrea, and Bella had chocolate cake with strawberry icing for breakfast the next morning. Charlotte had already planned to take off work the day after her baptism. Daniel showed up later in the morning, after the freeze had lifted and left a sunny haze across dewy grass that glistened in the morning sun. Charlotte met him in the yard wrapped in her coat, donning black gloves and a black bonnet.

"I think I can get used to you dressing like this." He pulled her into a hug before he kissed her with all the love Charlotte had dreamed of.

"*Danki* for my horse and buggy. I took the horse some dry oatmeal this morning. I figured it would do until you got here." She smiled up at him.

Daniel nodded to the buggy he'd arrived in. "That's Annie's buggy. Mine won't be ready for another week."

"I guess I'll be carting you around. After you teach me the ropes, pardon the pun."

He laughed, but his expression turned serious. "I love

you. I want my life to be with you. Is that what you want too, Charlotte?"

"More than anything in the world. I feel like I'm finally home. It's not just my *house*, but a home."

Daniel smiled. "You've been home all along. It just took you awhile to get here. To this place. And to me."

She snuggled into his embrace just as their own personal ray of sunshine shone down on them from heaven, as if approving the life they were meant to share. *Thank You, God.*

Epilogue

ONE YEAR LATER . . .

Dear Ethan,

It's been awhile since I've written, but I've been busy in my new life. And, Ethan, I'm so happy. I'm finally "home," and I have the big family I've dreamed of. Our lenient bishop here in our district allowed Annie and Jacob to get married outside of the normal fall season, and Daniel and I got married a month later in July. Both were beautiful and blessed events. I wish you could have been here.

Ethan, your house has provided refuge for Janell, me, and now it shelters Andrea and Bella. I bet you could have never guessed when you purchased the small house that your family would be making such good use of it. Andrea has turned her jewelry making into a nice business, and she's able to support herself. And I'm happy to report that

she has been dating a nice young man who works with
me at the newspaper. He's a handsome Christian fellow
who has been really good for her. She attends his church
on Sundays, and occasionally she goes with me to church
but dislikes that the Amish service is three hours long.
And the first thing our sister did when she'd saved enough
money was to put electricity in the house. We bake cakes
and bread often together, and it warms my heart to see her
making such a good home for Bella.

As for me, I'm living with Daniel at his parents' house,
along with Annie and Jacob. Daniel was able to get Jacob
a job with him, building storage sheds, and Daniel often
says Jacob runs circles around him. Jacob has grown and
matured into a fine young man and a hard worker.

Daniel is building a house for us on the property, and
Jacob is refurbishing the *daadi haus* on the back acreage.
Neither Lucas nor Eve's parents ever utilized the house,
but Lucas wants to make it his home eventually. Annie and
Jacob will keep the big house. They need the room! Annie
is pregnant with twins and has also assumed the maternal
role of her sister, Gracie. Lucas adores his younger daughter, but he has slipped into more of a grandfatherly role
with her. So, for now, we are one big happy family enjoying
God's abundant blessings.

Lena left us not long after Easter. She missed the birth
of Hannah and Isaac's baby boy, but I feel sure she was
watching and smiling from heaven. There are still days
that I miss Lena terribly, longing to sit at her kitchen table

sipping coffee, eating buttered bread, and having long talks. But even though I miss her so much, I'm forever grateful to her for showing me motherly love, in a way I hope to pass on to my own kinner. It's hard to stay down for long with all the happiness and new life around us.

Speaking of new life, guess who else is having a baby? Ya, that would be me, and Daniel and I are thrilled beyond words.

I miss you so much, Ethan. I think about you every time I see a butterfly and when I wade in Pequea Creek on a sunny day. You are on my mind as I watch Bella grow into a beautiful little girl. She has your eyes. But I will see you again when I make my final trip home someday.

> Love you to heaven and
> back again,
> Char

Discussion Questions

1. Charlotte is afraid to commit to Daniel and God for fear of failure. What character speaks to Charlotte in a way that helps her to see that failure is part of our journey?

2. Daniel and his family don't want to take Eve off of the machines keeping her alive. What are some of the happenings that sway their decision? Have you or a loved one been in a position when you had to make such a monumental decision?

3. Charlotte isn't Amish at the beginning of the story, but in many ways she is living the life of the Plain People. What are some examples of this, and what do you think is the hardest thing for her to finally let go of when she makes a commitment to the Amish church?

4. What do you think that Aunt Faye said to Daniel's father, Lucas, in the hospital? Faye convinced him to leave Eve's side for a few days, but we never hear that conversation. Aunt Faye continued to have a big influence on Lucas's decisions. Why do you think that is?

5. Charlotte and Andrea both had bad starts in their lives, evidence that a person doesn't have to stay on a path unfit for him or her. But where do you think Andrea was headed if she hadn't found Charlotte? What were Andrea's initial reasons for seeking out her sister? How did Andrea change as her relationship with Charlotte grew?

6. Ethan's little house provided shelter for Ethan while he was alive, but also for Janell, Charlotte, and Andrea. Each person ended up there for different reasons. With the exception of Ethan, who was deceased already, who do you think benefitted the most from that setting?

7. Lucas won't leave Eve's side in the hospital until Aunt Faye convinced him to do so. He also wouldn't interact with his newborn daughter. What are some of the emotions Lucas must have been feeling as he watched his wife being kept alive on life support? See if you can dig deep, beyond the obvious.

8. According to recent estimates, only 5 percent of Amish teens or young adults leave the community for good. Jacob left to pursue a life in the outside world, but longed to come home. What do you think was the big influencer as related to his choice to return? Was it Annie? The fact that he didn't find success, only trouble, in the outside world? Did he long for the Amish lifestyle? Perhaps all of these, but would he have had the courage to come home if his mother's cancer hadn't returned?

9. Edna isn't a very likeable character. She kisses Daniel while married to John. She also had a relationship with Ethan when he was alive. But later in the story, we see Edna's vulnerabilities, and toward the end of the novel,

we see an unlikely friendship forming between Edna and Andrea. Why do you think this is?

10. Charlotte's truck—Big Red—is practically a character in the story, and the old Chevy holds sentimental value to Charlotte since it was a gift from Amos. How did you feel when Charlotte gave Andrea the truck? Do tangible items like houses and vehicles hold a special place in your heart, or are they just things to be bought and sold as needed?

11. If Charlotte had ultimately chosen not to convert to the Amish way of life, do you think Daniel would have left his church district to be with her? Since he had been baptized, he would have been shunned. Would Daniel have resented Charlotte and the forced detachment from his family?

12. What were your thoughts about the cake and icing analogy? Have you ever felt a sense of heaven on earth brought on by events or powerful faith in an afterlife? And if so, what was the defining moment when you knew beyond a shadow of a doubt that there is heaven to look forward to?

Acknowledgments

With each story I write, my faith continues to grow, solidifying what I know to be true—that there is a beautiful world waiting for us when we leave this earthly existence. When I hear that someone has doubts about this, it hurts my heart, and I long to *show* that person the peace that comes along with this knowledge. But, my journey is my own, and others have to find their own way to this wonderful understanding about what awaits us. It's my hope and prayer that at least one non-believer will explore the possibility that heaven truly is for real.

God blesses me with stories to tell. None of them are exclusively mine to claim, so dear Lord, thank You again.

To my publishing team at HarperCollins Christian Fiction, you all are amazing, and I'm so blessed to be a part of this publishing process, hopefully entertaining and ministering to those who can benefit from our team effort.

Natasha Kern, you are special in so many ways. As an agent, you tirelessly guide me with regard to my career, but you are also a trusted friend. Peace be with you.

To my assistant and dear friend Janet Murphy, you are appreciated and loved more than you know. I'm sure I don't tell you that often enough, but please know that you hold a special place in my heart, and on a personal and professional level, I'd be lost without you.

I'd be remiss not to mention my husband, Patrick. Dear, you keep the ground steady beneath my feet. Thank you for loving me. I love you to the moon and back . . . forever.

Friends and family, you continue to bless and support me on this wonderful journey, and I thank you from the bottom of my heart.

About the Author

 eth Wiseman is the award-winning and bestselling author of the Daughters of the Promise,
Land of Canaan, and Amish Secrets series. While she is
best known for her Amish novels, Beth has also written
contemporary novels including *Need You Now*, *The House
that Love Built*, and *The Promise*.

The Daughters
of the Promise Series

Visit BethWiseman.com

Also available in e-book formats

THOMAS NELSON
Since 1798

9781595548870-A

What would cause
the Amish to
move to Colorado,
leaving family and
friends behind?

The Land of Canaan Series

Also available in e-book formats

THOMAS NELSON
Since 1798

ENJOY THESE AMISH NOVELLA COLLECTIONS FOR EVERY SEASON

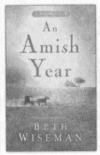

VISIT AMISHLIVING.COM
facebook.com/AmishLife

Available in print and e-book

THOMAS NELSON
Since 1798